HEART *Sick*

TRACEY RICHARDSON

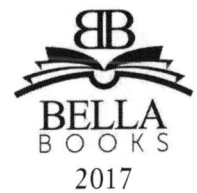

2017

Copyright © 2017 by Tracey Richardson

Bella Books, Inc.
P.O. Box 10543
Tallahassee, FL 32302

All rights reserved. No part of this book may be reproduced or transmitted in any form or by any means, electronic or mechanical, including photocopying, without permission in writing from the publisher.

This is a work of fiction. Names, characters, businesses, places, events and incidents are either the products of the author's imagination or used in a fictitious manner. Any resemblance to actual persons, living or dead, or actual events is purely coincidental. The publisher does not have any control over and does not assume any responsibility for author or third-party websites or their content.

Printed in the United States of America on acid-free paper.

First Bella Books Edition 2017

Editor: Medora MacDougall
Cover Designer: Judith Fellows

ISBN: 978-1-59493-564-0

PUBLISHER'S NOTE
The scanning, uploading, and distribution of this book via the Internet or via any other means without the permission of the publisher is illegal and punishable by law. Please purchase only authorized electronic editions, and do not participate in or encourage electronic piracy of copyrighted materials. Your support of the author's rights is appreciated.

Other Bella Books by Tracey Richardson

Blind Bet
By Mutual Consent
The Campaign
The Candidate
Delay of Game
Last Salute
No Rules of Engagement
Side Order of Love
The Song in My Heart
The Wedding Party

Acknowledgments

Thank you, as always, to the talented and professional women behind Bella Books for their continued belief in me and for the quality work they do. I can't say enough about my editor, Medora MacDougall, so to sum it up, I'll simply say she rocks! Thank you, readers…you are the biggest reason I do what I do! And last but not least, thank you to my writing community, my close friends, family, and to my wife for not only supporting what I do, but giving me a place to refuel and regenerate. A writer's heart and soul are tender things that need nourishment from many different sources, so thank you to all those who have left their fingerprints on me.

About the Author

Tracey Richardson is a retired newspaper journalist. *Heartsick* is her eleventh romance novel with Bella Books. Tracey is a two-time Lambda Literary award finalist and a first-place Romance Writers of America Rainbow Romance winner for contemporary romance. Tracey is also a (Word By Word) short fiction winner and a member of The Writers Union of Canada. She is married and lives in the Georgian Bay area of Ontario, Canada.

CHAPTER ONE

The ambulance's swirling blue lights bounced off the wet pavement, creating a kaleidoscope of rhythmic, shimmering motion. Angie Cullen blinked against the colorful onslaught as she guided her rig to a stop at the side of the road a good dozen yards from the car wreck.

For an instant, her heart stopped at the dark car that looked as though a can opener had ripped it nearly in half, its white airbags visible past the jagged metal, the shattered glass, the gaping holes where there should have been no holes. It had hit a light standard, which now sat folded over the trunk like a limb split from a tree. Brooke, Angie's lover of four years, was supposed to drive to the airport tonight for a flight to a real estate lawyers' conference in Miami, and on calls such as this one, Angie found it difficult to extinguish the spark of panic that her victim might be somebody she loved. It wasn't that she was nervous by nature, but rather that she'd seen the worst in her eight years with the army's medical corps and knew that devastation chose its targets randomly, wantonly, formidably, and without warning. Too many times she'd seen death's fickleness. But Brooke's car—*thank God!*—was white.

Angie dashed from her rig without shutting the door behind her, ignoring the relentless chime warning of the keys in the ignition and leaving the engine running. It'd been a year since she'd been on active paramedic duty, but she knew exactly what to do—quickly assess the situation, assign tasks and get to work stabilizing the patients for transfer. She barked at her partner, a twenty-six-year-old in his second year on the job, to check the passenger side of the wreck. "I've got the driver."

Jackson Shattenkirk hurried toward the far side of the wreck as a Traverse City Fire and Rescue truck screeched to a halt beside the ambulance, its red roof lights merging with the blue of the ambulance's, the two colors dizzyingly illuminating the dark; the crash had knocked out the overhead streetlight. Angie unclipped her small penlight from her belt and shone it on the driver's face. A woman, her hair long and dark blond, sat blinking in the dark, her lips open and moving like she wanted to say something.

"Whoa there, Cull!" a firefighter called out, and she recognized the voice of Vince Robertson. She'd known Vince since high school—he'd tried to date her back then, and when she finally confessed she preferred girls, he'd gamely swallowed his pride and decided he liked her as a friend.

"Hey, Vinnie. We got a couple of vics here." There was an unwritten code that saw firefighters, paramedics, and cops call each other by nicknames, which almost invariably played on their first or last name. In the army, you were called by your full last name with no cute twists, which Angie preferred, because Cull sounded so childish. So did Vinnie, for that matter, but she was used to it now.

She stepped back from the wreck to talk to Vince. He asked if anyone was trapped. The passenger—a woman with a bloody face—was being attended to by Jackson. There was nobody in the back seat. "I don't think so, but I don't know if their feet or legs are caught up in anything."

She leaned into the wreck and spoke to the driver. "Ma'am, are you trapped? Do you think you can get out?"

The woman's eyes darted to Angie. There was fear in them, pain too, but they were alert. It was another moment before she spoke, as if she needed to gather herself first. "Yes, I think I can get out."

"Okay, good, but don't move just yet. Shatter!" She flicked a glance at her partner from across the crumpled metal. "What've you got?"

"Woman, three-inch laceration on her forehead, contusion also. She was talking to me a second ago, but she's fading on me. Pulse is strong."

"Fading isn't a term I understand. Is she responsive or not?"

"Sorry, ma'am. Unresponsive."

Angie hated it when the younger paramedics called her ma'am. She wasn't old—well, to *her* at least, thirty-seven wasn't old. She conceded that her experience made her an old-timer. Eight years as a medic with the army, including stints in Afghanistan and Iraq. Seven years since with North Flight EMS, although the past year she'd taken a leave to teach in Munson Heathcare's program for paramedics. Later she'd talk to Jackson. Again. Being the new crew chief didn't mean he should call her ma'am. Cull or Cullen was fine, even Chief if he wanted to address her formally. But this ma'am crap needed to stop.

"Ma'am," Angie said again to the driver. "Where are you hurt?"

"I...I...the car, it went out of control. It was wet, I didn't—"

"It's okay. Are you hurt?"

"My, my left wrist. H-hurts b-bad. The air bag...or steering wheel...might have...broken it." She moaned as if just now finally registering the pain. It wasn't uncommon for shock to delay recognition of pain.

"All right, we'll help get you and your friend out of there. What's your name?"

"Karen. Karen Turner. My...my friend..."

"Okay, Karen. Hang tight, all right? We're going to get your friend out first. Vinnie?"

"Yeah, Cull, I'm here." Shattered bits of glass no bigger than a coin crunched under his heavy boots. His firefighter partner, a tall, bulky man nearing retirement, joined them at the front of the wreck.

"The passenger is the priority," Angie said.

"Got it."

Vince and his partner sprang into action as Angie thumbed the call button on the radio clipped to her breast pocket and asked dispatch for an ETA on a second ambulance. Four minutes out, she was told. Time enough to get the two victims ready for transport.

Angie stepped back as her partner and the two firefighters worked to free the passenger, felt the entire wreck shift as they heaved the door off its hinges. She reached in and checked her patient's carotid pulse before shining the penlight on her face and eyes again and down her torso. The air was warm, the August heat rising from the moist pavement, but her patient shivered like it was October. She was going into shock.

Shit, hurry up, she said in her mind but not to her colleagues because she knew they were working as fast as they could. They'd applied a cervical collar to the passenger and were now carefully strapping her onto a backboard, which they would slide onto the stretcher. Their patient was moaning, regaining consciousness.

The second ambulance roared up, and Angie motioned to its crew to bring the second stretcher.

"What've you got, Cull?" Ben Merkel yelled as he hustled the stretcher over to her.

"Possible left distal radius fracture. Pulse is ninety. We'll need to cuff her for a b.p. reading once she's out, and I haven't been able to check for any other injuries. She's getting shocky."

Shock was a deceiving little bastard. For something that seemed innocuous—light-headedness, the shivers—it could kill a patient by crashing their vitals.

"Cull?" Vince's voice carried over the noise. It was uncharacteristically high, strained, and Vince wasn't a guy who became easily rattled. "You better get over here."

Now what? she thought, impatient to get the two casualties locked and loaded and on the way to Munson Medical Center.

Jackson and Vince should be able to handle things, though it was no surprise that they would look to her for guidance, for critical knowledge. She never talked much about her army career, but they knew she'd spent some time working at Walter Reed Medical Center in Bethesda, knew she'd been a medevac medic in the war. It took little for her to summon the memories of the choking dust kicked up by the helicopters, the gaping and gory injuries sustained by soldiers, the sniper weapons aimed at herself and her fellow medics and sometimes at their hovering Blackhawk during a medevac, the sickening fear of a hidden IED or an RPG blowing her up the times she had to ride in a Humvee. There were also the veterans she saw at Walter Reed who, months later, continued to suffer mentally and physically from their wounds. All of those things had dulled her from being shocked anymore, had sharpened her keen sense of calm authority in a crisis. A car wrapped around a light post? Kindergarten stuff.

"What do you need?" she said, trotting over.

Vince gave her a look she couldn't read. Then he nodded at the patient on the stretcher who was still moaning softly. Angie followed his gaze, felt her eyes widen and her mouth open against her suddenly constricted throat. She hadn't seen the other victim's face earlier because it was dark and the woman was bloodied, but now she looked. And felt everything—the noise, the lights from the emergency vehicles, the chaos—coalesce into a loud ringing in her ears. The woman was Brooke.

Oh, shit!

Dr. Victoria Turner watched as her patient drifted into unconsciousness. He was in his forties, a weekend athlete who, not being in the best of shape, had crashed into the boards playing ice hockey an hour ago and dislocated his shoulder. Of course, it hadn't helped his sense of balance that, by his own admission, he'd had a couple of beers in the locker room before stepping out onto the ice. And now he was in Munson's ER suffering the kind of pain that instantly and mercilessly yanks its victim into sobriety. Sobriety that, in his case, came a little late.

She'd already checked the x-ray, confirmed that the rounded ball of the joint had escaped from the socket. She wouldn't try to do the anterior shoulder reduction with the patient conscious; this wasn't a television show or a battlefield. She was conducting the procedure with the luxury of drugs—much better for all of them. Vic slid her hands down her patient's arm, tugged it with a hard snap, and felt the satisfying thunk of it settling back into place. He'd wake any moment and be on his way shortly, no worse for wear. She wouldn't waste her time lecturing her patient about the dangers of drinking and playing sports, especially a sport played on the hard and unforgiving surface of ice. He'd either learn from this experience or he wouldn't.

"Doctor?"

Olivia Drake, one of three nurses on duty in the emergency department tonight as well as the charge nurse, popped her head into the treatment room. She also happened to be Victoria's best friend. It was at Liv's behest that six months ago Vic and her wife had made the move from the bustle and growing violence of Chicago to Traverse City—the city by the bay, the gateway to northern Michigan. Because of its location, Munson ER took in all serious trauma cases from the northern half of the state. It was the only Level II trauma center north of Grand Rapids, something that very much appealed to Vic. She wasn't at a point in her career where she wanted a sleepy town and a tiny hospital that closed its doors at sundown, but there was no question she was enjoying the reprieve from the daily avalanche of gunshot wounds and stabbings. Steady but controlled was how she liked her chaos, and that was pretty much what she got at Munson.

"What's up?"

"EMS is bringing in two victims from a car crash. Priority Two."

Non-life threatening but serious injuries. Vic relaxed a little. "How many minutes?"

"About eight."

She winked at her friend. "That gives me time to complete my notes on Wayne Gretzky here. Oh, and what about my confused lady in Four? Any results back yet?"

A seventy-year-old woman had come in an hour ago exhibiting confusion and complaining of general unwellness. She was running a slight temperature, and while it was probably a urinary tract infection, Vic had ordered a chest x-ray, head CT scan, blood and urine tests. If it wasn't something sinister and if it wasn't a UTI, her next guess was low blood sugar. Solving little mysteries like this were exactly the reason she had chosen a career in emergency medicine versus something cushier and with more tolerable hours, like radiology or dermatology.

"X-ray and scan are normal. Still waiting on blood work. Urine shows a spiked white count."

Back to a UTI. "All right. Make sure Dr. Greene is free as well when the ambulance gets here."

Jeff Greene was a second-year resident. Victoria, Jeff, and another resident, Julie Whitaker, were the physician crew for the ER tonight. So far they hadn't been run off their feet, but that could change in an instant. Last night shift she worked, Vic had stumbled out in the morning light so exhausted, she could barely find her car in the parking lot. They'd had to deal with a near drowning, two drunks who'd gotten into a messy fight, another drunk who thought it was a great idea to fire up his barbecue late into the night and ended up burning nearly half the skin off his face, a pregnant woman who didn't make it up to obstetrics before giving birth, plus the usual treadmill of coughs, fevers, and broken bones.

Vic typed in the last of her notes on the dislocated shoulder, then paged medicine to examine her UTI lady for possible admission. The patient would need IV antibiotics and fluids for a day or two while they waited for more blood cultures to come back. It was also one more patient off her watch in case the two car crash victims consumed most of her shift.

"First ambulance is here," Olivia said, gliding past the computer station where Vic sat at the main desk. "Second one is a minute or two off."

Rising, Vic asked, "Where's Jeff?"

"Here," he said, rounding a corner.

The three of them trotted to the ambulance bay in time to see a paramedic—a tall, brawny woman with a grim set to her jaw—jump from the cargo hold. The thought that maybe the patient was worse off than she had been led to believe escalated Vic's heart rate a little.

"What've you got?" she said to the paramedic, flashing a look at her nametag. A. Cullen. Six months on the job meant Vic should have met all the paramedics and EMTs in the city by now. But not this one.

Dark brown eyes that should have been calm but weren't captured Vic's. "Thirty-five-year-old woman. She's hit her head in the crash. Laceration on her forehead. She's…her vitals are stable."

Vic moved beside the stretcher as A. Cullen and her partner set it down and briskly wheeled it toward the bay doors. The patient was conscious, her eyes jumpy but alert. Her forehead was bloody around the bandage that had been roughly placed over it—a seeping laceration. There was a small cut on her lip too. Not enough to rattle what should be a seasoned paramedic, but Vic knew enough from fifteen years in medicine not to assume, never to underestimate.

"I've got this," she said to her resident, Jeff. "You get the next one." She directed her attention to the two paramedics. "Did she lose consciousness at all?"

"For a couple of minutes, yes," responded Shattenkirk, whom Vic had met a number of times in the ER.

"Anything else I should know?" Her gaze swung between the two paramedics. Brown eyes caught hers again. There was something pleading in them, something the rest of the paramedic's face had dammed up. Her throat bobbed up and down as though she couldn't stop swallowing.

Great, Vic thought. *One of my paramedics's gone mute.* She touched the sleeve of Shattenkirk as she kept pace with the stretcher down the hall. "Room Two. Jackson, is there anything else I should know about this patient?"

Vic hadn't had many conversations with Jackson Shattenkirk that didn't involve an immediate patient. He was young, quiet, the type who seemed to mind his business. He shrugged one shoulder, like he didn't want to say much. *What the hell is going on with these two? Has there been a zombie invasion nobody told me about?*

Carefully, they moved the patient onto the treatment bed and Vic began asking her questions—easy questions. She kept her tone even, efficient. Where are you hurt? How did you hit your head? Are you dizzy? Nauseous? Any medication allergies? Her name, the patient said, was Brooke Bennett, and yes, she knew what day it was and where she was and what had happened. But her head hurt like a son of a bitch.

"Let's order a head CT, chest and neck x-ray," Vic said to Olivia, who'd already taken a blood pressure reading. "And I'll need a suture kit."

The paramedic Cullen stood off to the side, leaning against the wall for support, pale and looking like she might throw up. Vic caught Olivia's eyes as if to say "Are we gonna have another patient on our hands?" Jackson was gone, had disappeared like he couldn't get away fast enough, mumbling something about meeting the other ambulance.

"Angie?" Olivia placed a hand on the paramedic's considerable bicep. "You okay?"

"Brooke." Angie blinked once, twice. "That's *my* Brooke. My...she..."

Vic saw Olivia's eyebrows jump before settling back down. "It's okay. Why don't you sit down? It's going to be a little while for the tests, okay? You might even want to go get a cup of coffee if you don't have another call."

Angie shook her head. She'd stay, she said.

Vic motioned for Olivia to join her in the hall. "What the hell is going on?" she whispered.

"They're a couple. I know Angie, not so much Brooke. Angie's a sweetie." Olivia rolled her eyes. "Brooke doesn't travel in my circles."

"What?"

"Never mind."

"Do me a favor and keep an eye on your friend Angie. I don't need her passing out or getting upset. She can stay if she behaves. Talk to her, all right? If there's any problem, I want her out of there." Vic turned to go as a question occurred to her. "Why haven't I seen her around here before?"

"She's been on sabbatical the past year, teaching. Years ago she was a medic in the army, did a couple of tours in Iraq or something. You've been to her family's winery I think. Sunset Bay Wines?"

She had. The merlot, she remembered, was spectacular. As was the view over Lake Michigan's Grand Traverse Bay from the second-floor terrace off the winery's main building. She and Karen had visited it a couple of times over the spring and summer.

The second stretcher from the crash was being wheeled toward the neighboring treatment room, Jeff directing traffic. He quirked his head at Vic to join them.

"I'll get those tests going. And I'll talk to Angie," Olivia said before peeling back toward the room.

Vic followed the group guiding the second stretcher into Room One. "What's up?"

Without a word, Jeff's eyes fell and Vic followed his gaze to the stretcher. It was Karen. Her wife! Moaning softly in pain, her eyes pinched shut. But it couldn't be. Karen had left hours ago for the eight-hour drive to Chicago to visit her sister for a few days. She should be halfway there by now. What the hell was she doing here? In a crash? With this Brooke woman?

Vic quickly gathered herself. Her questions would have to wait.

"Karen. It's me, Vic. Where are you hurt?"

Karen's eyes flew open, and it was then that Jeff intervened. "I've got this, Dr. Turner. I just wanted you to be aware."

Vic didn't want to, but she stepped back. Doctors shouldn't, unless absolutely necessary, treat loved ones. The situation was too emotional, too volatile, and while she understood the concept, right now it damn well sucked. She sagged against the wall outside the treatment room. Her head spun. Or at least, the questions in her head spun like a top, although one stood out. *What the fuck is going on around here?*

CHAPTER TWO

The shock of finding her partner in a crash, in another woman's car, had finally, mercifully, worn off. It its place came burning questions. And a dread so thick in Angie's stomach that it felt like a rock had been placed there. She paced the small treatment room while she waited for Brooke to return from her CT scan and x-rays. She'd booked the rest of her shift off sick and sent Jackson on his way. Later she'd catch a cab back to the house she and Brooke shared on the north side of the city—a new three-bedroom house that Brooke had insisted be finished with granite counters and travertine floors. The walk-in closet that was the size of a bedroom on its own, the three massive bathrooms—none of it was to Angie's tastes, but Brooke loved the place. Just as well, since Brooke's earnings as a high-end real estate and corporate lawyer were paying for most of it.

The red Hermes purse belonging to Brooke sat on the counter, and it occurred to Angie that she should call Brooke's boss to let him know what had happened and that Brooke wouldn't be arriving in Miami as planned. Rules didn't allow

Angie to carry her personal cell phone on the job, so she dug around inside the purse, feeling only the smallest bit of guilt. She never went near Brooke's private belongings and vice versa. If either left their Facebook or Twitter accounts open on the house computer, they never snooped. Or at least, Angie never did. There wasn't any reason to. She pulled Brooke's phone out of the purse. Except it wasn't the familiar iPhone with the glittery phone case that Angie found so distastefully girlie. It was a cheap phone with no security password, no frills. She touched it and its screen sprang to life. She hit Contacts, but the only name that came up was Karen Turner. The woman in the car with her. Next she clicked on the text icon. A list of texts, all between Brooke and this Karen Turner. Not good, a voice inside her head cried out. Not good at all. She clicked on the most recent one and her heart stopped. *See u soon, lover. Can't wait to be alone with you for almost a whole week! OMG I can't even stand it! xoxo.*

A clatter announced Brooke being wheeled back into the treatment room, and Angie tossed the phone back into the bag. She swallowed. Hard. The sense of something catastrophic arising inside her gripped her, turning her insides to liquid. Some massive force seemed poised to crush her and she staggered a little, grabbing the back of a chair for support.

The doctor looked up at her. "You all right?"

Angie nodded, but of course she wasn't all right. Her partner was fucking someone else, for Christ's sake. How could she possibly be all right?

Where she'd looked calm and detached earlier, efficient without being callous, the doctor looked distracted now. Confounded. Maybe even a little pissed off. Her nametag said Dr. Victoria Turner. Was she related to Karen Turner? Her sister perhaps? That could explain why she seemed a little frazzled.

"Your partner's tests are all negative," the doctor said. "I expect she has a concussion." She turned to Brooke with a blank expression. "I'll stitch you up in a few minutes. Normally I'd suggest you stay here in the ER for a few hours so we can keep an eye on you, but since you live with a paramedic, I think—"

"Doctor," Angie said, finding her voice and hearing it sound like gravel under car tires. "Can Brooke and I have a few minutes alone please?"

"Of course."

Alone with Brooke, Angie fought the urge to throw something. Hard. Instead she retrieved the burner phone from Brooke's purse, with its incriminating evidence that made her want to puke. "What the fuck is *this*?"

Brooke wouldn't look at her, just slammed her eyes shut and pursed her lips as though by doing so, she could make Angie fuck off without her giving her the third degree. Screw that. Angie would pry those eyes and mouth open if she had to, because she wanted answers, dammit. She wasn't stupid and she sure as hell wasn't blind. Or at least, not anymore she wasn't. What she needed to know was why. And how long. And how often. And what Brooke's master plan had been. And where she herself fit into all this. Had Brooke planned to tell her? Was she planning to leave her? Was she the last fucking person in this fucking city to know what was going on?

"Ange, my head hurts. Please don't yell."

"Then tell me," she said in a voice as tight as a cable about to snap. "Who is Karen Turner and why were you in her car? You were supposed to be taking a cab to the airport and flying to Miami tonight for that conference. Where were you really going, Brooke?" She thought of the text she'd snooped at, wondered what was said in the other dozen or so texts on the phone she hadn't had a chance to examine. "And explain to me this fucking cell phone you have in your purse."

"Look, it's..."

Angie waited for Brooke to finish. And waited. Another minute later, her voice cracking, she said, "What, it's not what I think? Because we damned well both know it is *exactly* what I think."

The nurse from earlier, Olivia Drake, stalked into the room, looking sternly from Angie to Brooke, then back to Angie. "Angie, I'm going to have to ask you to step out of the room.

Brooke has a concussion and she needs to stay quiet." She held the door open and motioned like a traffic cop. "Please, honey."

"What about what I need," Angie said so quietly that Olivia asked her to repeat herself. "Nothing," she mumbled and stalked out.

Vic tried to snap out of her fog. Before suturing the cut on Brooke Bennett's forehead, she stopped at the main desk to check on her wife's progress and discovered that she had a broken left wrist, a few cuts and bruises but nothing more serious. An ortho had been called to come down and examine her wrist, but so far it looked like Karen would not need surgery.

Jeff told Vic that she could go in and visit Karen. Though he was a second-year resident while she was the ER chief, Karen was *his* patient, and Vic had not been asked to consult or interfere in any way, nor did she have the right to in this case. She was the patient's loved one first, a doctor second. She hadn't, however, been able to resist scrolling through the computer and checking Karen's chart.

"Hi, sweetie," she said, stepping up to the bed and gently placing a hand on Karen's shoulder. "How are you feeling?"

Karen looked at her with such sadness that Vic feared there was something Jeff hadn't told her. Something that wasn't in Karen's chart, either.

"I'm so sorry."

"Hey, it's okay. Accidents happen. Everything's going to be all right." Vic reached for Karen's good hand. Her own hand was sweating, tremulous.

Tears, big and thick and slow, rolled down Karen's face, and all Vic could think was that something was about to happen. Something momentous and quick, like a room being thrown into darkness when the power suddenly goes out. She commanded herself to breathe, to be calm. Told herself she could handle anything.

"Your wrist should be good as new in a couple of months," she said as a delaying tactic. "We're very lucky."

"No." The word came out muffled, like it had caught on something in Karen's throat.

"I had a look at your x-ray, and—"

"Vic, don't."

Don't what, she wanted to scream, but she was afraid to say it. Maybe if she didn't speak, this would all go away. They could go home together at the end of her shift in a few hours. She would take care of Karen, their life would return to its natural order in a few days, a few weeks at worst.

"Brooke." Karen disengaged her hand from Vic's and carefully wiped the tears from her cheeks. "How is she?"

"She's…I didn't know you were friends with this person. You must have been giving her a ride somewhere. That was good of you, honey." Her breezy tone sounded ridiculous to her own ears. God, she was being pathetic! And a coward, because she did not want to hear what Karen was going to say next. But like a storm eating up the horizon, she was powerless to stop it.

Karen's voice shook with urgency. "Is she—Brooke—is she okay? Is she hurt badly? Nobody will tell me anything."

"No, just a nasty cut on her head that required some stitches. And she has a concussion."

Karen closed her eyes briefly, the muscles in her face relaxing. "Thank God."

"Is she…" *Oh God*. Reflexively, Vic clutched her stomach. She wanted to go hide in a supply closet. Or go back to her UTIs and dislocated shoulders and unexplained fevers like nothing had happened. But avoiding didn't come naturally to her. She was actually terrible at avoiding unpleasantness; she couldn't do her job if she were any other way.

She pressed on. "Is she another real estate broker in your firm?"

Karen shook her head. More tears were pooling in her eyes, like a faucet with a perpetual leak.

"Sweetie, we don't have to talk about the accident anymore, all right? You're on pain medication and I know all of this must have been so scary for you. I'm sorry this happened, but you're going to be okay. You'll have to miss the visit with your sister and we'll get another car, but otherwise, no harm done. You'll get better, I—"

"Victoria, stop it."

A simple, emotionless command, but it was like a slap. God, Karen was so beautiful, even lying in a hospital bed. And even with her face twisted in anguish. "Angelic" was the word Vic thought described Karen best, with her long, dark blond hair, fair freckled skin, and eyes the color of melting ice. She was Vic's real estate broker when Vic was looking for a two-bedroom condo in Chicago almost a decade ago, and she hadn't been able to stop looking at her, thinking about her. Too shy to ask her for a date, she waited for Karen to suggest a quiet dinner for two to celebrate the completion of the condo deal, and they'd not been apart since. Three years ago they legally tied the knot, and still when Vic looked at Karen, she could hardly believe she was hers.

"I can't…" Karen's eyes grew wide and searching, as if trying to locate her through a heavy mist. Her breath hitched at a sob. "I can't do this anymore. With you. I can't…I can't…I don't want to be married to you anymore, Vic."

The words took a moment to register, like they were coming at her from some distance, from a transistor radio or from underwater. It was someone else talking, not Karen; the words were meant for somebody else, not her.

"I…" Vic had to clear her throat to be heard. "I don't understand. What are you talking about?" She knew the literal meaning of the words, but not what they were supposed to mean to *her*.

"You know," Karen said quietly, "what I'm talking about. I want a divorce."

A *divorce*? Had Karen hit her head in the crash? Had someone else taken over her body? Taken over her life? *Their* life? No, it didn't make any sense. Everything had been fine up until tonight. They'd finally settled here, had begun making friends, had explored and enjoyed the area's hiking trails and wineries and parks and beaches. Not six weeks ago Karen said she liked Traverse City, that she was thrilled they'd moved here. Of course, they'd both been busy with their new jobs these last few months, but still… Why on earth would Karen say something like this to her now?

She backed toward the door, needing space. But there was, for now, one question above all others that screamed for an answer. Her voice shook. "Is it…does Brooke Bennett have anything to do with you wanting a divorce?"

Karen wouldn't look at her. She turned her face into the pillow, but she nodded. Vic stumbled into the hallway, her vision blurry, her thoughts in disarray. *She* was the accident victim now, trying to assess the damage while still absorbing the blow.

Oh, Karen, what have you done?

CHAPTER THREE

By the time Angie reached her family's winery, she had no recollection of how she'd got there. The fifteen-minute drive along the peninsula, past the other half dozen or so wineries, was a blur, but a familiar blur, at least, since it was her childhood home and she could pretty much navigate her way there blindfolded.

She didn't know why she'd come, only that she needed a sanctuary. After taking Brooke home from the hospital, she'd sat up the rest of the night while Brooke lightly dozed on the sofa. Over a breakfast neither touched, they talked. Or at least, Brooke talked, and mostly because Angie prodded her for every last detail, every shadowed corner of what she had been up to with this Karen Turner woman. And with each halting answer, each extracted confession, a part of Angie wished she hadn't pressed. Wished she could walk away without knowing all the gory details. But that was not who she was. Walking right into the fire, right into the shitstorm, that was the way she rolled because she couldn't imagine any other way.

Brooke said she met Karen five months ago at some real estate shindig—the kind, Angie knew from accompanying Brooke to a couple of them, with champagne and exotic meats and cheeses and elegant music playing in the background while people wearing expensive perfumes and makeup clustered together in small groups. The kind of event where the lighting was soft and the clothes were low cut and finely woven and every whisper was charged with something forbidden. A week later the two met for lunch (Brooke's idea). A week after that it was cocktails at a piano bar while Angie was away on a field trip up north with her paramedic class (Karen's idea). That was when the affair started, when they started sleeping together.

"But why...this?" Angie asked. "Why didn't you just leave me if you wanted someone else?" It seemed logical, like a math equation, because one plus one plus one did not equal a couple. It added up to somebody being left out, and that somebody, clearly, was Angie.

"Oh, Angie, do you *really* think it's that simple?" Brooke said in that way she had of making Angie feel like she'd just said the stupidest thing in the world.

"Yes," Angie replied, because to her it was.

"Well, it's not. I still loved you. We'd made a life together. This house, our finances. Four years together. It doesn't disappear over—"

"Over a few fucks?"

Brooke's face colored. "I was going to say it doesn't disappear overnight."

"Do you love this woman, Brooke?" Angie steeled herself for the answer. Not that it mattered, really, because she could never be with Brooke again. Not after what she'd done.

"Yes. I think so."

"Jesus." So it was worse than she thought. Not just sex. "How long did you plan to keep both of us, huh? Another five months? A year?" Anger rose through her, breaching the dam of her emotions, threatening to swamp her if she didn't tamp it back down.

Brooke started crying, and Angie couldn't take it anymore.

"I'll stay at my family's for a few weeks." She looked around at the kitchen—white, expensive, contemporary—that had never been her style. "Then we can figure out what to do with this place."

And now here she was outside her family's farm, a couple of suitcases in her trunk and a smothering exhaustion that made even getting out of the car seem like a painful chore.

Her brother Nick's orange tabby, tail arching in greeting, trotted out to her.

"Hi, Beau." It was short for Beaujolais. "How's my good boy?"

She scooped him up with one hand, popped the hatch on her SUV with the other.

"Hey sis." Nick jogged to her, his face registering surprise. She'd not been around the winery since she'd returned to regular duties with North Flight EMS a couple of weeks ago. "What are you doing here? Jesus, you look like you haven't slept in a couple of days."

Angie winced. "I haven't. Wanna help me with my suitcases?"

"Of course, but only if you tell me what these are for."

Angie ignored him, hoping to delay an explanation for as long as possible. Truth was, she didn't want to have to explain anything while she was in this state. Brooke had blown up their relationship, and the concussive effects were every bit as intense as if she'd been knocked on her ass by an IED attack. Fog, numbness, feeling like she was standing apart from her own body, then excruciating pain followed by denial, grief, anger. All of those things and more rolled in on her relentlessly, one after another and sometimes all at once. But she could think of nowhere else to go. Oh, she could have gone to stay with Vince and his wife for a couple of weeks, or Jackie, another friend from high school. But Vince had a houseful of kids and Jackie was in Petoskey, which was an hour away and too far for the drive back and forth to work.

Besides, family was what Angie turned to when times got rough. When she returned stateside after her first tour in Afghanistan and her second in Iraq, it was the family property that grounded her, restored her again for a few weeks. The smell of dirt on her fingers, on her boots, the shiny, stainless steel fermenting vats that were as big as a compact car, the heaping plates of food her mother and Nick's wife Claire cooked.

"Where's Dad?"

"In the barn working on a tractor. Why?"

"I only want to go through all this once. Mom and Claire, can you grab them too? I need to talk to you guys."

Nick, thankfully, didn't press her for more. She must have looked sufficiently like shit for him to realize something serious was going down. She set Beau back on the ground.

"All right. I think they're in the kitchen."

Of course they were. Her mom and Claire baked and cooked all the munchies the winery's guests could order over a glass or bottle of wine in the massive tasting room or out on the deck that overlooked Grand Traverse Bay. It was Monday, prep day for the week ahead and the only day of the week the winery closed its doors to the public so the family and its gaggle of employees could get work done. Bad timing on her part, but it wasn't like it could wait.

"Thanks, Nick. The kitchen's as good a place as any to meet."

* * *

Vic could think of no better antidote, no more effective cure for her broken heart, than work. Lots of it. Work was the only cocoon she could feel safe in right now, the only thing that could make her forget, at least for a little while, the images that swam through her mind like shadowy predators. The same predators that stole her sleep and shoved her into an abyss that left her staring at the walls at night and crying until she could hardly breathe. Being alone with her thoughts right now was the worst thing she could do.

Karen had moved into a hotel, even though Vic, against her better judgment, told her she didn't have to. But that was before Karen had confessed that she was in love with Brooke Bennett. Vic couldn't stay in the same house if her wife was in love with somebody else, because that kind of apocalyptic rejection she wouldn't be able to live with. She tried to get more answers out of Karen, because Lord knew she had about ten thousand questions. But Karen didn't want to talk about it anymore. Karen wanted to get the hell out as quickly as possible now that everything was all out in the open. Later they would talk, she promised halfheartedly. Some other time, which might mean next week, next month, or maybe never. Or maybe it meant any more talk would happen between their lawyers. Who knew?

It was her second day of working a double shift, and even though Olivia kept giving her the stink eye over this self-flagellation, Vic was the chief of the Emergency Department and she could work as many damn hours as she wanted. There was a serious car crash victim coming in, a man who wasn't wearing a seat belt and had been thrown through the windshield of his car on Highway 31. A Priority One.

"You okay with this?" Olivia asked discreetly.

"Of course," Vic snapped, not meaning to, but between her lack of sleep and the buckets of coffee she'd drunk, her nerves were in tatters. Olivia gave her that look she'd been giving her all week—sympathy, concern, admonishment—but Vic turned away and pulled on her disposable gloves to await the ambulance.

It was quiet moments like these, caught between tasks, when her mind wandered. Karen saying she loved Brooke. Karen saying she wanted a divorce and saying it in a way that left no room to negotiate a different outcome. Vic could feel, with every word her memory summoned, the press of the shock against her chest, squeezing her, urging her now to replay it like some elaborate injury one has to relive over and over until its power to hurt diminishes. *How can this be happening to me? To us?* And then she remembered there was no us anymore. And that it had, indeed, happened.

She commanded herself to focus on the task at hand, allowed the sharp edge of nervousness to race up and down her spine. She was always a little nervous before a P-1. Which is the way it should be, she'd counseled medical students, interns, junior residents. It was good to be confident, vitally important to trust in your training and experience, but any good ER doc knew that doing everything right didn't guarantee success in the treatment rooms.

Conversely, she often repeated the wise advice of a former med school mentor, who preached that you should never go into emergency medicine if you couldn't live with yourself after killing someone. Vic thought she'd heard wrong at first. "You mean if you lose a patient?" she asked him. "No," he said, "if you kill a patient, because you will. You'll misdiagnose or miss diagnosing something altogether. You'll be exhausted some shifts, harried, pulled in twenty different directions…and somebody, someday, will die because of it." It was one of the most helpful pieces of advice, one of the most realistic things she'd ever heard, in her more than fifteen years in the business of emergency medicine.

The ambulance roared up and the sight of its dancing roof lights transported her back to the other night, when it was Karen on the gurney. Karen's lover too. It was the moment her life had changed. The moment four lives had changed forever. She watched the first paramedic exit from the driver's seat and scramble around to open the back doors, hoping to hell it wasn't Angie Cullen in back with the patient. She hadn't run into Angie since that night, which was exactly the way she wanted it. She didn't even know if Angie was back at work, throwing herself headlong into the job the way she was or whether she was taking some time off. Nor was she about to ask anyone. The less she saw of Angie, the less it would remind her of…everything.

Her heart pounded and then settled when she saw it wasn't Angie hopping out the back and sliding the gurney out.

"What've you got?" Vic said.

"Semi-responsive, possible internal injuries, possible head injuries too," said the first paramedic. "Probable collapsed lung. Pulse has been dropping and is down to eighty-eight. He's thirty-seven years old, alone in the car when it hit a transport truck. Wasn't belted, went through the windshield."

"I can see that," Vic mumbled, taking in the bits of broken glass visible on the man's suit. She could never fathom why anyone wouldn't wear a seat belt. Some fool once told her he figured the airbags would be enough to save you. Nice try. Airbags didn't keep you in the car when force and gravity sent flying whatever objects weren't latched down.

Olivia and another nurse arrived, along with a burly young intern named Raymond, to help transfer the patient to the treatment bed, which was also mobile to make it easier to move the patient for tests or for transportation to another department such as surgery. The patient, mouth open, gave a gurgling gasp, and without being asked, the two nurses began cutting off his clothing.

"Get me a tube kit," Vic said to Ray. She'd need to intubate before anything else.

The man's eyelids fluttered closed one last time. He was unconscious, which would make things a little easier for Vic and her crew. Olivia moved to start an IV while Deb, the second nurse, hooked the patient up to a heart monitor and blood pressure machine. Vic listened to his chest. His lungs were definitely compromised.

"Ray, you want to trying tubing him?"

The intern hesitated for just a moment, and it was enough for Vic to decide she'd do it herself.

"Liv, give him twenty milligrams of etomidate and one hundred milligrams of succinylcholine." She wanted the man's throat muscles good and relaxed. "Ray, hand me the laryngoscope please. And Deb, get x-ray and ultrasound in here. I want him to have a head CT as soon as we're done with the other." He could have landed on his head or smacked it hard on the windshield.

"Right away, Dr. Turner."

Intubating patients came easy to Vic after the thousands she'd done in her career. Steady and calm, she pulled the man's jaw open and placed the L-shaped scope inside his mouth, pushed his tongue aside, spotted the vocal chords. Then she fed the hollow plastic tube into his trachea. "We're in," she said out of habit.

She stepped back to allow the x-ray tech to haul the portable machine in to take some pictures. A flat screen attached to the machine showed what came as no surprise to Vic and explained the man's collapsed lung: three broken ribs. Then it was the ultrasound tech's turn. On the screen of the portable machine, she saw the telltale swirling dark shadows of bleeding around the spleen, pointed it out to Ray, and ordered Deb to call Surgery. This man was going to need his spleen out because it'd been crushed in the accident, but first she needed to deal with his lung.

She handed Ray a scalpel. "Don't worry, I'll walk you through it."

Her steady gaze seemed to settle him, and he made a two-inch slice between the man's ribs where she'd circled with a Sharpie. She handed him the small, clear tube and told him to push it in a couple of inches until air hissed out, then watched as he connected it to a suction machine. It was almost miraculous to see the patient's lung refill again, and Ray smiled his relief.

"Surgery's ready for him," Olivia announced. "You still want him to have a head CT first?"

"Yes, please. The transporters can take him up now," Vic said in a voice thin with exhaustion. "Thank you everyone."

She threw her disposable gown in the trash, pulled off her sterile gloves and trashed them as well. As the others hustled the patient out of the room, she leaned against the wall and rubbed her temples.

Olivia hung back. "Sweetie, why don't you come over to our place for dinner tomorrow. It's Saturday and your day off. Unless you've done something stupid and signed yourself up for work again."

"Thanks, Liv, but I'd rather be alone."

"You've had all week to be alone. Beth and I would love to have you over."

"Thanks, but no. I'm terrible company right now."

They hadn't talked much about what had happened. Vic wasn't ready to, and Olivia seemed to sense that time and space was what she needed right now.

"All right, but promise me you won't spend the whole weekend moping around the house."

It was exactly what Vic was planning to do, and yes, it was probably a terrible idea. She'd done a rotation in Psych a long time ago, was smart enough to know she needed to shake things up to pull herself out of this funk. And yes, Liv was right. She should do something enjoyable, go somewhere different, anything to break up this pattern of work and sitting in the dark at home between shifts.

"All right, all right. I'll do something, I promise."

"Good. Any ideas?"

"Wine. Something definitely involving copious amounts of wine."

"Now you're talking!"

CHAPTER FOUR

Of course her family would put her to work.
Angie shook her head at the thought, but inside she was secretly relieved. Her boss had forced her to take a couple of shifts off work this week, so she was happy to fill the void with working at her family's business. It was therapeutic, distracting. And at the winery, there was always something to be done. There were 120 acres of vines (comprised of a dozen grape varieties) that needed regular monitoring and tending and equipment ranging from tractors to heating units to filtering systems in the distillery that required regular maintenance. The tasting room was always begging for another hand or two, which was where her mom, Suzanne, had assigned her today. Angie would rather be in the fields or in the barn with her brother Nick, mindlessly fussing with some piece of equipment or other, but Saturdays were the busiest day of the week in the tasting room. And you didn't say no to Suzanne Cullen.
Angie felt nowhere near as spunky and bright as her cobalt blue bow tie, matching vest, starched white shirt and black

pants were—all part of the dress code of working the tasting room. What she felt like was a boxer who'd taken a thunderous blindside hit and was still down on the mat—dazed, bruised, trying to survive the ten-count. It was a wallop Brooke had given her, but she wasn't willing to play the role of helpless victim any longer. She'd had a week to stew in the juices of self-pity and anger, and she was sick of it. Brooke could go fuck herself if she thought she'd dealt Angie a lethal blow, because Angie was done gathering up all her broken parts and was ready to fight back. Whatever fighting back might mean. That part, she hadn't figured out yet.

"Ready for a tasting?" Angie asked a couple in their twenties who'd been meticulously studying the floor-to-ceiling oak shelves that cradled a variety of bottles of wine. If Angie had to guess, their careful consideration was more from ignorance than knowledgeable discrimination.

"This room is so beautiful, I might never want to leave," the woman said, casting her eyes around in such a way as to take in all of the room at once.

She was right. It was beautiful, and sometimes it took a stranger's eye to remind Angie. Oak floors, twenty-five-foot cathedral ceilings, a thirty-foot-long tasting bar finished with birds-eye maple and black walnut, stained glass windows high up that featured various scenes of water, vegetation and bird life, and on the walls that didn't have built-in shelving, large windows looked out onto the rolling vineyards and the bay beyond.

It had been her sister-in-law Claire's idea to give the room a library feel. There were leather wingback chairs the color of deep red wine, end tables with Tiffany lamps, a tan leather fainting couch from the Victorian era and leather-bound classic books interspersed on the shelves with the bottles of wine. Somehow, the room even smelled of leather and ink and old books. Many people commented that the room felt like one they could spend all day in…which was both desirable and undesirable. The Cullens wanted people to feel at home, spoiled, but constant turnover produced more wine sales.

"Well," Angie reassured the young woman. "There is absolutely no hurry. Would you like to sample some of our selections? Or go straight to a glass or bottle to share?"

"Let's sample the reds first," the man said, looking a question at his companion. "Then we'll order a glass."

With an efficient but impressive flourish, Angie poured them each an inch of Sunset Bay merlot, explaining that the wine was made right here from their own grapes. Next it was a shiraz, followed by a cabernet. After more questions about the wine (2016 was a very good year for the grapes, she said, because of the dry summer), the couple ordered a glass each of merlot and claimed a table for two in a corner near a window.

So far it had been steady for a Saturday, but the tasting room had been far from overrun. It was the first weekend of September, and tourist traffic was beginning to taper off for the season. Angie was topping up the glasses of a couple in their fifties at another table when, from the corner of her eye, she noticed a tall blonde take a seat at the bar.

"Welcome to Sunset Bay Wines. Can I—"

Oh, shit! It was Victoria Turner, the ER doc, the wife of Brooke's lover, and about the last person she wanted to run into…well, other than Brooke or Karen. Angie could only guess at what the hell was she doing here. Had she come to grill her? Pick a fight with her? Angie felt heat rush to her cheeks. Whatever it was, it wouldn't be happening today and certainly not here.

Victoria turned sharply, her eyes widening and then dimming at the sight of Angie. The flash of panic in her face was so brief, it was almost as though it'd never been there. "I…Miss Cullen, I…I forgot this was your family's winery. Would you like me to leave?"

Yes, Angie was about to exclaim—wanting never, although she knew it was impossible, to see this Dr. Turner again. They couldn't avoid each other forever at work, she supposed, but she was damned if she wanted such a stark reminder of Brooke's infidelity thrown in her face right here on her own territory.

The doctor started to rise, but something in her eyes, in the slump of her shoulders, in the slow, languid, almost painful movements of her body, gave Angie pause to reconsider the unforgiving line she'd mentally drawn. Clearly, Victoria Turner was lonely. Hurting. Vulnerable. Which was a little shocking, given, in Angie's experience, that emergency medicine physicians were typically control freaks or adrenaline junkies who didn't fear a hell of a lot. They were bossy, sometimes dismissive, always distracted because they were either in a hurry or they were multitasking. Instead, Victoria Turner possessed the stunned look of someone who'd been slapped around. Figuratively, anyway.

"No, wait. Sit. Please."

"Are you sure?"

"Of course." Angie took a deep breath and found her business demeanor—courteous, efficient, pleasant without being too friendly. She didn't particularly want Victoria Turner sitting here drowning her sorrows—the very same sorrows Angie knew all too well—but it would be rude, not to mention bad business, to turn somebody away for personal reasons. Besides, her mother would have her hide if she was anything besides polite. "What can I get you, Dr. Turner?"

The doctor resumed her seat and ordered a glass of merlot, which moments later Angie placed in front of her on an orange and red Sunset Bay Winery coaster. She left her there, intentionally seeking out other chores, other customers to check on. The last thing she wanted was to hover around Victoria or, worse, have a conversation with her. It wasn't as if they'd be able to ignore the elephant in the room and chat about the weather or the varieties of wine available. No. Not when that very same elephant had stampeded through their lives seven days ago, razing everything recognizable, destroying all they thought they knew about the person they loved most. She could almost—but not quite, because she knew better—equate it to the battlefield, where, after a firefight, it took a considerable mental recalibration to get your bearings back, to resume what was considered normal.

By the time Victoria started in on her third glass of wine, Angie started keeping an eye on her from the other end of the bar. The Cullens didn't encourage people to sit here and get drunk; it wasn't a bar, after all. The tasting room had gradually begun to empty; closing time was six o'clock, thirty minutes away. The doctor raised her glass to signal to Angie for a fourth.

"I don't think that's a good idea, Doc."

"Please," Victoria said, raising glassy eyes to Angie that were devoid of emotion. Angie had seen that look many times in battle-fatigued soldiers. "Do me a favor and stop calling me doc unless we're at the hospital."

"All right. Ms. Turner or Victoria?"

There was a sharp edge to her laugh. "Call me Vic. I hate Victoria. It sounds far too formal. And Ms. is definitely…" She waved a limp-wristed hand in dismissal or defeat. "One more and I promise I'll get out of your hair."

"I'll call you Vic if you call me Angie. Deal?" She waited for Vic to nod. "You're not a seasoned drinker, are you?" The woman shouldn't be this loaded after three glasses of wine.

A smile, endearing in all the right ways, produced dimples Angie hadn't noticed before. "No, I'm not generally a lush, if that's what you're getting at. Certain recent circumstances, of which you're all too aware, seem to be turning me into one, I'm afraid."

Vic laughed then, which only made Angie frown. Nothing about any of this was funny. Before her sat a woman whose pride had been visibly steamrolled. A woman lost, directionless, bleeding her pain. Angie too felt adrift, at the whim of whatever emotional currents assailed her at any given moment. And yes, it was tempting to disappear into a bottle of wine. Hell, she had access to giant vats of the stuff if she wanted to tie one on. But since she'd survived combat medic tours in both Afghanistan and Iraq without resorting to buckets of alcohol, she'd find a way to survive this too.

"Come on," she said in a tone that left no room for resistance. "I'm driving you home."

"Oh no. There's no need for that."

"There is."

"I'll get a cab then."

"They're not out this way much. You'd probably have to wait close to an hour for one, especially at dinnertime on a Saturday evening."

She shook her head. "I'll wait."

"You won't. I said I'll take you and it's closing time anyway. Let's go." She called to Charles, a college student who worked part-time doing odd jobs around the place, and asked him to close up. Angie cupped the doctor's elbow.

"I don't need your help!" Vic jerked herself away, stumbling in the process.

"I'm not the enemy here," Angie hissed, touching her lightly this time. She'd dealt with nasty drunks before. Had dealt plenty often with people who were in a miserable place. She could be infinitely patient when it came to people's suffering. Not so much with herself, but that was another matter. What she needed to do was focus on the uncooperative Dr. Turner—er, Vic—and get her home.

* * *

By the time Angie had stuffed her into the passenger seat of her SUV, Vic had resigned herself to the inevitable. She didn't like relying on others. Worse, she'd made a fool of herself, and with her wife's lover's partner. Well, ex-partner. *God!* Could she be any more pathetic? Angie was going to think it was no wonder Karen had left her.

Without being obvious about it, she studied the woman at the wheel. Angie Cullen drove with expert efficiency, neither too fast nor too slow, and handled the car like it was an extension of herself. She wore no expression, though she glanced occasionally at Vic with clinical curiosity. *Probably to see if I'm asleep or slobbering or getting ready to argue.* She'd merely given Angie her address and didn't have to direct her further to her two-story Victorian duplex a couple of miles from the hospital. *Probably knows the city like the back of her hand,* Vic guessed, as Angie pulled expertly into the driveway. Her silence was unnerving, and Vic grabbed for the door handle. She couldn't get into her house fast enough.

"Wait," Angie said. "Let me help you in."

"I don't need your help, thank you." An icy declarative, but it was the truth. And she certainly didn't need *this* woman's help.

But Angie raced around the front of the vehicle and caught Vic as she nearly tumbled out the door. *Dammit!* I am not helpless and I am not a drunk, she wanted to scream. She tried to pull away, but Angie Cullen was a strong woman and was having none of it. She was as tall as Vic, but meatier, much stronger. Where Vic resembled a marathon runner, Angie looked more like she was into rugby or field hockey or lacrosse or something that required a lot of muscles.

"Let me help you," Angie urged, gentler this time. "You don't want to end up in your own emergency room, do you?"

That got Vic's attention. She'd die of embarrassment if she ended up hurt and in her own ER having to be patched up by gossipy colleagues, so she let Angie guide her to the mammoth oak and leaded glass double front door and handed her the key to let them in.

"I'm not," she started, "you know, normally…in need of assistance like this."

"I know. Let's get you comfortable somewhere."

Vic pointed down the short hall and to the left, which opened to the living room. She heard a tiny intake of breath from Angie. It was a spectacular room, with a fourteen-foot high ceiling, gleaming oak hardwood floors, a working fireplace framed on either side by full built-in bookcases, leaded glass French doors separating it from the dining room, and a big bay window that let in just the right amount of light.

"I feel like I should offer you a drink or something," Vic said, her voice tight. She wanted Angie out of here, away from her as quickly as possible, but didn't want to be any more rude than she'd already been. The situation was awkward as hell. In fact, awkward didn't even begin to describe it. It was almost incestuous—no, appalling—to have the woman who was Karen's lover's partner in her home like this, just the two of them. But Angie had gone out of her way for her, had done her a favor, and Vic hated that she was being so ungrateful about it.

"Thanks, but I need to get back to the farm. I can let myself out."

"You're sure?"

"I'm sure." Angie seemed as uncomfortable about the idea of an innocent little chitchat right now as Vic did. *Thank goodness.*

Vic flopped down unceremoniously on her leather sofa, impatient suddenly for Angie to get on with it and leave.

"You know, don't you," Angie said, spinning around suddenly, "that it's not our fault, right?"

Vic snapped her eyes shut, pretending to be asleep already. *Go away*, she bellowed in her mind.

CHAPTER FIVE

Angie was sweeping the cement floor of the large fermenting room when her sister-in-law Claire appeared with a sly smile on her lips and asked who the knockout blonde was.

"What knockout blonde?"

"Tall, fit-looking, late thirties, maybe early forties. An hour or so ago, she came and retrieved that Mercedes that was in our parking lot all night."

Angie leaned against her broom and rolled her eyes. "Don't ask."

"Too late, I'm asking. Don't tell me you're already dating? Not that I'm judging. You know we all thought Brooke didn't deserve you."

"Thanks for the vote of confidence. I think." She knew her family had never especially cared for Brooke, had behind her back labeled her snobby, among any number of disparaging descriptions, although they'd been nothing but superficially polite in Brooke's presence. Their conclusions had been proven right, it seemed, but she wasn't in the mood to concede yet. "And no, I'm not dating."

"Too bad." Claire leaned against a massive stainless steel vat filled with what would eventually become a rich, smooth cabernet sauvignon. A yeasty, pungent smell permeated the room. "She'd have my vote. So, do you know her?"

Crap. She started sweeping again, mostly to try to kill time and hopefully derail Claire. But Claire followed, stared at her like a drill homing in on its target. "All right, fine. She's Victoria Turner, an ER doc at Munson."

"Turner." Claire wrinkled her nose. "Not related to the homewrecker Karen Turner, is she?"

Angie had come clean with her family about her breakup with Brooke. And about Brooke's affair. She hadn't wanted to spill it all, not while her wounds were still raw and oozing, but she knew they'd drag it out of her eventually. Better to rip off the Band-Aid in one swift pull. Painful as the confession had been, it finally allowed her to breathe without feeling like a truck was sitting on her chest.

With more than a little reluctance, Angie explained who Vic was and why her car had been left overnight.

"Ooh, what's she like?" Claire's relentless curiosity had sprung to life and she moved closer.

"Don't know and don't care."

"That's kind of harsh. She must be hurting pretty bad too. I mean, they were married, weren't they? Together for a number of years?"

"Yes and I suppose so."

"Jeez, Ange, don't take it out on me. Or on the nice doctor."

"Take what out on you?"

"Your shitty feelings toward Brooke. Which she totally deserves."

"Fine. I'm sorry." Angie leaned her broom against the wall and rubbed her temples, where a headache threatened to take up residence. "And what makes you think the doctor is nice, anyway?"

"I don't know. She looked nice. And why wouldn't she be nice?" Claire shot her a sly look. "Unless she was a terrible wife, a rotten person. Maybe that's why her wife set her sights on Brooke."

Angie rolled her eyes. "I doubt it's that simple. And besides, I'm not letting Brooke off the goddamned hook. Even if this Karen needed rescuing, and I'm not saying she did, Brooke should have kept her hands off her. Brooke alone is responsible for making the decision to cheat on me."

"Of course she is, sweetie. I think what I'm trying to get at is, have you had a heart-to-heart conversation with the doctor? You know, to get her take on what happened?"

"Why the hell would I do that?" *Jeez!* Could she just be left alone with her own misery for once?

"To try and get some answers, some closure. I'm sure she's feeling all the same things you're feeling as well. It might be good to talk to someone else who's going through this. You know, to—"

"No!" Angie snapped. The thought of talking about the affair with a stranger…worse than a stranger, with the wife of Brooke's lover, was a terrible idea, the worst. In fact, she'd rather rip off her own fingernails. "Look, Claire, I know you're trying to help. But I really don't want to talk about Brooke or Karen or Dr. Turner anymore, okay?" Vic, she remembered, not Dr. Turner. Vic with the beguiling gray-green eyes left shadowed and shattered by pain.

Claire put her arms around Angie and pulled her in for a hug. "I'm so sorry, Ange. I'm not trying to make things worse for you. I just want you to be okay. We all do."

"I know. And I will be. I promise."

* * *

There were certain calls on the EMS radio that instantaneously galvanized everyone in the ER. Vic remembered one such call, almost four months ago, when the paramedics were bringing in a teenager who'd suffered life-threatening head injuries while backing his mother's car out of the driveway for her. It was a ritual he did every morning before school—he'd start the car and back it out of the garage and down the driveway a few yards, then when his mom arrived he'd get out and head over to the passenger side and let her drive. But that particular morning, he'd hadn't firmly placed the transmission in park, and when he tried to exit the car, it continued rolling back. The boy slipped and got his head jammed between the car and another car parked at the end of the driveway.

During the eight-minute rush to the hospital, Vic, two other doctors, and three nurses stood transfixed as they listened to the paramedics describe the boy's ongoing condition, the ambulance's siren an impatient and constant wail in the background. The boy's pupils were fixed and dilated and gray matter was visible, the paramedic said in an urgent and breathy voice. A pin could have been heard to drop in the ER at that moment; they all realized this boy had almost no chance of survival.

The call crackling through the radio now was almost as bad, though the chances for a better outcome were much greater. It was a seven-year-old girl who'd choked on a piece of candy at a birthday party. Vic recognized Angie Cullen's voice on the radio, and her heart sank a little. It'd been a week since the winery fiasco, and Vic inwardly cringed every time she remembered being tipsy in front of Angie, of needing to be escorted home like some drunken loser. God, how stupid she'd been that day. Pathetic came to mind. She'd not run across Angie since, nor was she anxious to, given that her level of embarrassment was still a code red.

"Unconscious but not moving much air. We've bagged her, but it's not helping much," Angie was saying over the two-way radio. "Pulse is still one hundred and we've started an IV."

Vic grabbed the mic before Liv could get to it. "Did you try the Heimlich?"

"Yes. Several times."

"What about suction?"

"We did, but it didn't work." There was a faint tone of annoyance in Angie's voice. "We're about four minutes out. Anything else you want us to do?"

"No, just get here!"

Vic caught the raised eyebrows and pointed expression from Liv. "What?"

"I'm sure they're doing the best they can."

"Whatever." She didn't have time to hold the paramedics' hands. "Dr. Whitaker." She touched the sleeve of Julie Whitaker's white coat and began hustling her toward the trauma room closest to the ambulance bay, Liv hot on their heels. "We're going to need to prepare for an emergency trach. Liv, please set up a trach tray." She yelled over her shoulder for the secretary at the ER desk to page whatever surgeon was on call.

"I haven't seen a tracheotomy performed on a child before," Julie said in a tight voice, and Vic gave her a steadying pat on her arm. Working on children was trickier and always more emotional than treating adults.

"We've got this, Julie. Just hang close."

Julie Whitaker was a second-year resident and a favorite of Vic's. She was smart, a quick learner, confident with the right amount of humility for a doctor still training in her specialty. She was not quite thirty years old, and on a quiet shift in the ER one evening in early summer, she'd come out to Vic and Liv as a lesbian. It wasn't much of a stretch for Vic to identify with the young resident, because she'd *been* her a dozen years ago. Working her ass off while trying to navigate a social life *and* coming out at the same time.

She explained to Julie that with the girl's oxygen compromised, they didn't have much time. They needed to get her airway open as quickly as possible, and a tracheotomy was probably their only option, since nothing the paramedics tried was working. "We'll need to make an incision right below her Adam's apple and insert a tube into her trachea, hopefully below the lodged piece of candy…" If the candy was lower than that, only surgery could save the girl and she might not make it to the OR. But Vic didn't voice her thoughts. She felt her own pulse racing as the ambulance's siren grew louder and louder until it finally stopped outside the hospital.

Snapping on a pair of sterile gloves, Vic stepped out of the way as Angie and her partner deftly transferred the patient to the trauma table.

"Name?" Vic asked without looking at Angie.

"Emily Johnson. Her parents should be here any minute. They were following us."

"Emily, can you hear me?"

Nothing.

Vic said to the room, "When her parents arrive, I don't want them in here. Got that?" The last thing they needed were hysterical parents on hand, distracting them, bringing an emotional energy that would act as invisible tripwires to Vic and her colleagues.

"Out, out of my way," Vic barked at Angie. Then felt bad, but only for a second or two because there was work to be done and her mind was already there.

Pulling on her stethoscope, she listened to the girl's chest. Faint breath sounds, which was hopeful but not great. "Hand me the laryngoscope," she said to Julie. "And where the hell is the on-call surgeon, anybody know?"

"He's busy on an appendectomy," Liv replied. "Going to be a few more minutes."

Great, Vic thought. They were on their own. She opened the girl's mouth and inserted the laryngoscope, using the small light at the end of it to have a look around. And there it was, a red gooey mess lodged at about her vocal chords. She would need a tracheotomy for sure.

Julie handed her a piece of gauze soaked in Betadine. Vic swabbed the girl's throat with it, took a scalpel from the trach tray and, about an inch-and-a-half up from the sternum, drew a quick and steady incision. With a clang she returned the scalpel to the tray, reached for a blunt instrument so she could separate the tissues covering the trachea, then slid in the plastic tube. Once it was taped into place, she watched Liv attach the other end of it to an oxygen bag.

"Start the O-2 compressions."

They watched as the girl's chest wall began to move easily up and down. A minute later she was taking breaths on her own.

"She's coming around now," Julie said.

"Emily?" The girl's eyelids fluttered open. Vic smiled, softened her voice. "You're in the hospital, but you're going to be okay. You choked on a piece of candy. Just hang tight, honey, and we'll get your parents for you." Vic patted her shoulder. "You're doing great."

Out in the hall, Vic took a deep breath, exhaled the tension and adrenaline that had stiffened her neck and shoulders. There was always, in every serious case, a moment of doubt, when she wasn't sure which way things might go, when it became a tug of war between herself and some other force, the patient the prize at the end of it. The moment things turned on a dime, when the outcome turned predictable and positive, was a moment that could compare to nothing else. It was triumphant, it was validation, it was justice and joy and relief all rolled into one. Most of all, it was a tangible reminder that all her training and education, the sacrifices she'd made, were worth it.

The second best part, she remembered, was telling loved ones that everything was going to be okay. With a spring to her step that she knew would desert her before the next serious call, Vic headed for the waiting room, casting a final glance back at her team. "Nice work, everyone," she said, noticing, for the first time, that Angie was no longer around.

CHAPTER SIX

October ushered in nights that were cooler and longer. In the Cullen family, autumn was a welcome time because the backbreaking fieldwork of grape harvesting and putting the vines to bed was over for another season while the winemaking—the fun part—was in full swing. Most years, the patterns at the winery didn't register much with Angie. Out of high school, she'd gone away to college, then it was eight years in the military as a medic. The last seven, her work as a paramedic with North Flight EMS had pretty much consumed her.

And then there was Brooke. Brooke had demanded an inordinate amount of her attention, her energy. One of their cars needed to go into the shop or a plumber needed to be called, it was always Angie who saw to it. Birthdays that needed remembering, bills to be paid were all details left to Angie. Along with the laundry and most of the cooking and cleaning. Brooke was always too tired for this or that or too busy with her own *important* work (as if Angie's wasn't), her own friends.

Angie's buddy Vince, not trying to sound like a judgmental ass but nevertheless coming across as exactly that, asked her point-blank one day why the hell she put up with Brooke. "Is she that good a lay or what?" Of course Brooke wasn't—not that Angie would admit that to Vince. Her attraction to Brooke wasn't easy to explain. How could she put into words the bright light and its magnetic warmth cast by Brooke when she was in the mood to be fun, adventurous, spontaneous, affectionate? Alternatively, that same dazzling light was mercurial sometimes, too hot, too arbitrary, too unpredictable.

But Angie had been willing to pay the price, to make the sacrifices, because she'd gotten things out of the relationship. Of course she had. Every day she got to look at someone and not see a soldier whose legs had been blown off by an IED. She got to look at someone whose eyes didn't reflect back the bodies destroyed by war or by car crashes or by drugs or illness. Brooke was from a different world, and Angie was nothing if not loyal; she'd made her bed and she would lie in it.

Until Brooke decided to toss a hand grenade into their relationship.

She rolled her window down an inch to let in some of the cool air. It was late, she needed the little jolt to stay awake. Shattenkirk was in the ambulance's driver's seat tonight, and they'd just come from a call that turned out to be a waste of time. It had come in as a stabbing, but when they arrived at the scene, there was no sign of anything. The people had either scattered or it was a hoax, leaving the two of them and a couple of cops milling around for a few minutes looking like they were having a coffee break in the middle of the street.

A be-on-the-lookout bulletin for all emergency services in the city crackled on the radio. A middle-aged suicidal woman had fled Munson's mental health lockdown on foot. A description followed.

Jackson groaned. "Must have missed her happy pill tonight. I mean, I know budgets are tight, but jeez, do they really need to cut back on the meds for the suicides?"

Angie grunted her agreement. She was not only used to the ribald humor in her line of work, but often a participant in it. Cops, firefighters, ER nurses, and doctors shared it as well, this defense mechanism against the ugliness and insanity of their jobs. Making light of a dark situation was sometimes the only thing that buffered them from the pain.

"North Flight to four-three-seven."

Angie picked up the mic. "Four-three-seven, go ahead."

"You clear for a call?"

"Ten-four, North Flight."

A Priority One drug overdose, the dispatcher said, and gave them the address of what Angie knew was a three-story dilapidated rooming house that she'd been called to before. When they arrived, they found an unshaven man in ragged clothes bent over a young woman in a hallway that looked like it hadn't been swept in years. The woman was half sitting, half lying against the stained wall. Angie plugged in the eartips of her stethoscope and put the diaphragm to the woman's chest. Shallow breath sounds. Pulse sixty. Completely unresponsive.

"What did she take?" she said to the man, who wouldn't look her in the eye and who smelled like rancid food.

"She might-a been snortin' heroin earlier. I dunno, man."

"How long has she been like this?"

He tapped a wrist that bore no watch. "Beats me. A few minutes?"

Angie ordered Jackson to prepare a dose of naloxone. When he presented her with the syringe, she stabbed it into the woman's upper thigh and depressed the plunger. Within a minute she stirred, opened her eyes, started mumbling.

Wide-eyed, the man mumbled in surprise, "It's a miracle. A fucking miracle."

"Sometimes it is," Angie replied, taking the woman's vitals again. She was coming around quickly, almost back to normal—whatever that was.

She told the woman she needed to be transported to the hospital to get checked out, but her suggestion was met with a stream of profanity. Jackson looked at Angie with raised eyebrows and Angie shrugged back. They couldn't force her, not without the cops and a special form.

"Suit yourself," Angie said, leaving the young addict with a hard stare and a warning to stay off the drugs. She knew it was wasted breath.

Minutes later, driving near the Eighth Street bridge near Boardman Avenue, Angie spotted a woman on the bridge. The wrong side of the bridge. She was on the concrete ledge, not holding on to the railing, teetering a little, hugging herself against the chill.

"Holy shit, isn't that the suicide from Munson?"

"Yup. Fits the description," Jackson said.

"Stop the rig. And call it in. Get the cops here."

Angie opened the door, but Jackson tugged the sleeve of her jacket. "Wait, where are you going?"

"I think we got a jumper." Angie pulled away from his grip and sprang from the ambulance, figuring her short declaration explained everything, even though she didn't exactly have a plan. She sprinted to the bridge, which spanned the Boardman River. It wasn't more than eighteen, twenty feet to the water, not enough to kill you, but the water had teeth this time of year.

"Don't do it, ma'am," she yelled into the darkness. "I'm here to help. Give me a minute to try to help you, all right?"

The woman, little more than a bundle wrapped in a pink jacket too light to be of much help, disappeared into the dark abyss. "Wait!" Angie's heart pounded against her ribs at the sound of a heavy splash. "Goddammit!"

"Dr. Turner, we've got two patients arriving in about two minutes," Olivia Drake said to Vic through the intercom. She'd been happily dozing in the doctors' lounge but was now instantly alert.

"What've you got, Liv?"

"Our Code White from a couple of hours ago. She jumped off a bridge into the Boardman. Plus we've got a paramedic."

"What?" She rubbed the last of the sleep from her eyes and swung her legs over the cot. A paramedic was one of the patients? She didn't wait to press Liv for more. "I'm on my way."

By the time she reached the emergency department, Julie Whitaker and a nurse had escorted the mental patient into a treatment room. Liv pointed Vic to Room Two. Inside stood Angie Cullen, shivering and wet, a blanket loosely around her shoulders. Her EMS partner was dry, but he paced around and nearly jumped out of his skin when Vic greeted them.

"What happened?"

"Nothing, Doc," Angie said with the kind of expression that said she'd rather be anywhere else but here as a patient. "Nice night for a little swim, that's all. Everything's fine."

"She saved the woman who jumped," said Jackson, his voice infused with adrenaline. "Jumped right in after her and pulled her out of the river!"

Why does this not surprise me? Vic thought. Angie had been to war and was a seasoned paramedic, which meant she was most definitely the hero type. A little cold water wasn't going to scare her. Nor even, probably, the prospect of getting seriously injured. "All right. Jackson, I'm going to need you to step out of the room so I can examine Angie."

Angie held her hand up like a traffic cop. "Oh no, I don't need to be examined. I'm fine. I'm only here because of protocol."

"Protocol or not, we need to make sure you're all right. Jackson? Please inform your supervisor that there'll be a delay in getting you two back into service."

"Um, actually, Doc, Cull here is our crew chief."

Vic shook her head at Angie's nickname. *Really, can't these guys do better than that?* Then she tilted her chin defiantly at Angie and leveled her with her no-bullshit look. "I'm not clearing you to return to work until I check you over. So it's either that or you two can sit here all night until your shift ends."

Angie huffed and sat down on the exam table, making a show of her displeasure. "All right, fine." As Jackson shut the door behind him, she added, "You don't play nice, do you?"

"I play exactly as nice as you."

"That's what I was afraid of," Angie mumbled.

"I want you to take off those wet clothes and put on a disposable gown. I'll go find you some scrubs to wear after we're done. What are you, about five-foot-nine? A hundred and fifty-five pounds?"

"Add half an inch and another seven pounds." Angie almost smiled. "But not bad, Doc."

"I'll be right back."

From the supply closet, Vic grabbed a set of pale green scrubs slightly larger than her own. As much as she didn't want to be reminded of the night when Karen's affair with Brooke had come to light, it seemed she couldn't escape it. Certainly, she couldn't escape it as long as she saw Angie here, in uniform, looking exactly the way she'd looked that night in late August—strong, capable, yet slightly frazzled and out of sorts at the same time. Which, she was sure, was probably driving Angie nuts. Anything that wasn't controlled chaos probably drove her nuts, and that was why she wanted to get straight back to work, wet clothes and all.

Back in the treatment room, Vic set the scrubs on a chair, noticing that Angie was trying not to shiver in the thin paper gown. As much as she wanted to dislike this woman, to not have to be reminded of that shitty night two months ago whenever she saw her, the sane and sympathetic part of her understood that they were both innocent victims. Angie had done no more wrong, had done nothing to deserve what had happened, than she herself had. It was Angie who had reminded her of that when she'd driven her home from the winery a few weeks ago, and now it was her turn to put on her big girl pants.

She retrieved a heavy flannel blanket from a cupboard behind the exam table and handed it to Angie, the other, thinner blanket now saturated with moisture. "Tell me everything that happened tonight. From the beginning, please."

In a calm voice but with slightly chattering teeth, she said she tried to talk the woman off the bridge, but then she jumped without warning. It wasn't a huge drop, but the woman was flailing around in the water, yelling something about not being able to swim. There wasn't time to run around to the riverbed on foot, so she jumped, then hauled the woman to shore.

"Does it hurt anywhere?"

"No, I don't think so. I'm…it's too cold to tell for sure."

With her stethoscope, Vic listened to Angie's heart and lungs. "Did you ingest any water?"

"I don't think so, not much anyway."

Vic took an electronic thermometer from the wall and had Angie insert it into her mouth. While she waited, she placed her hands gently on Angie's jaw and turned her head from side to side, then up and down. It was then she noticed an abrasion behind her ear.

"Do you remember what you hit your head on?"

"No, it was nothing," Angie said around the thermometer in her mouth. "There was a tree limb in the water. It wasn't very big, but it was dark and I didn't see it."

"Headache?"

Angie shook her head as the thermometer beeped. Vic read it. Her body temperature was too cold by more than two degrees.

She examined her back, her shoulders, had her move her limbs, checked her reflexes, and with a scope she looked in her mouth, nose, ears, and eyes.

"Okay, I think we're done. You do know that jumping off a bridge isn't perhaps the wisest thing to do?"

"Save the lecture, Doc. There wasn't an alternative."

If this patient were anyone but a former soldier, given what had happened in Angie's personal life lately, Vic would suggest a psych consult, because her heroics could be an indicator that she cared little for her own personal safety, that she might be depressed or despondent. But she strongly suspected it was simply the way Angie was wired. The woman was action-oriented, consequences be damned.

"So am I going to live?"

Vic sighed lightly, not at Angie but at herself. She'd come to a decision and one that she didn't particularly like. "Yes, you're going to live. But you may have a concussion. You're also a bit hypothermic." She glanced at the wall clock. It was 12:31 a.m. "I want you to put those scrubs on and book the rest of your shift off sick. And then you're coming home with me."

"Excuse me?" Angie's draw dropped open; it was almost comical.

"I'm done with my shift in twenty-nine minutes. You're not well enough to return to work and I don't think you're in any condition to drive home either. I also don't think you should be alone the rest of the night."

"What? Why?" Angie wasn't buying it, but it didn't matter. She either did as Vic said or she could stay overnight in the hospital. And likely on a bed in a busy hallway because the place was crammed with patients tonight, every room occupied.

"Because, as I said, you may have a concussion and you're hypothermic. You need monitoring and you need to stay warm."

Angie clutched the blanket tighter around her, resentment hardening on her face. "Look, all right. I'm cold and wet, but that's it. And I've got a scratch on my head. Other than that, I'm fine, I swear."

Vic was used to patients trying to negotiate with her and she smiled at the futility of it. "Sorry. Not changing my mind no matter what you say. Look, Angie, it's important that you have someone with you for the next six or eight hours. If not me, then I can call someone else for you."

"I'll go straight home."

Vic shook her head. "No, no driving with a concussion. Are you still staying with your folks at the winery?"

"Yes. I'll get a cab."

"And wait for an hour? Maybe longer? Besides, your family is probably all in bed and you should be under observation for a few hours."

"I could sit in the waiting room for a couple of hours. The nurses could keep an eye on me."

"That's not how the protocol works around here and you know it. Besides, the nurses have better things to do than to pop in and out of the waiting room keeping an eye on you. You also need more than a couple hours of monitoring, so nice try."

"I..." Angie shifted uncomfortably. By the defeated look on her face, she knew there was little point in continuing to resist. "Look, I appreciate the offer, but for the record, I don't think it's a good idea."

Vic sat down on the exam table beside Angie. Good idea or not, the offer had been made and she wasn't about to retract it. "Angie, I know things aren't exactly comfortable between us.

And for good reason. But you did help *me* out of a bind, in case you're forgetting."

The tremble in Angie's voice was barely audible, but it surprised Vic. "You don't owe me anything, Vic. Especially since you can barely stand the sight of me."

Vic gasped. Barely stand the sight of her? Where had that come from? It was Karen and Brooke she couldn't stand the sight of. She and Angie were collateral damage. Two unfortunates stranded on the same island of betrayal and pain. They weren't friends, no, but they were hardly enemies. Had no real reason to dislike each other.

Quietly, she said, "Where did you get the idea that I can't stand you?"

"Forget it. Forget I said anything."

Vic thought back to the last time she'd seen Angie. It was last week, the choking child Angie and her partner brought in. She had been curt to Angie. Rude. Even angry. But she'd chalked it up to the stress of the situation. Reaching back further, she remembered how ungrateful she behaved the afternoon Angie drove her home from the winery. She could no longer deny the pattern, because whenever Angie was around, something in her wanted to snap, wanted a place to lay some blame, and it was wrong of her.

"I…" Vic had to swallow to keep her voice from breaking apart. "I'm so sorry, Angie. It's just…I don't know what to do about…what happened. I don't quite know yet how to live with it."

They sat for a couple more minutes before Angie broke the silence. "Me either."

CHAPTER SEVEN

Angie wasn't given a choice of what she wanted to drink, though whiskey would have been her first choice, given the circumstances. You need liquids, warm liquids, Vic had emphasized, and now she set two mugs of herbal tea on the coffee table, one for each of them.

It was hard to get her mind around the fact that she was in Vic's house. Again. "We seem to be kind of stuck with each other lately," she conceded, her mug steaming in front of her. The tea smelled of wildflowers. Or maybe weeds. Something she wouldn't normally drink and that didn't hold a lot of appeal. Coffee was her hot drink of choice. Thick, strong coffee with a healthy dollop of cream, no sugar. It always cleared out her cobwebs.

Vic, at the other end of the sofa, wouldn't meet her gaze. The only light was from a Tiffany lamp in the corner, its colored glass like fine, dazzling jewels.

"I never saw it coming," Vic said so quietly that Angie had to tilt her head to hear clearly. "Did *you*? See it coming, I mean."

"Nope." She sipped her tea, knowing exactly what Vic was referring to. The tea still tasted like the weeds that grew along the edges of the vineyards at her parents' farm, and her brain was no less foggy because of it. "Too stupid to, I guess. Or blind. Or maybe I didn't actually give a shit."

"I like to think we were trusting, not stupid or blind, and that we did give a shit." Vic's eyes glistened with unshed tears and she studied her mug like it was a Picasso. "All of those things—it's how you're supposed to be in a relationship. Isn't it?"

"Tell that to them."

Vic laughed bitterly. "I would, but I can't seem to get Karen on the phone. Her lawyer, however, seems to have all the time in the world to talk to me."

"Figures. I'm sure Brooke put her on to one of her power-tripping lawyer friends. But you know what? I say 'Sayonara, baby!' Good riddance to them both. Let your lawyer talk to her lawyer. That's what I'm doing with Brooke. Hell, you couldn't pay me a million dollars to talk to Brooke right now." What was done was done. There was no sense in rehashing something that was over. Brooke and Karen had insured they'd be granted the last word. And they could have it.

Vic not only wasn't on the same page, she wasn't even reading from the same book. She looked at Angie as though she'd done something as reprehensible as poke a pin in a voodoo doll likeness of their exes—which come to think of it wasn't such a bad idea. "Well, I'd prefer to keep the lawyers out of it. I'd like to just talk to Karen. Find out what's going through her mind, why she…why they…how this happened. I'd like to know what went wrong. Between Karen and me. Don't you want some answers from Brooke?"

Anger swamped Angie like a massive wave pushing her under its surface, rolling her over, pounding her. "Answers? The only answer I need is that Brooke fucked around on me and supposedly fell in love with somebody else. I don't need the whys and hows to know that it's over between us. I don't need to know the reasons for her shitty behavior."

"But sometimes solving a mystery like this detracts from the pain. Makes it easier to heal."

"Maybe for you, but I'll tell you what. On the battlefield, you don't have time to ask why the enemy hates you. Why they're trying to kill you. You have to survive, and to do that, you have to shut everything else down and focus on *only* that, because nothing else matters but what's happening at that very moment."

Vic's lips parted in astonishment. "Angie, this isn't a battlefield."

"Really? Could have fooled me." God, Vic was being naïve. Too many psychology classes in med school. Too much just-talk-it-out-and-you'll-feel-better training.

"And hating them won't make the pain go away."

"The fuck it won't."

Vic drank her tea as though she too found it distasteful, her face twisting into something unpleasant. "Well, hating Karen won't make it any easier for me. What *would* make it easier is figuring out what happened, what went wrong, how Karen feels—felt—about our marriage. You don't just throw ten years out the window because of…because of…"

"Because of fucking around with somebody else for months? Falling in love with someone else? Or lust, or whatever the hell they think it is? Jesus, Vic, they probably screwed right here in this house while you were working nights and I was out of town. You ever think about that? You ever think about them making their little plans to be together? Getting their lies straight? You think they gave two shits about *us*?"

The words were like darts, poison ones, and Vic's tears were proof they'd hit their mark. *Ah crap*, Angie thought. Her head pounded again, and not from the concussion this time. It wasn't easy to make an ER doc cry. Wasn't easy to make a soldier or a paramedic cry either, come to think of it. Well, *she* certainly wasn't going to cry over Brooke and Karen. They could go fuck themselves before that was going to happen.

"Look, I'm sorry." For Vic's sake, Angie tried to soften her voice. "I know being angry like this isn't, I don't know, the healthiest way to handle things. But it's what works for me. At least right now." The anger was the only thing keeping her from breaking apart.

"Is it?"

"What?"

"Working for you?"

She picked up the warm mug again and cradled it between her hands. At least she wasn't shivering anymore, thanks to this dreadful tea and probably because of the quilt Vic had made her wrap herself in and the hot water bottle snugged within.

"Honestly, I don't know if anything would make me feel better right now. But I do know I can't stand the thought of seeing Brooke right now. Or talking to her."

Vic's tears had dried in streaks down her face, her expression unreadable as she gazed blindly into the dim light. Was she feeling regret? Nostalgia? Grief? Hope? The sudden haze of calm about her brought instant alarm to Angie.

Oh no. "Don't tell me you want Karen back?"

Vic took one look at Angie with her short brown hair sticking up at every possible angle and nearly laughed out loud. She would be cute if she wasn't, well, Brooke's ex.

"How are you feeling this morning?"

"Like a truck ran over me."

Vic frowned and took a step closer. "Maybe I should get you back to—"

"No." Angie held up a forestalling hand. "I don't want to go back there. It's only like a pickup truck ran over me, not an eighteen-wheeler. I promise, I'm fine."

"Coffee?" Vic directed her to the kitchen table for two and at Angie's nod began pouring for each of them. "Cream?"

"Yes, please. Thank God you're not forcing me to drink those melted weeds again."

Vic laughed. "It was only chamomile. Not exactly some kind of witch's brew, you know." She placed a small pitcher of cream on the table before Angie. She sat across from her and took a sip of her black coffee while Angie added cream to hers and stirred slowly. "Tell me about your life as an army medic. You were deployed overseas?"

"Twice. Afghanistan and Iraq. Worked out of the main hospital in Kandahar on my first tour. After that I trained as a flight medic. Got tired of doing medevac flights to Landstuhl, Germany, so on my second tour in Iraq I was attached to an Airborne unit doing helicopter medevacs in the field."

Vic couldn't help wincing. "Guess you saw a little bit of everything over there."

"Yup." Angie sipped her coffee and stared at nothing, her eyes opaque shields.

This woman was an enigma, full of shadows, dark corners, bright lights, fury and serenity in constant battle with each other. It was Vic's first clue as to why Brooke might have strayed. Perhaps she'd gotten tired of chipping away at the emotional barriers that Angie had undoubtedly constructed early in their relationship. Ex-soldiers were not the easiest nuts to crack, not the most emotionally available people.

But then neither were front-line emergency medical personnel, Vic knew. How much had she ever revealed to Karen about her work life? About the losses, the near-losses, the heartbreaks or even the successes? She rarely ever talked about her work with Karen, not in any emotional way, because she preferred to shut it off by the time she left the hospital parking lot. It was the only way to separate work from the rest of her life, to keep the drama and pain of the ER from swamping her—or so she'd always told herself. Perhaps what she'd thought was so necessary to her own well-being was the very thing that killed her relationship with Karen.

She thought back to the Karen she'd first fallen in love with. The young, uncomplicatedly ambitious, completely transparent Karen. Then the Karen who grew more distracted, more distant, more self-involved. And more recently, the Karen who, it was obvious now, was merely going through the motions, pretending to be satisfied with her life, with their marriage. All of these versions of Karen rushed at her, reaching through the fog of her grief and misery until she realized she didn't know her wife at all anymore. And by extension, she wondered if she even knew herself very well. After all, hadn't she too grown more distant, more cynical, more self-involved, less emotionally available over the years? Had they both driven each other away without intending to? And then there was Angie, whom Vic had secretly and high-handedly been blaming for driving Brooke into Karen's arms, because she hadn't wanted to acknowledge her own shortcomings as a partner.

"I think I owe you an apology," Vic said on a long sigh.

"For what? I'm the one who owes you my thanks. For taking care of me last night."

"It was the least I could do. Because I don't think I've been treating you very well."

Angie raised her eyebrows but said nothing.

"I think," Vic continued, carefully setting down her mug, "that I was looking for somebody to blame. I wanted it to be your fault that Brooke got involved with Karen. But that's not fair to you, and it doesn't explain Karen's part in it."

"Maybe we're both the bad guys and got what we deserved."

Vic studied Angie's eyes, could see right away that she was playing devil's advocate. "You don't believe that."

"You're right. I don't."

They sat in silence for a few minutes, sipping their coffee, each immersed in the bitter brine of their failed relationships. Vic knew better than to expect a simple, solid, sensible answer for why Karen had done what she did, yet she grasped for one like a lost hiker searching frantically for a trail marker.

Angie broke the silence first. "One thing I learned on my tours is that blame is a waste of time, a waste of resources, a waste of emotional energy. Over there, you didn't always know who your enemy was, because they usually hid in plain sight so that you couldn't tell if someone genuinely wanted to help you or kill you…The market vendor who wouldn't meet your eyes, for instance. I mean, what was he planning? Or was he just scared? And even if the enemy did present himself, it was always a mystery to me why he wanted to kill me. I mean *me*, Angela Cullen. Killing is a very personal thing, you know? Why me?"

She shook her head before continuing. "It was personal to me, but it wasn't to the guy who wanted to kill me. Sometimes it was for ideological reasons, sometimes the killer was being paid to lay down a bomb or coerced into wearing a suicide vest. You did what you could to survive over there and you didn't waste time trying to figure out the whys and hows. And I'm sorry I didn't explain that very well last night."

"So Brooke and Karen, it was more about them and not us? That it wasn't personal? Is that what you're saying?"

"Oh, it was personal, all right. Or at least, the result was. But, yes, the more I think about it, the more I think that what happened was more about them and not about us."

"Huh." Vic finished her coffee. Maybe Angie was right. Maybe Brooke and Karen answered something in one another that had nothing to do with her and Angie.

"Can I use your shower? And wear these scrubs home?"

"Of course."

"I should get going. If I have medical clearance, that is." Angie winked to undoubtedly smooth the bumpy road their conversations last night and this morning had taken.

"You do, but I don't want you to go back to work for a couple of days."

"I don't know about that. Work is kind of my salvation right now."

"I hear you. It is for me too, but you need to rest for a couple of days, make sure you don't have headaches before you go back, all right? And if you develop a fever, I want to see you right away."

Angie turned to head up the stairs but halted before the first step. "Vic?"

"Yes?"

"Do you think we're becoming friends?"

The question came as a surprise. Were they? And if so, was it such a terrible idea? They'd both been deserted, left behind to pick themselves up and lick their wounds, a couple of soldiers in a foxhole who'd have to make their own way out across the minefields and back to friendly territory.

"I think," Vic said, "that I could kind of use a friend."

"Me too." Angie's smile was a revelation; Vic didn't remember if she'd ever seen her do it. Her whole face relaxed into it, even her eyes, until it made her look kind, loyal, as though she were fully prepared to pick you up and carry you to safety through enemy fire, if that's what it took. Vic found that her breath had stalled somewhere in her chest, so slammed was she by this new side of Angie.

"So," Angie continued, "since we're friends and all, are you available Monday to come out to the winery for a private tour? We're closed to the public that day, but I happen to have the keys to the place."

"I'll make myself available." Vic grinned, feeling a tinge of embarrassment in her cheeks. "If I'm welcome back there, that is."

"Of course you are. Make it noon."

"All right. And I promise I won't need you to drive me home this time."

Angie laughed. "After last night, I'd say we're even."

CHAPTER EIGHT

Angie wasn't surprised her luck had run out. She'd managed to tour Vic around a couple of the fields on a two-seater ATV and then into the storage room where the red wine was fermenting. They were about to head to the tasting room when her sister-in-law Claire rounded a corner and practically collided with them.

Claire had the good grace to quickly hide her shock at seeing Vic again. Her slick manners were one of the reasons why she was the company's unofficial ambassador and public relations whiz. But Angie should have known better than to think she'd get away with squiring a woman around the premises. Especially when that woman was Victoria Turner.

"You must be Dr. Turner." Claire smiled and warmly shook Vic's hand. "It's my pleasure to meet you. Welcome. Again. I'm Claire Cullen, Angie's sister-in-law."

"Nice to meet you, Claire, and thanks, but please call me Vic." She cast her eyes around, surveying the massive steel tanks, their various tubing and spigots. "I love it here, it's gorgeous. And I especially love that view to the bay. It's so quiet here."

"It's only this quiet on Mondays, but I agree, it is gorgeous." Claire was adept at engaging people's trust, and Angie noticed Vic lean in almost imperceptibly as Claire added, "Angie's told me a bit about you."

And here comes the inquisition, the part where Claire takes over as new best friend and confidante. Angie fought to suppress her irritation, surprised to realize that she wanted Vic all to herself. "We're going to the tasting room for a glass of wine and some munchies. I'd ask you to join us, but I'm sure you've got a lot to do." She shot her sister-in-law a private look that told her to get lost in the nicest possible way.

"Oh, yes, you're right, I do have things to do. Especially with Nick and your parents away today." The three had gone to check out a cherry orchard north of Petoskey that the family was considering purchasing, thanks to their new plans to start making cherry cider. Claire whispered to Angie, "You almost got away with sneaking her in."

"'Bye, Claire," Angie said pointedly before steering Vic toward the tasting room. "Sorry about that."

Vic hopped up on one of the leather-upholstered barstools. "What are you sorry about?"

"My nosy sister-in-law." Angie pulled down two wine goblets. "What's your pleasure?"

Vic leaned her elbows on the bar, the kind of mischief in her smile reminiscent of a kid playing hooky from school. "Ooh, I love the merlot, but what else do you recommend? And I like Claire. She obviously cares about you. You're lucky."

Angie rarely thought about how lucky she was to have family so close and so involved in her life. More often she considered them smothering, overly involved in her business, constantly inviting her to family dinners, regularly pressuring her to become a partner in the business (although they mostly stopped doing that after she hooked up with Brooke). She paused at the double refrigerator that held several dozens of bottles of red wine, keeping them chilled at sixty degrees. "The 2012 pinot noir is pretty spectacular."

"That sounds enticing. I'll try that."

Angie poured them each a generous glass. From a jar underneath the bar she dumped out some of her mom's famous spiced and roasted pecans into a pottery dish. "I take it your family's not as involved in your business as mine is."

"You can say that again." Vic tilted her head back and slowly, pleasurably, swallowed a mouthful of wine. Her neck was long and smooth—silk came to Angie's mind—and it was one of those moves that was sexy without meaning to be. "Oh, this *is* spectacular."

Angie came around the bar and claimed the stool beside Vic's. She swirled the wine in her own glass before taking a healthy sip. It was perfect. Medium body with hints of raspberry, cherry, and chocolate with a fruity finish. "Is your family back in Chicago?"

"I'm not sure. I guess so."

Angie raised her eyebrows questioningly but didn't speak. She resisted prying into peoples' lives, mostly because she hated it when people pried into hers. It was up to Vic to share her history—or not.

"I didn't know my father. My mom raised me. My first year of college, she walked in on me kissing another girl. That was it for her. She kicked me out. I put myself through the rest of college and then medical school."

"Jeez, that must have been rough. I'm sorry. Did you ever try to reconcile?"

"Once, yes, right before I graduated from medical school. I went to her house. She slammed the door in my face and I haven't seen her since."

"Wow. Harsh." Angie sipped her wine and tried to imagine having nobody. At least, nobody who'd known her all her life. Nobody who supported and loved her unconditionally. When she came out to her family at the end of high school, they were protective, worried for her, but they never stopped loving her and certainly never thought less of her. "I'd have thought your mom would be proud of you, being a doctor and all."

Vic laughed without pleasure. "My mother can only see one thing, and that's that I'm a lesbian."

"Wow," Angie said again, knowing how inadequate her response was, but it was stunning how people could be so close-minded, so mean, to people they were supposed to love. "I'm surprised you're not a raging alcoholic."

"How do you I'm not?"

"Ah…"

Vic threw her head back and laughed. "I'm not, don't worry. But I do find comfort in other things. I play tennis. I love to sail."

"Really? You have a sailboat?"

"I do. She's in dry dock now for the winter. Just a little twenty-one footer. I call her *Genome*. Genie for short."

"Genome, that's cute. I've always wanted to sail."

"Then let's do it next spring, when I get her back in the water. Come sail with me!"

There was a spark in Vic's eyes when she talked about sailing, the gray in them now edged with green the color of a bright sea.

"I'd love to. But only if you teach me everything you're doing."

"Absolutely." Vic sipped her wine and kept her eyes on Angie. "Now that I've told you mine, what's your salvation? Besides work?"

Angie didn't have a lot of hobbies besides running. And reading. "Here I guess. The farm, the winery."

Vic glanced around. "I can see why. It's wonderful here. You never wanted to join the family business?"

"Not really. Believe me, they tried. Everything from bribery to guilt until they finally figured out I'm more of an adrenaline junkie than a farmer."

"Gee," Vic said with a teasing note in her voice, "I wouldn't know anything about that."

Angie laughed. ER docs were every bit the adrenaline junkies that paramedics, soldiers, cops, and firefighters were. She looked at Vic, really looked at her as though trying to memorize every line, every curve, every subtle movement. Claire was right; Vic was nice looking. And not simply because of her pretty eyes and the alluring dimples when she smiled, but because there was something honest in her face, something straightforward, uncomplicated, an unspoken contract that said the outside matched the inside. Which meant somebody good, decent, somebody you wanted to know. *What a waste*, Angie thought, *that this woman should have spent so many years with someone who didn't appreciate her.*

She cleared her throat and decided it was time to push Vic on the question she'd tried to ask her the other night. "So. You didn't answer my question the other night. At your place."

Vic figured she'd successfully dodged the question and her heart sank at its resurfacing. She decided to play dumb. "Which question is that?"

"About Karen. Whether you want to try to get back together."

She tried to gauge Angie's tone and how much judgment was in it. In her eyes too. She wavered for a moment, wondering if the question was academic or serious. Then it struck her that Angie wasn't the type to ask rhetorical questions.

"I don't know." It was the truth.

Something flared in Angie's eyes, but it was gone before Vic could get a read on it. Probably condemnation. Angie hadn't disguised the fact that she wanted nothing more to do with her ex, that the damage and the hurt exacted by the affair was irreparable. And unforgivable. But that was Angie and she was entitled to her own feelings. Life, Vic had learned a long time ago, wasn't that simple. Or at least, people weren't. There was a lot more gray in the world than black or white.

Angie contemplated her drink. "Then I'm guessing that means you'd like to try."

"Maybe, maybe not. I honestly don't know because I haven't been able to exchange more than a couple of words with her since everything went down." Vic took another sip of wine, then popped a couple of nuts into her mouth. "What are you and Brooke doing with your house?"

"She's buying out my share. I've already moved my stuff out and put it into storage."

"Does that mean you're staying here awhile longer?"

"Only until I find a place of my own. I have to decide whether I want to rent or buy. What about you? You're obviously keeping the house."

"Karen wanted out of everything we bought together. Wants a clean break, I guess. I understand that she's moved into an apartment across town." She tried to picture the place and wondered how much Karen had invested of herself in it. Or was it merely window dressing to make it look like she wasn't living with Brooke? Which she probably was. Vic had driven past Brooke's house a few times, Liv having told her where it was, and sure enough, Karen's car had been there.

"I guess that tells you right there what her intentions are."

"Maybe, but I don't give up easily. Marriage means something to me, you know? Relationships, years together, shared memories. They matter. You don't throw all those away for nothing."

"Nothing?" Angie's face tightened. "You call what they did to us nothing? Months of carrying on behind our backs? They're a couple now, for Christ's sake. They want nothing more to do with us. Which is exactly fine with me."

Vic had to swallow the roughness in her throat. It did not please her that Karen continued to hold this kind of power over her, especially in front of the take-no-prisoners Angie Cullen. "You've made it clear how you feel. But I want to be sure it's over between us, that's all. I…I can't put it behind me until then."

Angie's mouth slid open. She closed it with a loud crunch of her teeth. "Suit yourself, but it's obvious that barn door has closed, as my father would say."

Heat blazed a trail through Vic's chest and into her cheeks and up to the tips of her ears. "Well, if you're so sure everything is in the past, why don't you start dating? Move on with your life?" *Instead*—Vic wished she had the guts to say—*of hiding out at your family's home and being so bitter?*

Angie smiled. A lazy, lopsided smile that reminded Vic of a cowboy with one leg on the fence rail and a blade of grass tucked firmly between his teeth. The look was brazen, ballsy, unapologetic. "What makes you think I haven't?"

Vic felt her own mouth drop in surprise, the way Angie's had a moment ago. "You *are*?" *Jesus.* She'd not been serious challenging Angie to date again, and it hadn't occurred to her that Angie could be so callous, so insensitive. It'd only been seven weeks! Well, seven weeks and two days, but who was counting?

Angie's smile fell away and she shook her head. "No, I'm not. But maybe I should. I'd have every right to. And so would you."

"The thought of it makes me nauseous."

Angie topped up their glasses. "Why?"

"Why? Are you kidding? I don't even know what dating is like anymore. And even if I was brave enough, which I'm not, I just…I can't imagine being with someone else. At least not yet. It's way too soon."

"You can date somebody without sleeping with them, you know."

Vic thought about that and her stomach roiled. Aside from Karen, she'd only slept with two other women—her first girlfriend in college and then another woman in her final year of medical school. She wasn't ready to think about sleeping with somebody. And as for the whole dating thing without sex, well, who did Angie think she was kidding? It was like wine without cheese. A boat without a sail. A book with no pages. It simply didn't ring true. "I thought sex is supposed to be the whole point of dating."

Angie looked at her, then broke down in laughter. Deep, howling laughter. "And I thought you said you didn't know anything about dating. Oh, wait, I get it. You watch *The View* every day and read *Cosmo* religiously."

"Ha, ha, very funny. I don't know anything about dating and I don't watch that TV show or read that silly magazine, but I do have ears, and that's the way everyone at the hospital talks about it. That you're not really dating if you're not sleeping with the person. Everything seems to come down to sex. *Always.*"

"Not always." Angie grinned. "This isn't. What we're doing."

Vic forgot to breathe. She'd gotten comfortable hanging out with Angie and not thinking about sex. But now it was out there and couldn't be reeled back in. It was like someone reminding you as you obliviously hiked through the mountains that you were fourteen thousand feet up and that falling over the edge that was just visible beyond the thin stand of trees would mean certain death.

"Sorry." Angie seemed to sense her discomfort, and it was as though the light in the room had suddenly been extinguished. Both, it seemed, understood that talking about sex, sex that wasn't and wouldn't happen between them or with anyone else in the near future, served as a reminder of what their exes had done and were doing together. Sex was a subject between them that would have to remain off limits.

"It's okay. Really."

They sipped their wine, the silence broken only by the crunching of the roasted pecans being chewed. Finally, Angie said, "All right, let's make a deal. Let's at least start taking notice of cute, single women."

"Oh no, wait, I don't—"

"Seriously. I'm not talking about dating. In fact, forget I even said anything about dating. I'm talking about looking. Sort of. Like, not *looking* looking, but secretly looking. Like pretending you're staring at the computer when you're really looking at the cute woman standing beyond it. Or you're staring out the window and a woman walks by and she doesn't even know you're looking. Or if she does, she thinks you're lost in thought. If that doesn't work and you get caught, like, *nakedly* staring at a woman, like totally undressing her with your eyes, you apologize and say you thought she was somebody else."

"You're funny, you know that?" Vic hadn't expected Angie to have such an engaging sense of humor.

"I can be, I guess, though I haven't felt very funny the last few weeks." She held her glass up. "Now let's clink glasses and be merry and seal our little deal."

With only the slightest bit of hesitation, Vic touched her glass to Angie's. *What the hell. Looking never hurt a damn thing.*

CHAPTER NINE

Angie didn't flip on the siren, but with the roof lights engaged, she swung the ambulance around in a U-turn and sped toward the mall parking lot she and Jackson had been dispatched to. The call wasn't a Priority One, but it was the type that could go south if they took too long getting there. It came in as a twenty-year-old woman who had been struck with an asthma attack while shopping with friends.

The patient was sitting on a curb, hunched over, flanked by her two friends. Worry etched on their faces as they rubbed her back and whispered encouragingly to her.

Angie knelt in front of the patient. "Hey there, I'm Angie Cullen. You're not feeling too well, huh? What's your name?"

Pale, her chest rising and falling starkly with each breath, the young woman squeezed out, "Danielle."

"Danielle, can you make it into the back of the ambulance with us, or do we need to get the stretcher?"

The woman started to rise, a good indication, and let Angie and Jackson guide her to the bench in the back of the rig. But she struggled to breathe, and her bottom lip looked bee-stung.

"What happened before you got sick?" Angie kept her voice calm and steady but insistent. "Were you exposed to anything like perfume or lotion? Did you eat anything unusual?"

"I...I...ate a couple of peanuts."

Jackson took Danielle's pulse and wrapped a blood pressure cuff around her arm. "Are you normally allergic to peanuts?"

She shook her head, crying softly.

You are now, Angie thought, and asked Danielle if it was okay to unbutton her blouse. When she pushed the fabric aside, right away she saw the raised welts on her stomach. "All right," she said to Jackson. "Let's get her on a Ventolin mask. I'll start an IV so we can get some epi and some Benadryl in her." To the patient, she said, "Danielle, you're going to be okay. You're in anaphylactic shock, but we're going to get some medicine in you to counter it. And the breathing mask will help you too. We're going to take you to the hospital as well so they can check you out, okay?"

She nodded through the wheezing and Angie patted her shoulder reassuringly.

At the hospital, Julie Whitaker took the handoff. She and Angie had not exchanged more than a few pleasantries and some small talk since Angie had rejoined regular paramedic duties in August. Now, as Angie took a closer look at her, she wondered why she hadn't tried to engage the young doctor in more conversation. Julie seemed nice. And she was definitely cute. And she was supposed to start noticing these things, as per the deal she'd struck with Vic. "These things" being cute women. Well, preferably cute, *single* women, of course. She wasn't Brooke with her apparent weakness for married women. *Christ.*

"Nice work," the cute doc said to her a few minutes later, her smile friendlier than usual.

"Our patient going to be okay?"

"Absolutely. But she would have been in real trouble if you hadn't helped her when you did. Even five more minutes might have made things real interesting."

"Well, I'm just glad her friends called for help right away. But thank you." Angie's tongue began to thicken, as though she were suddenly the one in anaphylactic shock. She'd never been nervous in front of Julie before, but now she was. And all because she'd decided she was cute. And because she was supposed to take note of cute women. *Damn it, why did I ever suggest that stupid deal?*

"You, um, enjoying being back on regular duties?"

It took Angie a minute for the question to register, so caught up was she in the embarrassment—and the flicker of enjoyment—of noticing an available woman and engaging in conversation that strayed into the personal. Maybe, *maybe*, there was hope that she could move on from Brooke some time in the not-too-distant future. She'd been full of bravado talking with Vic about dating and noticing women a week ago. False bravado, phony confidence. But now it actually seemed like a possibility, and though it was one that scared her, it didn't actually terrify her anymore.

"I am." *Say something besides one-syllable words, you dork.* "I mean, teaching was a challenge I really enjoyed, but the street is where I feel I do the most good. The classroom's not really the place for me. It's too…stagnant. Too boring." Her ears began to ring at how rehearsed her words sounded, but Julie kept looking at her as though she'd actually said something interesting.

"Good, I'm glad. We like having you around here, you know."

"Ah, there you are." It was Vic, rounding a corner and making a beeline toward them. "I heard you'd brought a patient in."

"I did. And Dr. Whitaker here was just telling me what a fine job I did."

"Well, I wouldn't want to interrupt *that*." Vic's smile reached right up into her eyes. It was the happiest Angie had seen her since, well, everything. Maybe she too was beginning to turn a page, and Angie was dying to ask her if she had started noticing other women. Had maybe even begun flirting with them too.

"No," Angie teased. "It's not every day a doctor tells me I did a good job. I have to savor them, they're so rare."

"Ah, you poor thing," Vic teased. "Starved for affirmation and compliments from us mean doctors, huh?"

"Yes. I should make you two buy me lunch one of these days to make up for all your ball busting."

Julie brightened, opened her mouth to say something, then clamped it shut. It was uncanny how much the two women looked alike standing next to one another. Julie was a decade younger, her blond hair a shade lighter, her eyes more hazel than gray, and she was a couple of inches shorter than Vic. But they could be sisters. Or cousins. So if she thought Julie was cute…*oh shit*. Did that mean she thought Vic was cute too? And if so, was she even allowed to think of her that way? What the hell did the rules say about thinking your ex-girlfriend's new girlfriend's ex-wife was cute? Her head spun. *Damn it, why did I have to start looking at women again? And why can't doing so be uncomplicated?*

"Come on," Vic said, touching the sleeve of Angie's jacket. "I'll walk you back to your rig. I'm afraid lunch will have to wait for another time. We've just had one of the docs on the next shift call in sick."

She waved goodbye to Julie, who waved back with that enthusiastic smile still on her face. It felt like trouble. But it felt kind of good too. "Thank you for rescuing me."

"Rescuing you from what?"

"Another couple of minutes and I think I might have asked the cute Dr. Whitaker out on a date. Or she might have asked me. And we're only supposed to be looking, right?"

"What?" Vic looked like she didn't have a clue what Angie was talking about.

"Julie. She's cute. And we made a deal, remember? We're supposed to start noticing cute women. I can't believe I never really noticed her before."

"I…*Julie?*"

"Yes. Julie. As in Whitaker. As in cute. That's all I'm saying."

"Oh."

"What?" Had she said something wrong?

"I…" Vic was a million miles away. Or she was annoyed with her. "Nothing."

Angie studied her, hoping to solve the puzzle of why she was so obviously displeased by the subject. Surely she wasn't upset that she found Julie cute. That would be…weird. Possessively weird, as in jealous. So, no, that couldn't be it. *She's probably just having a busy day, distracted by a hundred things.*

"Well, there's my bus," Angie said, pointing to her ambulance sitting in the bay and Jackson standing impatiently next to it. "Call me some time. Come up to the peninsula and we'll drink more wine. Or do something healthy like go for a run. It smells so nice with the leaves falling." Angie didn't want to go and yet she wanted to get the hell away as fast as she could.

"Oh…right." Vic pulled together a smile. "Sounds great."

Even though it was dinnertime, Vic wasn't hungry. Mostly because it'd been too busy this afternoon for her stomach to have time to register the fact that it hadn't had any food all day, and now she couldn't muster the interest in food. Julie and Liv had been run off their feet too, all three of them working a couple of extra hours, thanks to a flu bug knocking down staff like flies. Not only had a doctor called in sick for the evening shift, but so had one of the nurses. Vic chose a garden salad for her tray. And a much-needed cup of coffee.

"Honey, you need to be gaining some weight back, not losing more," scolded Olivia, in line behind her and watching her like a hawk.

"I'm forty. Trust me, my skinny days are behind me for good."

Olivia made a face and asked for the hot turkey on a bun with fries and gravy. "Well, so are mine, but what the hell. You only live once. I can be skinny again when I'm dead."

In spite of her gray mood, Vic laughed. She wasn't sure why she felt like a balloon that had been punctured by a pin the size of a tire iron. She'd been content most of the day—and content these days felt like the next best thing to happy. Now she felt like shit again—grumpy, exhausted, joyless—and yet it wasn't fair to blame it on Angie. Angie was being…normal. Angie was noticing other women. Flirting with other women. She was moving on with her life, and good for her. It was right that she should, wasn't it? Just because she herself didn't feel like—

"Oh, look, there's Julie sitting alone," Liv said. "Let's join her."

Julie moved her tray to make room. "Boy, isn't this turning out to be a day?"

"Hey, thanks for agreeing to stay late," Vic said. She could have ordered Julie to help out, but Julie had volunteered. It was better that way.

"Not like I have anything else to do on a Saturday night."

"Well, I do," Olivia supplied. "My wife is sitting at home with a glass of wine that has my name on it."

Vic patted her friend's hand. "It was good of her to let us keep you. Tell her I'll buy her an entire bottle of wine."

"Ooh, a bottle of Sunset Bay wine?" Olivia waggled her eyebrows. She knew Vic and Angie had become friends.

Julie leaned in. "That's the winery Angie Cullen's family owns, isn't it?"

"It is," Vic said. "It's good wine too."

"Well, I wouldn't expect anything less." Julie looked all dreamy and dopey suddenly, like a high school girl with a secret crush. "She sure is *hot*, isn't she?"

Olivia coughed on the milk she'd just gulped. "Like, hell yeah! I can see her muscles under that uniform. Mmm-mmm. And those brown eyes you could absolutely curl up in, like wrapping yourself in a warm blanket on a cold night." She nudged Vic. "Don't you think so, V?"

"What? Angie?" It was…inappropriate talking about her that way. And, and…weird. And, just, no! It was not how she wanted to think about Angie Cullen. Not at all!

"Well," Julie said. "She seems nice too. And I was thinking, like, you know, maybe I'd ask her out on a date some time."

Vic's insides turned to molten lava. She pinned Julie with her eyes, not meaning to, but it was too late as she watched Julie shrink before her.

"I mean, if you think it's not too soon. Or, you know, too weird or something." Julie's body language, her eyes, pleaded with Vic not to skewer her simply for giving voice to the idea of dating Angie. "I wouldn't if it would make anyone uncomfor—"

"Honey, I think it's a fabulous idea," Olivia said. "That girl needs to move on from…" She glanced quickly at Vic to include her too. "From all that awfulness. You can't stay in a place of hurt and betrayal forever. I think you should go for it. And if it is too soon, I'm sure Angie would tell you."

Wait, Vic wanted to say. It *was* too soon. How could anyone think otherwise? Two months. Two crappy little months after years of being with the same person. Was eight weeks the current shelf life on grieving for the end of a relationship? On healing from such devastating hurt? And if so, who the hell had decided all that? And why hadn't she gotten the memo?

She pushed her half-eaten salad aside and stood, her appetite gone. "Sorry, I just remembered I'm supposed to check on the patient in Three."

She pushed her chair out and made her retreat before Olivia and Julie could say anything to stop her. And she refused to glance back at Liv and see the alarm on her face, or worse, pity. She hurried down the hall, the colored stripes on the wall that directed visitors to various areas of the hospital a blur as her rubber-soled sensible shoes squeaked on the polished floor. There was no actual urgency in her task, so before she got to the Emergency Department, she ducked into a supply closet and leaned on a plush pile of towels and blankets that still smelled of detergent.

What the hell was wrong with her? She had no right to be rattled by Julie wanting to ask Angie out on a date. No right whatsoever. She was being…what? Jealous, territorial, childish, petty? Or was she simply being cautious, careful, protective of herself and, by extension, Angie? She liked to think it was the latter, yet why did her stomach feel like a washing machine on spin cycle? And why the hell did it matter so much that Angie seemed so eager to move on while she herself stayed stuck in… in this miserable place?

She brought a towel to her face, smelled it, held it to her cheek. Angie Cullen could go ahead and date whomever the hell she wanted, because Angie and Brooke hadn't been married. Angie hadn't been with Brooke for half as long as she and Karen had been together. Angie obviously hadn't loved Brooke the way Vic had—or thought she had—loved Karen. No, she told herself, there was no comparison. And as much as she thought Angie understood her and sympathized with her, she was wrong. She was in this thing all by herself.

The absence of Karen ambushed her with such force that her breath caught and her eyes began to fill with tears. She'd never felt so alone.

CHAPTER TEN

Coffee. That's all it was, Angie told herself. Although, admittedly, it was coffee with a good-looking, single woman. So. Okay. Maybe it could be construed as more. Like, a date. Which it wasn't. Not really. She sipped her overpriced mocha latte and tried to focus on what Julie was saying. Something about taking flying lessons.

"What do you like to do in your time off?" Julie asked. "For hobbies?"

Oh, Jesus. This was the part where she got to feel inadequate with her lame interests that couldn't come close to exotic hobbies like flying lessons. "Um, well, I…Let's see. I like running. And I'm a big reader. And I help out my folks a lot at the winery." She liked to dabble in fiction writing, but that was her little secret. Well, Brooke knew a little bit about it, but Brooke hadn't been particularly encouraging. "You realize," she'd said in that razor-sharp tone she'd honed to perfection practicing law, "that there is no money in writing." Like money was all that mattered, the only thing of value.

"Ooh, a woman who reads." Julie's eyes glinted with fresh interest. "What do you like to read?"

"Ah…" It hadn't been this hard talking with Vic about the things she enjoyed doing, especially reading. This was more like a job interview. Or a matchmaking questionnaire. "Um. I like biographies and histories. I just finished one on the Civil War."

A frown formed on Julie's forehead.

"And Zadie Smith," Angie added, hoping to score a point. "I love her fiction, especially her most recent." So did Vic. They'd exchanged texts last week about Smith's novel, what they liked and hadn't liked about it, even rating it (five out of five stars from Angie, four-and-a-half from Vic).

"Can't say I'm familiar with her." A tenuous smile. "I guess with my line of work, it's mostly medical journals I read. Short stories, now those I'd probably have time to read."

So why don't you? "I see. Any favorites?" It was mean of her to push the topic, but Angie wanted to punish Julie for not sharing her love for books.

"Sorry?"

"Short story authors."

"Oh, um, not really."

"Alice Munro? George Saunders? Flannery O'Connor? Julian Barnes?" Angie had read them all.

Julie shook her head, the names clearly failing to register. "I guess I haven't read much since high school."

Angie sipped her latte, shifted a little in her seat, wishing for a way out of this. She could be home with a bowl of popcorn watching an old Katharine Hepburn comedy, for God's sake, or cracking a new novel from her to-read pile. Julie was most definitely nice, so that wasn't the reason she wished this little date was over. Good-looking too. In fact, she looked damned amazing in her tight jeans and a scoop-necked sweater that hinted at the gentle swell of the goods below. Her hair, shoulder length, was pulled back in a youthful, delightful ponytail. But the more the silence between them stretched, the more Angie felt like she'd been tossed into the middle of someplace she didn't belong. Or at least, with some*one* she didn't belong.

Julie, apparently, possessed no such reservations. She kept looking at Angie with a glint in her eye, with an expectant kind of interest. With thoughts, Angie was sure, that coffee was merely the appetizer, the warm-up to something a little more intimate. And could she blame her for thinking that way? She'd kind of led Julie down the garden path, what with wearing her brand-name designer jeans and square-toed leather boots and her most expensive sweater, the one she liked to think showed off her shoulders to maximum advantage. They'd both showed up at the café looking very much like this was an official first date.

"I don't mean to pry," Julie said quietly. "But you and Vic Turner seem to have become friends."

"Yes. We have."

"I guess it must, you know, help to be able to talk to someone in the same situation? I mean…I guess it makes sense."

It was a nuisance that everybody at the hospital and at her workplace knew her business. Each sympathetic glance, every whisper in her direction, was a personal affront to her. Traverse City was really more like a small town. Ditto for the hospital and emergency services. Everybody, sooner or later, came to know everybody else's business, good or bad, and everybody's turn came round eventually as the subject of all that burning gossip. It was inevitable that her and Vic's situation would be talked about. Talked to death, probably, until it lost its power to entertain or arouse and something juicier came along. It was what it was and Angie had no control over it, nor had she the interest anymore in letting it get her down. It was wasted energy to worry about what others thought or said.

She shifted again in her chair. Julie wasn't being judgmental. She was actually being kind of nice about it, but it didn't inspire Angie to want to disclose much. "It does help a bit."

When it was clear that was all she had to say on the matter, Julie smiled nervously and said, "Good, I'm glad."

Each woman retreated into her own thoughts until the silence became a chasm between them. Then they both started talking at once.

"You know, it's very kind of you to—"
"Do you think maybe you would—"
They both laughed.
"I think what I'm trying to get at," Julie said around a smile, "is that I'd really like to get to know you better. If, you know, you'd be interested in that. If it's not too soon to, like, go on a real date."

A real date. Angie pondered the meaning of that. Dinner? A movie? And what about afterward? Would sex be an expectation? A fine bead of sweat began to break out on her forehead.

"Um…"

Vic shuffled along behind her shopping cart, surprised to find herself surrounded by shelf after shelf of canned soup. It was a veritable mountain of canned soup—vegetable soups, creamed soups, stews. The only soup she ate was the freshly made kind from the deli section. Which showed, she thought with renewed frustration, that work seemed to be the only thing she was capable of focusing on these days. When she wasn't at work, her thoughts crashed around like a pinball. And it wasn't just the supermarket where she found herself dazed and confused, losing her train of thought or forgetting her purpose. Two days ago she'd gotten momentarily lost while driving home from work, ending up in some new subdivision that seemed to have endless cul-de-sacs and streets named after every possible kind of tree.

Enough already, she told herself. *Enough brooding and feeling sorry for yourself.* It had been nine weeks, and while she knew there was no magic number, no jail sentence with a finite date, she was tired of spinning her wheels, of alternating between hoping Karen would come back to her and silently begging to be free of the specter of their relationship. She wanted all this behind her once and for all, and yet she knew how unlikely that was to happen anytime soon. The settlement continued to grind its way through the lawyers and Karen, *still,* chose to ignore her messages. And so Vic's purgatory continued.

She rounded the corner, her cart bumping into another cart with a shrill metallic clang. Her mouth opened to apologize as her eyes rose. And settled on Karen. Karen and Brooke. For a moment, time seemed to stand still. Vic was paralyzed with indecision. Turn and run like hell or acknowledge the situation?

"Vic." Karen broke the awkwardness, her smile tight, like a string pulled to the breaking point. "Close call, huh? Sorry, I, we...weren't paying attention."

No, Vic thought, you weren't. *You weren't paying attention to a lot of things, Karen. And neither, apparently, was I!*

Brooke, her lipstick and eye makeup perfectly applied, her perfume faint but smelling undeniably expensive, extracted herself with a feeble excuse—she needed to hit the produce section before the cantaloupes got picked over, she said—and disappeared. Karen looked over her shoulder a little too frantically, a little too panicky, as if willing Brooke to return to her side. *Pathetic*, Vic thought with a small measure of satisfaction.

"Karen, why won't you answer my calls? All I want to do is—"

"What do you want me to say, Vic? What is there to talk about that our lawyers can't deal with?"

"What is there to talk about?" Everything, Vic wanted to shout. *Ten years worth of stuff, if you want to be more precise, including three years of marriage. But if you really want to narrow it down, we could just talk about why you started screwing around with Brooke.* Oh, she wished she had the guts to say those things, but decorum won out. This wasn't the time or place for a good verbal jousting.

Karen clutched her cart tightly, as though it might shield her. "Look, I'm sorry, all right? I'll rent a billboard if you want. But I'm where I want to be. I'm *with* the person I want to be with. And I am sorry it came as a shock to you, but I'm moving on and I wish you would too. It's the way it has to be."

Moving on? Was that the salient point in all this? The only thing to do? "I see. The Best Before date on our marriage had expired so it was time to move on?"

Karen's face tightened, the ropey muscles of her jaw working in protest. "We're not doing this here."

"Then where? Since you won't answer my calls."

"I'm not answering your calls because I don't want to be dragged into doing some kind of autopsy on our marriage," she hissed. "It's pointless, Vic. It's over."

Vic felt her mouth curl into a vicious smile. Now she got it. "You're a coward, Karen. That's why you won't talk to me. You're afraid it might burst your little pleasure bubble with Brooke. That it might force you to take some responsibility in all this, to have to examine your own flaws."

Karen began to move away, jerking her cart around, her eyes madly searching for Brooke.

"Fine," Vic said to her retreating back. "Run. You're good at that."

Her groceries abandoned in the store, Vic sat in her car trying to calm down, trying to dam up the tears that felt the size of a golf ball in her throat. She had been prepared to measure the months-long affair against the decade of their relationship, to weigh one against the other, the scale heavy on one end, ridiculously light on the other. Forgiveness had been creeping into her heart. Until now. Now she felt stupid, naïve, gullible. A victim, a child. And she hated feeling this way. Loathed it.

She started her car just as Brooke and Karen emerged from the double glass doors, holding hands, laughing at something, Karen pushing their grocery-filled cart with her free hand. Their wide smiles, the looks they were giving each other, jabbed at some place inside Vic that was so raw and broken that she felt it a grave danger to look at them any longer.

She pulled her cellphone from her bag with trembling fingers and keyed in Angie's number, her sluice of emotions obliterating her conviction that Angie had gotten over Brooke, that Angie was past the indignity and the sting of something as inane as seeing Karen and Brooke together. All she could think was that she needed the only other person who was in this crazy accord with her.

CHAPTER ELEVEN

The thought of ignoring her ringing cellphone occurred to Angie for all of half a second. She wanted to be rescued from this *date* with Julie. Because the way Julie was looking at her—a little moon-eyed, a lot too smiley—there could be no question her interest in Angie was intensifying. When she saw that it was Vic calling, she couldn't press the answer button fast enough.

"I can meet you at your place," she said into the phone after hearing the tears in Vic's voice. Vic halfheartedly discouraged her, but when she quickly explained to her that she'd just run into Brooke and Karen, Angie wouldn't take no for an answer. "Be there in ten minutes."

She jammed her phone back into her coat pocket and hastily gathered her things. "Really sorry, but a friend needs me urgently."

Julie had the good manners to say it was okay and to look like she meant it. But before Angie could make her escape, Julie lightly squeezed her wrist and caught her eyes. "How about the real date we talked about? I'd still like to get to know you better."

"Sure." Angie swallowed, not certain at all, but there was no time to explore her feelings further. Or to give Julie an honest answer. "Call me some time."

Moments later, she pulled into Vic's driveway just as Vic was exiting her car.

"You okay?" She wasn't, obviously, so chalk that up as stupid question number one. Vic's face was puffy and blotchy, her mouth set in a grim line. It was clear she had been crying.

"No, but I will be."

Vic unlocked her front door. Angie followed her inside and shed her shoes and jacket.

Vic turned to her before they got any further. "Look, I'm sorry to have dragged you here, Angie. I really didn't mean for you to—"

"No, please don't apologize. I'm glad you called me. It's what friends do, right?"

"You're sure?"

"I'm sure. Stop worrying."

"Come on in then." Vic led her into the great room. She flipped a switch and the gas fireplace leapt to life. Instant warmth cut the autumn chill, and the light from the flames bathed the room in an orange glow. "Have a seat. Would you like a glass of wine with me? Or something stronger?"

Wine didn't look like it was going to cut it tonight. "How about something stronger. Surprise me?"

Vic winked and disappeared, giving Angie time to examine the framed photo on the mantel. It was Vic and Karen on a Ferris wheel together. The giant Navy Pier one in Chicago, by the looks of it. They looked happy, in love. She wondered how long Karen had *not* been in love with Vic, because if she'd been in love with her, she couldn't have been in love with Brooke too.

As for her own feelings about Brooke, well, she was under no illusions about that. Brooke had acted the part of loving partner, said and did the right things (most of the time), but ever since the honeymoon stage of their relationship expired, they'd been going through the motions, forcing a square peg into a round hole. Brooke flitted around in her own social circles, went to yoga and the spa regularly, took calls on her cellphone at all hours of the day and night with an apologetic sigh, while Angie read her books and fooled around writing short stories, went for runs or stopped in on her family. Hell, she wasn't even missing Brooke. Not really.

Vic returned, her face darkening as Angie placed the picture back on the mantel. "I've been meaning to do something with that. Like run over it with my car or maybe throw it off the nearest cliff. Here." She handed Angie a chunky crystal glass identical to her own. "Canadian whiskey with a splash of ginger ale and a slice of lemon."

"Looks heavenly, thank you." Angie sat down on the leather sofa that was much softer and more comfortable than it looked.

Vic sat too, leaving space between them. "I didn't realize when I called you that you were practically around the corner or something. Please tell me I didn't drag you away from anything important?"

"Important, no. Uncomfortable, yes." The whiskey was a welcome change from wine, although Angie felt slightly adulterous drinking it. "Julie and I were just—"

"Oh, shit. You were on a date, weren't you?"

"Sort of. I don't know. It was coffee, but it felt like Julie thought it was a date. Or wanted it to be."

With a thunk, Vic set her drink down, stood and started fussing with a piece of paper in her pocket. She was rattled, something Angie had never really seen before. "I went to buy groceries earlier and…dammit, I just realized I still don't really have anything in the house. I didn't…I walked out without buying anything after I ran into Karen and Brooke, and I really should offer you—"

"It's okay, Vic."

"No, really. Stay and finish your drink while I—"

"Vic, wait." Angie set her drink down too but didn't get up, choosing instead to lean forward with her elbows on her knees. "You're upset and I'm sorry. It's not…you're not upset that I was out with Julie, are you?" Something small but deep inside her hoped so, though she had no right to.

"Of course not, don't be ridiculous." Vic's tone didn't match her words. "I mean, you pretty much warned me you were going to start dating. And so you should, if that's your thing. You can do whatever you want, Ange. I'm not your…your…oh, shit." Her mouth collapsed in anguish. Her hands rose to angrily wipe at the fresh tears streaming down her face.

Angie sprang from the sofa and wrapped her arms around Vic, pulling her into her. She expected resistance or at least a stiffening against her. But Vic surprised her by melting into her, so much so that Angie was pretty much the only thing holding her up.

"Oh, God, I'm so sorry about this," Vic mumbled into her shoulder, but her crying had not abated. "I'm not…I don't…I'm being a fucking idiot."

"Shhh, it's okay, and no, you're not being an idiot. You don't have to talk. And most of all, you don't have to apologize."

Something in Angie's heart broke loose as Vic quietly sniffled against her. She soothingly rubbed her back in concentric circles, noticing how soft Vic felt beneath her hand, soft and hard at the same time. And God, she smelled nice. Something citrusy. Something that made her instantly think of warmth and sunshine. *Jesus*. She corralled her thoughts into a more appropriate direction. Thoughts that soon yielded to anger. How could anyone hurt this woman? Make her cry like this? Make her weak, unhappy? Vic hadn't done anything wrong. She didn't deserve this.

"Come on over here," Angie whispered, her voice thick with emotion. She steered them back to the sofa. "And tell me what happened."

Vic did. She left out nothing, including how happy Brooke and Karen looked.

"Well, fuck them," Angie spat, the rocky bank to Vic's river of tears. "I don't give a rat's ass what they do or if they're happy or miserable. Though my vote would be for miserable. And you shouldn't give them a second thought either. They don't deserve…" Angie spread her hands out in exasperation. "Our tears. Or anything else from us."

"Including anger?" Vic began composing herself, wiping away the last of her tears.

"Oh, I'm not ready to give up my anger." In fact, this conversation was only making her hotter. "Not until they get what they deserve." She took a long, bolstering drink and began to think of horrible things that might happen—or should have happened—to Brooke and Karen. Like if they'd died in that stupid car crash. Or were insanely miserable together now that the forbidden nature of their relationship was gone.

"Ange, don't." Vic's hand crept toward hers, then into it. "Anger doesn't change anything. Or make anything better. Though I wish to hell it did."

"Fine. But neither does feeling sorry for yourself and playing the victim."

Vic's loud, ragged intake of breath forced Angie to look at her. Tears were pooling in her eyes again. *Shit.* "Aw, Vic, forgive me. I didn't mean that. I'm being an ass."

"Maybe feeling sorry for myself and being a victim is all I have." She blinked hard, then pounded back the rest of her drink as Angie intently watched her throat swallow back the liquid. She had a nice throat, a nice neck. One that smelled nice too.

"No, it's not," Angie said. "It's the least of what you have."

"Then tell me what's wrong with me, goddammit."

"What do you mean?"

"That she—Karen—doesn't want me. I mean, what did I do that was so terrible? What is it about me that's so awful, so—"

"There's nothing wrong with you. You're giving her way too much credit. And power. Jesus, Vic. You're a good woman. You're smart, you're kind. You're everything she should have wanted."

Vic's mouth trembled, but her eyes were steel. There was a dare in them that made Angie blink in surprise. "Then kiss me."

Vic's humiliation was complete—Angie refused to kiss her. Which meant she'd been right; there *was* something wrong with her. She decided the best thing, the only thing to do, was to fix them both another drink.

Wordlessly she handed Angie her glass and took a gulp from her own. Unaccustomed to the relentless salvos of alcohol, she blurted out, "The more I think about it, the more I think you're right."

"About what?"

"About dating. That it's the thing to do to move on." Somebody out there must want to date her, Vic decided.

"Whoa, wait. Did I say that?"

Fuzziness edged into Vic's brain, a curtain of gauze slowly descending. "I think so. Something like that."

"So you're ready to date now, is that what you're saying?"

Oh, God, was it? She'd do it if she really believed it would put Karen—and her betrayal—behind her. But she wasn't that naïve. "Shit. I don't know." She took another drink. "I mean, you're doing it." She tried to keep the edge from her voice, because something about Angie dating felt like an annoying pebble in her shoe. It wasn't exactly painful, but it was an irritation.

"One date isn't dating. And I'm not even sure it was a date. It's not like there was a kiss at the end of it."

Vic's neck tingled at the mention of kissing, and when she looked at Angie, her cheeks were aflame too and she couldn't meet Vic's gaze. That small evasion made Vic want to wring answers from her. "But you'd like to kiss her."

"No. I—I wouldn't. I don't want to. I'd rather…"

"Kiss someone else?"

"Yes. I'd rather…" Angie's eyes were slow to find Vic's, but when they did, the soulfulness in their depths immediately made Vic want to surrender to them. "I'd rather kiss you, if I'm being honest."

Vic's heart leapt into her throat. Her head swam and she unconsciously slid further away on the sofa because this couldn't be happening. Not when five minutes ago Angie said she was flattered Vic had asked her to kiss her but that she couldn't. The rejection had flattened her, humiliated her, but it was entirely reasonable, given the circumstances. "You…wait. We can't. You said so yourself."

"Right. We can't. Shouldn't. But it doesn't mean I don't want to. Is that crazy?"

"Yes. It's crazy." Vic erupted in laughter. Cynical, ironic laughter now that it was clear the idea of them kissing wasn't unappealing to Angie, the way she'd feared. "Wouldn't that be the ultimate revenge? You and I. Oh, God, could you see their faces?"

"It'd almost be worth it, wouldn't it?"

As their laughter faded, the reality of kissing, or rather the absurdity of it, produced instant sobriety in Vic. And shame. To think that kissing Angie would somehow exculpate her from her own self-loathing and blame. That it would make everything instantly better, brighter. Well. It was a misguided idea. A stupid one, and she couldn't believe she'd actually asked Angie to kiss her.

"I'm sorry," Vic said tentatively.

"For what?"

"For thinking, for suggesting that kissing you would magically allow me to move on, to feel better about myself. I don't know what I was thinking. It…I lost my head."

Angie smiled her forgiveness. "It was a bit rash, but not the stupidest idea I've ever heard."

"It wasn't?" There was her heart doing crazy things again, like doing a tap dance in her throat.

"Nope. Not even close. But I am getting a little bit drunk, which means stupid ideas just might start appealing to me." Her eyebrows danced suggestively. "So what do you say we order in a pizza and then forget that most of this conversation ever happened?"

Relief came swiftly. Angie wanted to kiss her, and for that she was grateful. But the exerting of common sense, a return to sanity, was exactly what she—they—needed. She reached for the cordless phone. "Let me place an order."

Minutes later, she settled back on the sofa. *Whew*. They'd gotten this kissing/attraction thing out of their systems. Maybe now they could get back to normal.

CHAPTER TWELVE

Angie signed the last of the papers from the neat pile that had been placed in front of her—the pile a testament to the last four years of her life. She placed the pen on the polished table, but what she really wanted to do was roll the pages into a crinkly ball and throw it in Brooke's face. She could almost picture it bouncing off Brooke's flawless forehead or off her two-hundred-dollar haircut. She almost smiled.

"Ms. Bennett has asked for a few minutes alone with you," Angie's lawyer said to her with an apologetic smile.

For confirmation, Angie glanced at Brooke's lawyer, a thirty-something-year-old man who looked like he'd walked out of the pages of *GQ*. He gave her a curt nod, efficiently swept the papers off the conference table and prepared to leave. "All right," she said, though she wasn't sure it was a good idea at all.

Seconds later, it was just the two of them. Finally.

"I figured you'd save your theatrics for an audience," Angie murmured. She knew she was being a child, but Brooke fucking deserved it.

Brooke artfully dodged the comment. "No need to be petulant, my dear. I thought it was time we had one last civilized conversation. In private."

"I don't have anything to say to you. You've got the house, I've got my share of the equity. You're lucky I'm not hitting you up for alimony, given that you make twice the money I do. And then some."

"You're not sour about money and you know it, so don't play the money card with me."

"Fine. How about I play the lying, cheating, fuck-around-behind-my-back card?"

"Ange, don't."

Angie sat in silence and tried to gather herself. Clearly, there would be no justice for the wrong Brooke had dispensed to her. Brooke had everything she wanted. And she looked far from miserable. "What do you want from me, Brooke?"

"I..." Brooke seemed to be at a rare loss for words. And suddenly flustered, though it was obvious only to someone who knew her so well.

Always flawlessly put together, perfectly composed, impeccable in manners and speech, Brooke Bennett was a woman whose every word and every movement was well orchestrated. She was a woman acting out her own life, who wanted her life to be neat and tidy and perfect and enviable to others.

Angie felt sick. What had she ever seen in Brooke? It was true that when Brooke turned all that dazzling, exquisite, high-octane attention on her, she felt special. Lucky. But when that spotlight switched off? That was when Angie felt alone, lonely, friendless in their relationship. Which was most of the time. She'd lost count of the number of evenings she spent alone reading or attempting to write some fiction while Brooke flitted between social engagements and work events. True, Brooke sometimes asked her to accompany her. She rarely did, however, because she had no patience for small talk, no tolerance for Brooke and her friends alternately talking shop and gossiping. Angie far preferred her own company to that, but she also understood that all that alone time wasn't the way a relationship was supposed to work.

Brooke tried again. "I just wanted to say I'm sorry it ended this way. We…had some good times, but…well. There it is."

There it is? Angie resisted a good eye rolling. Clearly, no meaningful apology was coming. And so what. She had been hurt, of course she had, but now she realized it'd mostly been her ego that had taken a beating and not her heart, because Brooke didn't possess the ability to shred her heart.

"Brooke, why did you choose me?"

A well-manicured eyebrow rose, then settled. "Because you were real."

"Real? I don't understand."

Brooke sighed impatiently. "You didn't have pretensions, hidden agendas. You didn't act like someone different than who you were. You never made a promise you didn't keep, you never said things you didn't believe with all your heart. You were who you were, and it was a refreshing change."

Angie swallowed. "And that wasn't good enough?"

"It might have been. But I couldn't reach you, Ange. I could never really get through to you. It's like you would have been perfectly happy to go live on a desert island all by yourself with your books and those notepads you're always writing in." Brooke rose, brushing a speck of lint from her blouse. "You never needed me. You never even needed my money."

All one had to do was look at her seven-year-old SUV in the parking lot to know that last bit was true.

Angie watched Brooke pack up her briefcase in silence and slip out the door. Sadness edged into her heart—not so much for what she'd lost, but for herself. Was it true she didn't need anyone? That she was happiest alone? She did love nothing better than to sit someplace quiet and read or to dabble with her short stories (she was too scared to start a novel yet). But she loved her family. And she enjoyed her once-a-month billiards and beer night with Vinnie and some of the boys.

Her gaze slid to the window, where a wet snow shower blurred the view. Brooke was wrong. She wasn't a loner. Thanksgiving was around the corner, which meant time with her family. And she had a proper date lined up for the weekend—dinner with Julie.

There was Vic too, although Vic was sort of the reason Angie was going out with Julie again. Vic and that damned smooth, sexy neck of hers that kept resurfacing in Angie's mind. Same with the vision of how her mouth turned up when she laughed, the way her eyes looked more green when she was happy, gray when she was sad or upset. And the way she used her hands to express herself when they talked about books. Those were the things she couldn't stop thinking about. They were also the things she *needed* to stop thinking about. Seeing Julie again might help her with that.

* * *

Vic didn't mind working night shifts; they beat the hell out of being home alone. Before bedtime was always the worst; no Karen brushing her teeth, humming Madonna or Prince tunes while washing her face. And then there was the bed, cold and empty. Totally uninviting.

Julie sat at the nursing station, in the process of logging out of the computer and handing things off to Vic.

"How was your shift?" Vic asked.

"Easy peasey. Except for the guy in Five."

Olivia appeared, so preoccupied with cleaning her glasses that she nearly collided with Julie. "What's up with Five?"

Julie rolled her eyes. "Thirty-six-year-old male. Wants opioids for his back. Says he fell on some ice."

"Did you check him in the database?" Vic asked.

"Yup. He was here three weeks ago looking for the same thing. His excuse that time was falling off a ladder. And a month before that he was at the ER in Gaylord complaining of a sprained ankle. I was just about to go in and tell him to take some over-the-counter NSAIDs."

Vic grabbed the patient's chart off the counter. "I'll do it." She could tell Julie was in a hurry to get out of here, the way she was fidgeting.

"Ooh, now I remember," Liv said to Julie. "Big date tonight with our favorite paramedic, huh?"

Irritation engulfed Vic. She sure as hell hadn't forgotten about the date. In the hallway at the hospital the other day, Angie had told her about her date with Julie almost as an afterthought. She'd looked slightly embarrassed about it, like she wasn't sure it was a good idea, but not to the point that she'd canceled it, it seemed. It was a mystery Vic couldn't quite figure out, or rather, Angie's vibes were the mystery. Did she actually want to date Julie, or was she only going through the motions, like it was some kind of obligation or dare? What was most puzzling was why she wanted to date Julie when she admitted it was Vic she'd rather kiss. Women, dating, it was all some giant, annoying riddle that Vic couldn't begin to unravel.

"Yes, and I don't want to be late."

"So what are you two doing?" Liv pressed, oblivious to the heat rushing to Vic's face.

"Just dinner." Julie glanced nervously at Vic, then away. "And a place where they have some live acoustic music. Nothing much."

Liv seemed to suddenly notice Vic's discomfort. "Right. Okay, well, um, behave yourself now."

Minutes later, the patient in Five sent on his way without a prescription, Vic said pointedly to Liv, "You know, I'm not that delicate. Or precious."

"Hmm? What do you mean?"

"Don't play dumb. We've been friends too long for that."

They were alone at the nursing station. Liv collapsed into a chair and pushed her glasses up onto her head. "I'm sorry, all right? I thought…I don't know, that you might be less than thrilled that Julie and Angie are dating. I shouldn't have been talking about it in front of you."

"They're going on a date, not *dating*. And what makes you think I have a problem with it?"

"See? That's exactly what I mean. You're defensive about it." Vic started to protest but Liv cut her off. "We've been friends too long, remember? You just said so yourself. Now. Tell me why those two seeing each other bothers you, and I know it does."

Vic hesitated, but she knew how persistent Liv could be. "She said she wanted to kiss me."

"What? She wants to kiss you? She *said* that?"

"Don't look so shocked. And yes, she said that. But don't worry. We didn't. We can't."

"But you want to?"

Ah, now that was the tricky part. She didn't actually know what she wanted, mostly because it didn't matter. Angie Cullen was off limits. Period. And she told Liv as much.

"What?" Vic said after a moment, trying to read the inscrutable look on Liv's face.

"You're being way too sensitive about this," Liv said. "Or maybe moral is the word I'm looking for. You don't have to be a nun, you know. It's okay to date. You're single, and you've been single for almost three months."

"Jesus, I'm not a tub of margarine that's about to expire."

"I know. Look, sweetie. I want to see you happy, I want to see you move on, that's all. And for the record, I think you're being too hard on yourself."

Vic sat in the chair beside Olivia, raised her arms over her head to stretch out the knot between her shoulder blades. Talking with her old friend, she could already feel a clarifying effect. Liv had a way of restoring her to herself, a deep and intuitive understanding of her nature that she seldom encountered with others.

"I don't want anyone getting hurt, including myself, that's all."

"I get that. But Angie's a big girl and so are you. If you want to date her, then it's time to make your intentions known."

Vic laughed. "That sounds like something out of a Victorian romance novel. 'Make my intentions known.' Like give her my calling card or something? Ask a chaperone to set something up?"

Olivia swatted her lightly on the arm. "No, silly. Like shove Julie out of the way and get in line before that one's taken."

"But she's Brooke's ex, for God's sake." She didn't need to spell out that there was something icky, something incestuous about the idea of dating her ex-wife's current girlfriend's ex. "It'd be...weird."

"Oh, get over yourself, Vic. That kind of thing happens all the time in the lesbian dating world."

Vic wasn't ready to concede. "But it's *my* dating life, not the entire lesbian dating world we're talking about. I don't care what other people do."

Liv snatched her reading glasses from the top of her head and put them on, then turned her attention to the computer. She shot Vic a final, impatient glance.

"What?"

"If there's chemistry between you and Angie—and I know there is—then go ahead and explore things a little. You don't have to move in with her or even sleep with her. You can simply see how things go. Hell, you might even discover you have nothing in common except your exes, and then you can move on with no what-ifs."

Things should be so simple, Vic thought. She didn't fear that she and Angie had no common ground. What she feared was making a fool of herself, of Angie rejecting her. Again. Dating Julie was a safe option for Angie and not the minefield it would be if she and Vic dated. Why would Angie want to subject herself to the kind of trouble that dating *her* would surely bring?

Vic dropped her face into her hands. Asking Angie on a date was a dumb idea. And moot anyway, because she was dating Julie. Man, this was some complicated shit!

CHAPTER THIRTEEN

Angie was too nervous to do much more than pick at her chicken Alfredo. By the time she and Julie hit the café where two musicians sang softly with their acoustic guitars under dim lighting, she was ravenous. Of course it was too late then; coffee and biscotti would have to do.

"They're good, aren't they?" Julie said as the musicians, two women in their twenties, stepped off stage for a short break. They'd covered James Taylor, Carole King, Adele—their harmonizing spot on.

"They sure are." She was enjoying the music. And the distraction. But she couldn't entirely eradicate from her mind Brooke's remarks to her at the lawyer's office the other day. She let them lash her all over again, the sting only slightly duller now. "I could never really reach you. I could never get through to you." It was those words Angie chose to dwell on, rather than the part about her being real, authentic, the fact that she didn't put on airs. Because Brooke had spoken them, she wanted to focus on the negative.

"Julie?"

"Yes?" Hazel eyes scrutinized her with a curiosity plainly anchored in attraction. She leaned close enough for Angie to smell her gardenia-scented perfume, angling her cleavage to a more advantageous view, a move that couldn't be more intentionally seductive. The staginess of it made Angie a little dizzy, like she'd suddenly stepped into an old black-and-white romance movie. She was flattered, but that was all.

"Do you ever…I mean, have you ever…would you ever get involved with someone who was really hard to get close to?"

Julie arranged her expression into one of bemusement. "Probably not, no. Do you mean someone who's emotionally inaccessible?"

Isn't that what I just said? It wasn't the first time Julie had taken something she'd said and rearranged it into something more complex in a superior sort of way, as though she could say it better, more cleverly. Perhaps it wasn't intentional, but it reminded her too much of the way Brooke spoke to her. Vic, now she would have given her a straight answer. "Yes," Angie added. "Someone who holds things back."

"Well, if they hold back important things, like feelings, then that's definitely a problem. If they're holding back how they can't decide between black tea or herbal tea, then, no, it's not a problem. Is this an academic question you're asking me?"

"Yes. Of course. Hypothetically. How would you handle someone like that?"

"Simple. I wouldn't." Julie screwed up her face like she'd eaten something distasteful. "The problem is, you'd keep thinking that person would change, that you might finally be able to break through." She sighed and sat back in her chair. "But they wouldn't and so it'd be a waste of everyone's time."

Angie pretended to wipe something from her mouth to keep from laughing out loud. It seemed Julie had become a relationship cynic already. "People can change," she added benignly. What she really wanted to say, because it was so crystal clear now, was that Julie was wasting her time with her. *I'm one of those people who's hard to get through to, one of those people you'd be wasting your time with, can't you see that?*

"Yes. I suppose they can. But I'd rather talk about something else." Julie leaned toward her again, the suggestion of sex in her eyes.

Ah, now she was getting it. Julie only wanted a fuck buddy and not a serious relationship. A relief, it should have been, because *she* wasn't in the market for a relationship either. Not with Julie, anyway. And yet it rankled being treated like meat, even though she'd preached to Vic that this was exactly the elixir for moving on from Brooke and Karen.

"I want to kiss you," Julie whispered, her breath minty from the Tic Tac she'd snuck into her mouth.

"Wait. I...I'm not sure about this, Julie."

She arched an eyebrow. "It's just a kiss. And maybe more, I won't lie. But I'm not looking for a serious relationship. And neither are you, if I'm not mistaken."

Angie's mouth was impossibly dry, the ability to adequately express herself having deserted her. "No, I...I'm not, but—"

"I promise you, it doesn't matter to me if you're emotionally inaccessible."

But it matters to me, Angie wanted to scream. *It matters to me that I'm only good for a good time. As in, ask Angie Cullen on a date because she's good in bed but lousy at relationships.* Did they gossip about her this way at the hospital, where they gossiped about everybody? That she was a relationship fuckup, damaged goods, but she could probably do casual sex?

"Excuse me," she said, pushing her chair back and standing up. "I really think I need to go. I'm sorry, Julie. You have your own car here, right?"

"Yes. Look, I'm sorry if I said the wrong thing."

"You didn't."

She left the café defeated. She was tough, hardened inside by her two tours of duty and her years of working on the street as a paramedic, so it wasn't a mystery to her that she was like a plant on a rock that didn't need much water or light to survive. But this instant, just for now, she wanted to be so much more than that. She wanted her roots to go deep and she wanted to bloom. Wanted the nourishment her soul was afraid to crave.

When she hopped into her car, it was only a couple of minutes before she did a U-turn and headed in the direction of Vic's house.

* * *

Vic plunged her hands into the soapy water and got to work scrubbing the pot she'd neglected before heading to work late this afternoon. The remaining spaghetti sauce had congealed and it was proving more obstinate than a broken femur that resisted setting. The last thing she wanted to do after work, even though the shift had been unusually light, was deal with this damned pot. It was almost midnight. She should be in bed with her book. The pot could wait until morning, but she knew the pattern all too well. As soon as she slipped into bed, she'd start thinking about Karen and everything that entailed—trying to dissect what went wrong, wondering how much of their relationship had been one big lie, worrying about what the future held for her. No. Far better to scrub this pot to within an inch of its life and put off her self-inflicted torture for another few minutes.

The doorbell startled her. She rarely got visitors since Karen's departure and certainly never this late. Even Liv had a habit of calling before she stopped by.

Leaving the chain attached, she cracked the door an inch. "Angie! What are you doing here? Are you all right?" She hurriedly released the chain and opened the door.

"Sorry for coming by unannounced. I'm fine. Did I interrupt anything?"

"Yes," Vic said severely.

Angie's face tightened. "Oh shit. Sorry."

Vic laughed. "It was very important. I was scrubbing a pot and hating every damned minute of it. Come in. Wait! Aren't you supposed to be on a date with Julie?"

"I was, yes."

Angie followed her into the kitchen, where Vic wordlessly poured them each a glass of wine. Wine from Angie's family estate. She felt guilty if she bought any other kind. "Well…did you have a good time?"

"No."

Vic motioned for Angie to join her at the small, round kitchen table. Their knees lightly touched as they sat. "That's all I get? A one-word answer?" Something must have happened for Angie to show up on her doorstep this late.

"I'm not going to see her again."

Vic's heart thudded as she realized she was happy about the news. She shouldn't be, but she was, dammit. "I see. Her decision or yours?"

"Mine."

"She was looking for something serious and it scared you away?"

Angie met Vic's gaze. "Nope. The opposite. She made it clear she wanted it to be casual."

"Well, then," Vic said, hating the way her voice was thickening into something emotional. "That's good, right? I mean, isn't that what you wanted?"

"I thought I did too, but…I don't think casual is for me, and that's what's pissing me off." Angie took a sip of wine. The sound of a distant clock ticked. "I'm not relationship material, Vic, and everyone knows it. I'm sure the gossip mill at the hospital is having a field day with all of this. Angie Cullen sucks at relationships, but she's good for a roll in the hay. And a roll in the hay is exactly what I *don't* want. Even if that's all I'm good for."

"Whoa, wait a minute. Where is all this coming from?"

"Come on, Vic. It's what I believe, and it's what you must believe too. Hell, everybody."

"No. Absolutely not. Nobody's saying anything like that. The only thing I've heard anyone say is that you're hot." Vic hid her cowardice behind a long sip of wine. She didn't disagree with that assessment. In fact, she wholeheartedly agreed, but she didn't want Angie—or anyone else—knowing she was as shallow as all that. Nor did she want Angie to get the wrong idea. *No. I am absolutely not hot for Angie Cullen.*

Angie sulked into her glass, unaware of the guilty thoughts rolling through Vic's mind.

"Look, I have the same feelings of failure," Vic said soothingly. "My ego's taken a massive hit too from what's happened. Don't you think I worry that I can't do relationships either? That I'm a relationship failure?"

"Yeah, but you were married. You were with Karen for ten years. That doesn't make you a fuckup like it does me. Brooke was the longest relationship I've ever had. I mean, have you heard of anything sadder? And it should never have lasted as long as it did. It shouldn't have lasted past the first six months. God, Vic, I'm almost thirty-eight years old and I haven't a clue how to make a relationship work. It's pathetic. *I'm* pathetic."

"Nah. I can out-pathetic you. Fucking up your marriage is a hell of a lot worse than fucking up your not-married relationship. Trust me, divorce isn't pretty. But anyway, tell me where this is coming from. What exactly happened tonight?"

Angie confessed that it had all started with what Brooke said to her at the lawyer's office. "And the worst thing about it is she was right. I don't let people in. I don't let people reach what's really inside."

"Maybe you just didn't want to let *her* in. Maybe she wasn't deserving enough. Maybe you never trusted her enough to completely give yourself to her."

"Maybe." Angie ducked her head and smiled something between gratitude and amusement. "You really are good for my tender ego, you know that?"

"Well, I'd rather we patch up each other's pride than throw a pity party."

"Good point."

"But, Ange?" Vic gently touched her wrist. "If you want to talk to someone, I can give you the name of an acquaintance. She's very good."

"You mean a head shrinker?"

Vic smiled. "If you want to call her that. She's a PhD psychologist."

"I did a couple of sessions with one through the army after each deployment."

"I'm not talking about something that you're ordered to do as part of your debriefing or decompressing or whatever they call it. I'm talking about doing this for yourself."

Angie studied the wine in her glass for a long time. "All right. Maybe."

"Good. I'll text you her contact information tomorrow."

Angie heaved a dramatic sigh before sinking into silence, which Vic understood came with the territory. Angie needed room to process, time to make peace with the decision to see a therapist. She wouldn't press her any further.

"There's one more thing," Angie said after a few minutes. "Can we not talk about Brooke and Karen anymore tonight? Actually, make it longer than tonight. Make it forever."

Vic picked up her glass and clinked it against Angie's. "Not sure I can promise the second part of that, but I can definitely promise the first part."

They finished their wine in silence. Then Angie rose, signaling it was time to go. At the front door, she turned to Vic and said, "Hey, are you doing anything tomorrow?"

"Not a thing. Well, probably still wrestling with that pot in the sink."

"Want to come house shopping with me? I could use another set of eyes. And a friend."

Vic leaned against the doorjamb and didn't attempt to hide her smile. "I'd love to. But I can't promise good advice." She tilted her chin toward the ceiling. "I'd probably talk you into buying some hundred-and-thirty-year-old fixer-upper."

Angie smiled back. "I wouldn't expect anything less."

CHAPTER FOURTEEN

Asking Vic to go house shopping with her had popped out of Angie's mouth last night like the cork from a champagne bottle. It was strange, this spontaneity that seemed to grow like moss on a wet stump when she was around Vic. Worse, confessing things to her that she'd never said to anyone else, like her failure to let others inside. Where the hell had that come from? She rarely talked about her insecurities to anyone outside of family, because only she could fix herself; only she understood herself. But now! Now she was actually thinking about visiting that shrink Vic had suggested and had already decided to call next week and make an appointment (if she didn't chicken out between now and then). She found herself trusting Vic that it wasn't such a terrible idea. That she could be better, and that it was time to start trying.

"So," Vic said beside her, affecting a cheery tone. They were driving to a three-bedroom townhouse in a gated community. "You never finished telling me how your date with Julie went."

"Oh, right. After the part where she said she just wanted a casual thing."

"Did you let her down gently?"

"Not really." Angie giggled at the memory of what she'd said to Julie before leaving the café. "I told her I wanted my next relationship to end in marriage and that I wanted three kids. Maybe two if I compromised."

Vic's hand flew to her mouth. "You didn't!"

"Actually I did." She didn't understand the devilish impulse that had come over her, but she'd decided to go with it. It'd been the most fun she'd had in weeks. "I thought she was going to start hyperventilating."

Vic laughed. "Well, I guess you don't have to worry about her asking you out again."

"Nope. It was either that little gem or tell her that I'm working on a novel where the main character is an ER doc who happens to have blond hair and is a babe."

"Okay, wait." Vic's face began to pink. "You're making this up, right?"

"Which part? Marriage or writing a book?" Angie deadpanned.

"Jesus, Ange. I think you might be serious about both."

"Actually…I think I am." Now she was scaring herself. Confessing that she wrote fiction and that she wanted to get married one day. And maybe have kids! *Why don't you just tell her you want to fly to the moon while you're at it?* Lately she seemed to possess the knack of making women run away from her. Which was a good thing in Julie's case, but not so much in Vic's.

Vic remained speechless as Angie maneuvered the SUV through the heavy Saturday afternoon traffic. She'd probably said too much. Yeah, definitely she'd said too much. Time to backpedal.

"I'm not actually writing about an ER doc, so you don't have to worry that I'm, like, watching every move you make or taking notes or something. I haven't even started my novel yet. So far it's only short stories. Scraps of paper where I scribble down something that occurs to me." Okay, now Vic was going to think she was ridiculous. "I mean, it's just for fun. It's not like I think I'm the next Jonathan Franzen or Stephen King or something."

"Why not?"

"Why not what?"

"Why can't you be a great novelist, if that's what you want to do?"

Angie pretended to fiddle with the navigation unit on her dashboard. "I don't know, I...It's just something I fool around with, you know? In my spare time. For fun."

Pursing her lips in concentration, Vic stared through the windshield. "I see. And do you just *fool around* with being a paramedic? With being a soldier? With making wine?"

"No, of course not. I had to learn those things. Commit to them."

"So learn the craft of writing. And then commit to it."

They'd reached the address. Angie pulled into the driveway, which was constructed of textured cement dyed the color of clay. The townhouse was new, two stories, vinyl-sided in a light mossy green. It had a long porch that reminded her of leafy streets on warm summer days, and a big wooden door with stained glass inlays.

"Wait, Ange," Vic said. "If you want to be a writer, then I think that's awesome. And it's not something you should diminish or excuse or apologize for. If you want to do it, then don't let anything hold you back. Not self-doubt and not other peoples' opinions."

Not used to talking about her writing, and certainly not used to Vic's brand of honest encouragement, it took a moment for Angie to accept that Vic was genuine. And that she was right. She'd never let fear, or what other people thought, stop her before from doing the things that were important to her. "All right. Thank you, Vic."

"For what?"

Angie shrugged. "For believing in me. For kicking my ass when I need my ass kicked."

Vic smiled. "It was a gentle kick, I hope."

"It was."

They locked eyes, and Angie could feel the force of mutual appreciation. They wanted, needed, to believe in each other, needed like oxygen this permission to be true to themselves, to be honest. She didn't often get that from people in her life and definitely not from Brooke.

Vic broke the spell with a collegial pat of her arm and said, "That's what friends are for. Come on, let's go see if this place is as nice inside as it is outside."

Friends, Angie repeated in her mind as a shadow crept into her heart. She had friends, other friends besides Vic, but none of them touched the parts of her that Vic touched. She imagined a snicker of cynical amusement from her buddy Vince if she ever told him about her dreams of being a writer. From her parents or her brother Nick, it would be more like humoring her in a way that would almost, but not quite, be condescending. But Vic. Vic seemed somehow to get her, to cut straight through her doubts and insecurities and affectations. Vic made her not only more aware of herself, but unafraid to *be* herself. It was a gift Vic had, and Angie was grateful.

The realtor, a perfectly coiffed woman in her sixties, greeted them in the foyer. She handed them each a sheet with all the home's particulars: square footage, cost of utilities and taxes, and other details. She was the chatty type, barely stopping for a breath as she extolled the virtues of living in a gated community.

"Of course, the nice part about it is that it's couples only, so it's very social without worrying about single people who like to party and make a lot of noise."

Angie glanced at Vic for confirmation that she'd heard correctly. "Couples only?" She didn't remember seeing that in the fine print.

"Oh yes, but I can see that's not a problem for you two." The woman's exaggerated wink swept them both up. "How long have you two been married?"

Vic drew closer and wrapped her arm around Angie's waist. "Only a few months." She gave Angie a squeeze. "Does it show?"

"Oh, absolutely! I can see that you're newlyweds, it's written all over your faces. Now, if you'd like to take a look upstairs, I really think you'll find the master bedroom and en suite to your liking."

"Wait, one more question," Vic said to the woman, and Angie cringed at what it might be.

"Yes, dear?"

"Children. Are they welcome here? Because, well, we don't have any yet, do we, sweetie pie?" She planted a loud, smack of a kiss on Angie's cheek that audibly sizzled like a branding iron. "But we certainly plan to."

"Oh, children are most certainly welcome here. It's a lovely neighborhood for kids."

Angie's stuttering kept time with her beating heart. "I, ah, we, ah, I mean, c-can we…" She gently removed Vic's arm from around her waist and began backing toward the door. "I'm sorry, ma'am, but I think you'd better sell this place to somebody else."

In the car, Vic burst out laughing. "Oh, my God, I'm sorry, but I so could not resist that. You should have seen the look on your face. It was absolutely priceless."

Angie shook her head. She had to admit, Vic had gotten her good. "Sweetie pie? Newlyweds? *Children?*"

"Well, you said last night you want to get married someday. And maybe have kids."

"Geez, I didn't think it would happen *that* fast."

"Since we're on this marriage and children kick, don't you think I should have met your parents by now?" Vic batted her eyes teasingly.

Angie backed her SUV out of the driveway. There were two more homes on her list. "Yes, as a matter of fact you should." Time to call Vic's bluff. "What are you doing for Thanksgiving next week?"

"Seriously?"

Ha, got ya, Angie was about to say, except she suddenly wanted nothing more than for Vic to join her and the rest of the Cullens for their Thanksgiving feast. "Yes. I'm deadly serious."

* * *

Vic hadn't been this nervous since taking her marriage vows. Before that it was her state medical board exams. *You're only meeting the family of a friend*, she reminded herself. A *friend*, not a girlfriend. It was a game she was playing with herself, a useless game, because however she wanted to label it, it was *not* the same as if she were going to a family dinner at Olivia's or Julie's. It was Angie. Angie who gave her a small ache in her chest lately whenever she thought about her. Angie who, whenever she touched her, sent an involuntary shiver of excitement through her.

"Hi," Angie said at the door, her face lighting up and mirroring none of the tension Vic was feeling. "Glad you made it. Did you bring your appetite?"

"God, I can't think about eating right now," she whispered, stepping into the foyer. "I'm too nervous."

Angie quirked an eyebrow at her. "Don't be. It's not like—"

"I know." *But it sure as hell feels like it.*

"Well, hello there." Angie's mom. Had to be, because she was the spitting image of Angie, only heavier and her brown hair was shot through with silver. "I'm Suzanne Cullen. Lovely to meet you, Dr. Turner. Welcome to our home."

Vic shook Mrs. Cullen's outstretched hand. "Please, call me Vic. And thank you so much for having me."

"Yeah," Angie supplied with a barely suppressed grin, "she's been so excited, she said she's starving."

Vic's eyes lobbed darts at Angie and she mouthed *I'll get you for that.*

"That's wonderful, Vic. We're delighted you could join us. And please, call me Suzanne."

"Will do. Oh." She fumbled with the bouquet of carnations and baby's breath in her hand and passed it to Angie's mom. Cheap, but the best she could do for a last-minute flower purchase on a holiday.

"Oh, thank you, dear, you didn't have to bring anything. And since you're hungry, follow me to the kitchen. That's where all the other hungry people have gathered. I think they're waiting for scraps to fall out of the pots or something."

Angie's dad, a middle-aged man with a slight paunch and thick silver hair, greeted her in the industrial-sized kitchen that featured a six-burner gas stove as well as a grill and three wall ovens. His smile was easy, his handshake firm. "Don't even think about calling me Mr. Cullen. It's Roger. Or Dad. I'm happy to answer to either."

Dad. A prick of emotion burned in Vic's throat. She didn't have a father. Well, she had a biological father somewhere, but she'd never met him and hardly knew a thing about him. Growing up, it was just her and her mom. Until her mother cast her out for being gay.

Claire stepped forward. "It's nice to see you again Vic. Welcome. And this guy..." She gestured at a tall, good-looking man who bore a striking resemblance to Angie, "...is my husband Nick, Angie's brother. And now that you've met us all, you don't have to be nervous," Claire continued. "Come on. Nick, pour this woman a glass of wine, would you?"

"Happy to," Nick said after shaking Vic's hand. "White or red?"

A quick scan of everyone's glasses told Vic they were drinking white. "I wouldn't dream of breaking with the crowd. White it is. You have a beautiful homestead, by the way."

"Thank you," Angie's parents said in unison.

"It's been a labor of love," added Roger. "Like anything worthwhile."

Nick handed Vic a glass of wine. "Don't get him started about the farm or you'll be here all night."

Fine with me, Vic wanted to say. It would beat the hell out of returning to her empty, drafty house, and she was interested in the winery—how things actually worked, because it was a bit like magic to her, the concept of planting grapevines and turning them into fine wine. "I promise not to overstay my welcome if you all tell me more about your farm. And the wine you make is spectacular, by the way. How many varieties do you make?"

It was awhile before Vic could get a word in edgewise after that, which suited her fine. She much preferred to listen. And to watch the Cullens talk about their greatest joy, which was the family business, but also to watch how they related to each other. They had a gentle way of teasing one another and of seamlessly seguing between subjects. There was a flow to the conversations, an underlying consciousness that none of them wanted to monopolize or be the center of attention. If someone had been left out for a while, Claire or Suzanne or Roger would reel them in by asking a question or including them somehow. Everyone got equal airtime, equal consideration of their opinions. Which totally threw Vic. She didn't know families could get along so well. Karen's certainly hadn't. Karen, her parents, and her four siblings were often squabbling—picking fights, taking sides, throwing down ultimatums. Vic could never keep up with who was on good terms and who wasn't.

"Hope you left some room for dessert, young lady," Roger said to Vic after she'd stuffed herself with turkey, mashed potatoes, squash, and fresh cranberry. It was the best Thanksgiving meal she'd ever had, bar none. Thanksgivings usually involved working or Karen Googling how to cook turkey for two. Neither she nor Karen resembled anything close to being great cooks. "Suzanne's pumpkin pie is not to be missed this side of the Mississippi. Isn't that right, Angela?"

Angie, seated beside Vic, said, "Don't worry about stuffing yourself, we'll go for a walk later." She leaned closer, her breath warm against Vic's ear. "And Dad's right. The pie really is to die for."

A shiver, a pleasant one that also had the promise of torture beneath it, raced down Vic's spine. She looked into Angie's eyes to steady herself, but the warmth and honesty in them only rocked her again.

"Actually," she said to Angie, "what if we had that walk now and saved the pie for later?"

"I think that's a wonderful idea." Angie rose first and made their excuses. "Don't worry," she said to her mother. "This way Vic will have even more room for a gigantic piece of pie. Right, Vic?"

"Hmm, well, maybe if you're planning to jog me around the farm."

Angie's eyes sparked with mischief.

"Don't even think about it," Vic hissed, earning a wave of laughter from around the table.

CHAPTER FIFTEEN

The light from Angie's flashlight played on the ground ahead of them. She knew every inch of the farm and didn't really need a light, but she didn't want Vic tripping over a tree root or a rock. In the cool air, their breaths rose in small milky clouds.

"Your family's wonderful. Although I would have been surprised if they weren't."

"How so?"

"Because they brought you up right."

Duty, loyalty, hard work, respect. It was true that she and her family prided themselves on those attributes. They were values she'd risked her life for in the military. "Warm enough?" she asked, touching Vic's elbow with her free hand.

"Yes, plus I have enough food in me now that I think I've gained a layer of fat."

"You haven't, but stick around here long enough and you will. Why do you think I run at least a dozen miles a week?"

"Nice try. You run because it's a stress valve for you. Am I right?"

"I suppose." Vic was right and there was no sense in denying it. "And guess what? I booked an appointment with that shrink you told me about."

"You did?"

"Didn't think I would, did you?"

"I…wasn't sure, to be honest. But I'm glad you did. And you know what else I'm glad you did?"

"What?"

"Confided in me about being a writer. That took guts, you know. And trust."

Angie kept her silence for a few steps. "When you trust somebody, it doesn't take a lot of guts to confide things. And I trust you, Vic." More than Vic knew. She couldn't understand how that trust had manifested so quickly or where it came from. But it was there, as solid as the John Deere that lay beyond the barn doors.

Angie couldn't see Vic's eyes in the darkness, but she could feel them on her. "Well, I'm not sure what I did to deserve that trust, but thank you. It means a lot to me."

They halted behind the barn. Angie leaned up against its rough boards and toed the half-frozen earth with her boot. "I'm just glad you don't think my little writing hobby is stupid. Brooke did, that's for sure."

"I don't think anything you do is stupid." Vic put her back against the barn too, her shoulder touching Angie's. "And I'm not Brooke, so please don't compare me with her."

"Sorry. That *was* stupid. I know you're nothing at all like Brooke."

"What attracted you to her? I mean, besides the obvious. If you don't mind me asking."

"Of course I don't mind you asking. It's not like I haven't been asking myself the same thing a million times over. I guess it was the whole opposites-attract thing. Except I didn't realize that once the flame starts to fizzle out, it's actually the sameness between two people that keeps the pilot light going."

"Huh. That's quite the metaphor."

"I'm a writer, remember? And don't you think it's true?"

"I do, yes. I think some differences are good, but I think the important things, like your moral system, your values, your outlook on life, the things you desire, need to be the same. And it helps to share interests for sure."

Angie thought about the love for books she and Vic shared. Their sense of humor too, plus the methodical, confident way they both went about their jobs. There was comfort and familiarity between them, whether it was in the emergency room or hanging out here at the farm. Being with Vic was like the buttery soft leather work gloves she always reached for because they felt like a second skin.

"This is how clueless Brooke was about me. Our first Christmas together, she bought me a Gucci purse. A fucking purse, can you believe it?"

Vic laughed. "No, I can't. And what did you buy her?"

Angie's indignation died with her answer. "I bought her a power drill. All right, look," she said over Vic's laughter. "I know I was every bit as bad and every bit as much to blame. She didn't get me and I didn't get her. That should have been our first and *last* Christmas together. But I figured I'd chosen her, so…"

"You had to stick with her?"

"Something like that. But I don't plan to repeat my mistakes."

"Ah…no more dating women with Gucci purses?"

"Nope. Or women who haven't read a novel since high school. Or whose annual clothing budget is enough to buy a compact car. I'm done with the whole opposites-attract thing. Doesn't work. At least not for me."

"So you're looking for salt-of-the-earth types. Loyal, honest, genuine. Maybe even somebody who wants a family someday?"

"Maybe." It wasn't really that simple. But it wasn't exactly complicated either, once put that way. "What about you?"

"Oh no. I'm not looking for anybody. Been there, done that."

"Ever?"

"I haven't decided yet. Ask me in ten years."

Angie moved to face Vic. Vic who was full of shit about not looking for anybody for at least ten years. Vic was every bit the marrying kind, more so than Angie. Companion, wife, a loyal heart were all stamped on her soul. She was exactly the kind of woman other women married. Vic Turner was built for the long term. Built to be a partner in every sense of the word.

And that was the major difference between the two of them because Angie, as Brooke had so succinctly put it, was incapable of being a true partner, thanks to her stubborn resistance to letting anyone in.

"Stop," Vic whispered.

"What?"

"Whatever negative thing you're thinking."

Angie wanted to ask Vic how she seemed to so easily search out the hidden corners of her mind, the same way she herself knew every hill, every valley, every vine on this farm. Instead she stepped closer and gently took Vic by the shoulders before she could second-guess herself. "You get me, Vic. I don't know how, but—"

Vic's mouth closed the distance between them, her lips brushing the side of Angie's mouth, like a breeze ruffling the page of a book. Angie's eyes fluttered shut because she didn't want to see, only to feel. She angled her face so that their mouths met. Soft, impossibly soft, were Vic's lips. Angie wanted to devour them, spread them with her tongue, taste and consume them with her mouth, but she didn't. The kiss was warm and sweet and full, and it rolled through Angie like a hot afternoon rain shower, forever changing the landscape it left behind. Vic's mouth pressed harder and Angie met the pressure with her own, understanding that they could never go back after this kiss, because with every heartbeat, the kiss was sweeping aside everything Angie thought she knew about herself and what she wanted and everything she thought she knew about Vic and their so-called friendship.

Angie's hands fell to Vic's waist and she pulled her into her. What she really wanted was to get her hands under that heavy jacket because a fire was raging in her core, a fire that needed more fuel. Vic began to moan softly, to press her body into Angie, and it was blissful agony, a pleasure pain that ripped through her body, a slow unfurling of heat that left her wanting more. It would be so easy to tug Vic right into the barn, to pull off her clothes, to take everything offered, to make love to this woman who…

Shit. Visions of Karen Turner, of Brooke, of the two of them together, stampeded through Angie's mind, like enemy troops suddenly breaching the secure perimeter she'd set up around her heart. Her libido came to a screeching halt, and in its wake came wave after assaultive wave of doubts and self-condemnation. *What the hell am I doing? I cannot do this. Not with Vic. Oh God, anybody but Vic.*

She pulled back and immediately began apologizing, stammering words that didn't make much sense and certainly did nothing to explain her sudden change of heart. Her chickenshit heart.

In the darkness she could barely make out the look on Vic's face, but it wasn't good. Inwardly Angie cringed. "I'm so sorry," she said lamely. "I—I don't know what…I—"

"Don't worry about it," Vic said, her tone polite but carrying a knife-sharp edge. "I'll go thank your family and then I'll be on my way."

"No, Vic, wait…"

But Vic was off, striding through the dark as if completely unconcerned about the minefield of tree stumps, rocks, and ankle-twisting divots in the soil. And something inside Angie's heart clanged shut.

* * *

Vic rushed to the ambulance bay to receive a fifty-two-year-old heart attack victim. He was reported as stable during the ride, but she knew how quickly such things could go south.

Angie leapt out of the back of the ambulance, athletic grace in motion. The sight of her momentarily forced Vic back on her heels. Her stomach clenched as the kiss outside the barn two nights ago came flooding back to her, swamping her. She remembered, had replayed in her mind, everything about it: Angie's lips, their soft persistence, their heat, the tenderness with which they took and gave.

And then there was her own visceral reaction and the tangle of her emotions—caution even as she silently begged for the kiss to continue. Each moment the kiss continued, Vic lost more territory because Angie stirred her, unglued something deep in her that didn't want to remain pinned down. How close she'd been to total surrender exactly at the moment Angie so jarringly, so humiliatingly, ended the kiss. But later, as her anger settled, Vic, truthfully, was relieved. It was too soon, too confusing, too complicated to be taking things further—a disaster that would spell not only the end of any romantic hopes between them, but their friendship too. Painful as it was, Angie had done them both a favor.

Angie met her eyes, but barely.

"Let me have a look at the EKG strip," Vic said, all business.

Wordlessly, Angie handed it to her before she and her partner, Jackson, pulled the stretcher from the ambulance with an efficient clatter.

"Good call. Looks like an MI. Let's take him to Room Three."

The man was conscious. Pale and weak, but alert. They wheeled him to the treatment table, and Olivia began hooking him up to the Emergency Department's monitoring equipment. Angie and Jackson stepped back, Jackson disappearing with the empty stretcher and the EMS equipment while Angie lingered near the door. Vic hated this awkwardness between them and was glad Angie had hung back. It was just a kiss, after all. A hot, bone-rattling, take-your-breath-away kiss to be sure, but nothing they couldn't walk back. Or maybe they could simply agree to forget about it, let time bury it.

"What's your name?" she said to the patient. Angie would have to wait.

"Chris," he said thinly. "Chris Manning."

"All right, Chris, we're going to help you. I want you to tell me what happened."

He explained how he thought he'd had indigestion all day. Had some shortness of breath the last couple of weeks too, come to think of it. Then about a half hour ago, suddenly it was as though an elephant was sitting on his chest.

"How is the pain now, is it worse?" Vic waited for a response. The patient's eyes were open but now vacant. "Chris?"

"He's in v-tach," Olivia announced, her eyes on the cardiac monitor. The patient's rhythm was chaotic—up and down, fast then slow.

"He's unconscious," Vic confirmed. "Call a code," she said sharply to Olivia. A code meant her patient was crashing and she needed more help. Olivia dashed for the wall phone.

From the shadows Angie stepped forward. "What can I do?"

Vic pressed the defibrillator paddles to the patient's chest. "Give me two hundred joules."

Once Angie adjusted the controls, Vic yelled "clear" and they watched the patient's chest heave as his heart kicked in again.

Olivia returned, followed by a second nurse and Ray, one of the Emergency Department interns. Vic ordered blood thinners and rhythm stabilizers to be administered intravenously and asked Olivia to call a cardiology consult and to book the catheter lab for angioplasty.

"Nice work," Angie remarked, backing out of the room.

"Wait. Can I talk to you for a sec?"

"Of course." Angie visibly swallowed. Clearly she was nervous about what Vic might have to say.

In the hallway, staff bustled past them and they had to flatten themselves against the wall. "Are we okay?" Vic said to her.

Angie gave a short, clipped nod, as something closed up in her eyes. "Yes. We're okay."

"Good. Because it kinda doesn't feel like it. But I want it to be."

"Vic." Angie dropped her voice as a loaded stretcher buzzed past them. "I'm sorry. It's all my fault that—"

"No. This isn't the place." A physician's assistant and a nurse sauntered past them, seemingly deep in conversation, but the hospital had ears. Everywhere. "What are you doing Saturday?"

"Nothing. Why?"

"I'd like for us to go out for lunch. We should talk." And have some fun. She didn't want their time together to always be dominated by heavy conversation, to always tug at their emotional strings. They could talk about the kiss and get it the hell over with and then *not* talk about anything serious for a change. "I was thinking maybe we could make a day of it. Drive over to Charlevoix or something." She didn't want to lose Angie, this friendship, because Angie *got* her. Angie could both read her and understand her. It was a potent attraction and one she found she needed. Most of all, she really liked her. *Please say yes*.

Angie's smile was slow and she crooked a teasing eyebrow, making her wait. *Damn you*, Vic thought, but she grinned even as her stomach somersaulted with anticipation.

"Only if you let me pay," Angie finally said.

"You're on. I'll pick you up at your folks' place."

"Jones-ing for another dinner invitation from my mom?"

Vic laughed. "Maybe."

CHAPTER SIXTEEN

Angie tapped her boot impatiently on the plush carpeting of the shrink's office. Melanie Scott, PhD, was old enough to be Angie's mother and as capable as her mother of giving her a good butt kicking. It was Angie's second session; during the first they'd gone through the history of her life until now, ending the session with Brooke's betrayal.

Melanie was asking her if she was still angry with Brooke.

"Hell no. Good riddance. She did us both a favor, though screwing around wasn't a cool way to go about it."

"Ah yes, the tough Angela Cullen couldn't possibly be hurt by anything Brooke could do to her. Tell me. What *could* hurt you, deep down, if not that?"

Angie took a minute to think about it. Someone in her family dying would hurt her. Her career coming to an end would hurt her. No, the psychologist clarified. Romantically. As in, what could a romantic partner do that would hurt her. Wouldn't infidelity be at the top of the list?

"Maybe if it was somebody I was actually in love with."

"So why weren't you in love with Brooke? You spent four years with this person. Lived with her. Do you always live with women you're not in love with?"

"Of course not," Angie said. She'd never lived with anyone before Brooke. Sure, she loved her or at least cared for, but she wasn't *in love* with her. They were never truly meant for the long haul. They were oil and water, opposites in pretty much every way.

"So why did you stay with her until she forced an end to it?"

"Doc, is there really a point to analyzing my relationship with Brooke? It's been over for more than three months."

Blue eyes the color of a frozen lake bored into her. "If you don't come to terms with what went wrong with your relationship, how can you expect to be a good partner to somebody else in the future?"

"By choosing a better partner in the first place?" Melanie wasn't cracking a smile at Angie's joke. "All right, fine. I stayed with her because I believe in commitments, in loyalty. I'm not a quitter."

"You may not be a quitter, but you're a coward, Angela."

Angie's heart hammered her shock and anger. "Excuse me?"

The therapist's eyes softened considerably, but not the set of her jaw. "There's nothing brave or honorable about sticking with a failing relationship. Do you dislike yourself that much?"

Fury continued to pulse through Angie. This woman knew nothing about her. "I don't dislike myself."

"Perhaps not, yet you felt the need to punish yourself by staying with Brooke all that time. Do you think you don't deserve better? That you don't deserve to be happy? Is that it? Because nobody deserves to be *un*happy."

She hadn't thought she was unhappy the last four years, though it was true she hadn't exactly been happy either. Going for solitary runs on the peninsula, hiding in her books and in her writing, those things made her happy, but those things were also her escape from unhappiness, she supposed. Her way of balancing the ledger.

After several moments of silence, she finally declared, "I do want to be happy."

The therapist smiled, but Angie didn't. A sob had begun roughly working its way up her chest and into her throat, lodging there like a golf ball. She coughed, choked on it and finally burst into tears. The first tears she'd shed, she realized, since that shitty late August night in the ER.

* * *

The lake, as they drove along beside it to Charlevoix, was gray and roiling angrily, resisting winter's trespass. Vic was at the wheel, Angie beside her, and she thought about the seasons, the slipping from one to the other. Her heart was still stamped with a winter chill, but she could sense a spring thaw approaching her soul. Karen wasn't going to leave her in a deep freeze forever, and the realization made her feel light, free, happy for the first time in a long while.

Angie was telling her about her sessions so far with Melanie Scott, cursing her out as a "tough old broad," but Vic could hear the respect in Angie's voice.

"Do you think seeing her will help?"

"It already has. And do you know one of the things I've finally figured out?"

"What's that?"

"That I'd gotten comfortable these last three-and-a-half months letting Brooke be the bad guy. She ended our relationship, and not in a nice way, but it needed ending. I should have ended it a long time ago."

"So why didn't you?"

An adorably self-deprecating smile. "Because I'm a stubborn S.O.B."

"Well, cheers to that. Stubborn can be a good thing sometimes. Like when you don't give up on a patient. Something we both know a little bit about, right?"

"Right. But not so good when you're in a shitty relationship."

They drove in silence, Vic sensing that if she was going to wait on Angie to bring up their kiss at Thanksgiving, it was going to be an awfully long wait. There was a strip of parkland up ahead, between the lake and the highway. Vic pulled off into it, Angie giving her a mild look of surprise.

She pointed the car toward the lake, parked it, shut off the engine. They were the only ones around.

"You want to go for a walk?" Angie asked.

"Not particularly." It was cold, barely above freezing, and the wind snapped like a wet towel. "But I would like to talk."

"Vic." Angie turned to her. "I'm so sorry. About the kiss."

"It was a mistake that we kissed, or it was a mistake that we kissed at that moment?" It was uncomfortable, but Vic pressed. She needed to get at exactly what Angie wanted to say, how she felt about it. "What, exactly, are you sorry about?"

"I'm not sure." Angie stared out the passenger window. "Except I feel like I should apologize, like we might have done something wrong." She turned suddenly. "What about you…do you feel it was a mistake?"

"Honestly? I'm not sure either." It should be a mistake. Kissing the woman whose partner had run off with her wife. Ex-partner, ex-wife. But still.

"Vic? I don't want it to be. A mistake, I mean. Do you?"

Vic felt the hard inquiry of her eyes. "But you did. Right after it happened."

"I know. I was scared. I was…confused."

"Confused?"

"Because I didn't know if what I was feeling—doing—was appropriate. Given the circumstances. And I was scared because I felt like I was kind of going out on a limb and—"

"And I wasn't?"

Through the windshield, Angie's eyes followed the heavy surf. "Yes. You definitely were too. All right, look. I was a coward. As my shrink likes to remind me." She made a face before looking at Vic again. "Vic, I want to be sure we weren't kissing as a way to get back at our exes. Or because we need to prove to, I don't know, the world, ourselves, that we've moved on, that we're okay. I wanted that kiss to be for the right reason."

Vic swallowed. "And what would the right reason be?"

Angie moved closer, the car's console the only thing between them. "The right reason would be that we're attracted to each other. That we like each other. A lot. That we want to explore things."

Angie's hand crawled gently to Vic's denimed thigh, as though it had been waiting to be there its whole life. Her fingers were warm, and Vic longed to feel them on her skin.

"I do like you." Vic was finding it hard to breathe, hard to scratch out her words, thanks to the little pulses of fire coming from Angie's touch.

"I like you too. And I would have liked you no matter how we met."

"But?" There was a definite *but* underscoring Angie's words.

"I don't want to screw things up with you because of my own issues."

Vic laughed. Didn't mean to, but there it was. "Like I don't have issues too?"

Angie watched her with sharp, steady eyes. "I don't want to hurt you. And I don't want to get hurt."

Vic took Angie's hand and removed it from her thigh with more force than she intended. She twisted the key in the ignition and the motor roared to life. This conversation was resolving nothing. Clearly Angie was paralyzed by her own fears, scared shitless of her feelings. If she'd only wanted to be friends, she wouldn't have put her hand on her thigh the way she had, wouldn't be letting her eyes settle on Vic's lips right now like she wanted to kiss them again. *Damn you!*

"Vic, wait." Angie stopped her hand before she could gear the car into drive. "Don't."

Vic sat back stiffly in her seat. "Don't you think I'm scared too? Do you think I want to get hurt? Or that I want to hurt you?"

"No, of course not."

"What," Vic finally said with what shred of patience she had left, "is it that you want? Because I think you need to decide." They both did. Friends…or something more.

Angie's hand took up its station on Vic's thigh again, and a bolt of lightning shot straight into Vic's crotch. *Jesus*! The raw power such a simple touch wielded over her was shocking. *I could be a slave to that touch*, she thought, and then immediately began to shrink away from the idea. As if her mind could wrestle her heart and her libido into knowing their places.

"What I want," Angie said, her breath suddenly next to Vic's cheek, "is to kiss you again."

No, Vic said in her mind. "Yes," she whispered, and Angie's mouth claimed hers. Triumphantly tender, as if the kiss were the very culmination of something years in the making. It was a kiss that said this was exactly perfect, that *this* was how they were meant to be, *what* they were meant to be to one another. And with each minute the kiss continued, Vic's need grew more insatiable. And then the kiss was done, the ghost of it lingering on her mouth, tingling and sweet.

They talked about mundane things for the rest of the journey into Charlevoix, but the kiss wasn't far from Angie's thoughts. She cracked the window, felt the cool air slice through her lungs and numb the fire that had turned her belly into a furnace. Now that she'd kissed Vic—properly this time, without regrets—she could think of little more than kissing her again. When? she wondered. After lunch in the car again? In the same little park on the way back to Traverse City? When Vic returned her to her family estate? Maybe near the barn again. Or maybe she could go straight back to Vic's house with her, and they could... *No, wait*, she told herself. It was a mistake to think of more, of doing and wanting more. Kissing Vic would have to be enough. *Baby steps*.

"What?" Vic said, lifting a smile at her.

"Nothing."

"You were thinking about something because your cheeks were turning red and you were smiling."

"Fine. You caught me. I was thinking about kissing you again."

It was Vic's turn to blush. "Angie, we have to do this slow. We can't just—"

"I know." Angie reached across the console and twined her fingers with Vic's. "But just so you know. I want to."

A deeper shade of red splashed across Vic's cheeks. "Happily noted."

This kiss, even more than the first one, was a game changer, an event from which they could not go back and could no longer apologize for or regret or question the hell out of. Strangely enough, this new plateau was good with her. And it was good with her that she had no idea where they were going next, if anywhere. Vic was easy to be with. Simple but good, like toast with butter, and it was enough for Angie. Well, that and more kissing.

They were in Charlevoix now, its main street littered with quaint, high-end boutique shops. Salt water taffy, handmade chocolates, name brand clothing, a gallery, a bookstore, a music store, a bistro. Vic pulled the car into an empty spot in front of an antique store. "Ooh, I love antique stores."

"I can tell. And you've got the kind of house for it."

"Speaking of houses, have you settled on one yet?"

Angie held the door for Vic, then followed her in. "No. Nothing's really captured my heart. What I'd really like is an old house like yours with tons of character. Just not sure I can afford all the maintenance it would take."

"It does take work, I'll give you that. I've got to get someone to paint the old girl's outside trim next summer. You going to stay at your folks' awhile longer?"

"I guess. I'll rent by spring, though, if I haven't bought a house yet."

Vic gave her a look that was full of longing. "I envy you your family, just so you know."

"Well, they're a pain sometimes, but mostly…yeah, I know. I'm lucky." Christmas was only a couple of weeks away, and Angie wanted nothing more than to invite Vic over for a family meal again. "You working a lot over the holidays?"

"Yup. Like crazy. I've never been big on Christmas. And especially not *this* Christmas."

"Well, if you're working, maybe I'll sign up for a couple of extra shifts too."

"I'm free Christmas Eve." There was a hint of a question in the declaration.

"Me too. How about a date?"

"All right. As long as it involves popcorn, wine and *It's a Wonderful Life*."

Angie couldn't have planned it out better if she'd tried. Forget the family dinner. "You read my mind."

She let her hand graze over the cast iron of an old sewing machine, then traced the fine wood in the cabinet of a radio from the 1930s. She could forgive the musty smell of the place because of all the cool stuff in here. Her gaze fell to a case of old books, which was a magnet to her. She scanned the titles, picked out a hard copy of *To Kill a Mockingbird* in fantastic condition. She opened the flap, saw that it was a first edition. Well worth the two hundred bucks. She thought of Vic, who'd said it was one of her all-time favorite books. She stuffed it back into place and sought out Vic, who was browsing the far end of the store.

"I'm going to need you to get lost for a few minutes."

"What? Why?"

"I think I need to do some Christmas shopping in here."

"On one condition. That when you're done, you text me and then *you* get lost for a while."

"Uh-oh. Seems like our minds are on the same track."

Vic's smile warmed her from the inside. "Well. You know what they say…"

CHAPTER SEVENTEEN

"You're almost looking happy these days, Vic." Liv slid into the booth with a weary sigh—the night shift had run them off their feet—and opened the menu. They'd decided to have breakfast at the diner across the street. "Don't tell me you've been sneaking home some of that medical marijuana."

"I wish."

"Better share if you ever do, that's all I've got to say on the subject."

As if they'd willed it in their minds, two huge mugs of coffee appeared in front of them.

"So?" Liv pressed. "Karen finally acting human toward you or something?"

Vic made a sound that was a cross between a sigh and a laugh. It was true, she had been feeling happy lately, and even the mention of Karen's name couldn't spoil her mood. "Actually, Karen has nothing to do with my mood. For a change."

Liv closed her menu. She always ordered the same thing—eggs Benedict—yet she persisted in going through the charade of trying to decide what to order. "Do tell, girlfriend."

"You have to promise not to tell anybody else. Other than Beth, of course."

"I wouldn't dream of squealing on you." She leaned closer. "This better be good."

"It is. Angie and I are sort of…you know…dating."

"Ooh, you weren't kidding, this *is* good!"

The server, an older woman who knew all the hospital staff on a first-name basis, took their orders and promised to get the cook to add extra to their plates.

"I mean, we haven't really been on an official date. Except for going to Charlevoix last week, and yesterday we went out for lunch, and—"

"Sheesh," Liv said. "Lunch? Going for a drive? That sounds way too exciting for me. I thought you said you two were dating?"

"We are. I mean, we've decided to call it that. I think." Vic was determined she wouldn't go down the rabbit hole of overthinking her and Angie's status. They were taking things slow, at a crawl really, but it was how it needed to be. And it felt good. "Anyway, we've been kissing like we invented it."

"Okay, now you got me. Kissing how? And where?"

Vic blinked. "The usual way. On the lips."

"No, I mean, *where*? Like, in your bedroom? Ooh, wait, in the back of her ambulance?"

Vic rolled her eyes. "We're going slow. S-L-O-W. No bedrooms yet and not for a long time. And definitely not in the back of an ambulance." They'd kissed again on the way back from Charlevoix—a long, slow, sizzling one that reminded Vic of long, hot, luxuriating bubble baths. Under cover of darkness they'd kissed in Vic's car in the doctors' parking lot at the hospital a couple of days ago. Snuck another toe-curling one in a supply closet the day before that. "We're having a real date next week. On Christmas Eve."

Liv's eyebrows danced suggestively. "A sleepover?"

"No!"

"Oh, come on. Live a little, Vic. It won't kill you. And she is hot, in case you haven't noticed."

"Oh, I've noticed, trust me." Vic sipped her coffee, let her mind wander for a minute to all the things she'd secretly thought of doing to Angie—and Angie doing to her. But she—they—weren't there yet. They needed to be cautious, to make sure they weren't rushing into anything either of them might regret. What horrified Vic the most was the idea that this all could be a rebound thing. "I need time, Liv. I need to make sure I'm not making a mistake."

"The way you made a mistake with Karen?"

"Exactly like I did with Karen."

"Well, I hate to break it to you, but you're human. And humans make mistakes. And maybe Karen wasn't a mistake at first. Maybe she *became* a mistake."

"Maybe. But I should have seen it coming and I didn't. I'm not sure I can forgive myself for that."

"Well, you'd better, or you're never going to trust anyone else again. And that would really suck, you know that?"

The server delivered their steaming plates while Liv mouthed the words, "You're too hard on yourself" at her. It was true, she was her own worst critic, but somebody had to be. She felt her cellphone vibrate in her pocket and pulled it out. A text. From Karen! Her heart stuttered in alarm. Weeks ago she'd stopped reflexively looking for texts from Karen, jumping every time her phone chimed or vibrated. Divorce was a series of small, internal earthquakes. Like not getting texts. Like not buying Karen's favorite cereal or picking up the scattered newspapers she left behind every morning like freshly fallen leaves. Divorce was all those little habitual things that were suddenly gone as if they'd never been there in the first place. And it was exactly those things, it occurred to Vic, that had made her happy in her marriage. The cereal, the newspapers, the long, lazy Sunday mornings of drinking coffee on the patio—sometimes together, sometimes alone—cutting grass while Karen mucked around in the garden. It had been enough for her but not, apparently, for Karen.

What's wrong with me that I found all that enough?

Out of curiosity she finally thumbed open the text. *Please call as soon as u can, need to talk.* Vic shoved her phone back into her pocket. What a laugh, Karen finally wanting to talk when Vic had begged her over and over for just that. Well, forget it. Karen had been right when she'd told her outside the grocery store that there was nothing more to talk about. She was simply holding Karen to her word now.

* * *

Angie let the cold air slice through her lungs, breathed in the sting of it as she jogged around the final bend and up her family's lane. She never minded winter. In fact, she loved its crispness, loved the bright assault on her eyes of sunshine and snow, loved how the cold and boniness of the season was like wiping away everything clean for a brand-new start in spring. She thought of Vic and her breath caught. She supposed this lifting of her soul might be the feeling of falling in love—like the world was a flower suddenly opening up to her. Feeling this way again was like unearthing a buried treasure. And then she remembered that she was still the same old Ange. Still the same failure at relationships, still the same architect who so successfully built those impenetrable walls around her heart. Thinking of Vic and love was getting way ahead of herself.

Just yesterday, her therapist, Melanie, had tried to drill down to what made her so afraid of letting people in. Probably because of the army, Melanie suggested. It was probably the fear of losing people she'd grown to care about. "I did lose people," Angie countered. "And did it hurt?" Melanie asked. Of course it hurt, Angie said. "Good. It's supposed to hurt when we lose people we care about. But being afraid to hurt is not a good enough reason to go through life alone." Well, those fears had kept her in good stead. Until now. Now she was sick of her own company, more frightened of the idea of being alone forever than of the idea of letting someone get close. As in *really* close. Maybe it was time to try.

Her mom found her in the kitchen over a cup of hot chocolate, brooding and staring into the steaming, chocolate froth.

"Lovely morning out there, isn't it? Ooh, that looks good." Suzanne set the kettle back to boiling and spooned some hot chocolate powder into another mug. "You know, honey, you really shouldn't look this miserable on a perfect winter day like this."

"I'm not."

"Could have fooled me. Listen, why don't you ask your friend Vic over for Christmas dinner?"

"Can't. She has to work. But thanks."

"All right. Then how about for Christmas Eve?"

Angie felt the familiar tickle in her stomach whenever she thought of Vic. "I…we, ah, have plans, actually."

"Are you…you mean a date?"

"Yes. A date."

Suzanne lit up like it was already Christmas morning. "Oh, honey, I'm so happy for you. I like her, she seems lovely. So why the long face?"

"I don't think I want to talk about this." *With you.* She'd never been one to confide in her mother about past relationships. Before Brooke there hadn't been anyone too serious, and Brooke, well, hadn't exactly been popular with her family.

Suzanne poured boiling water into her mug, stirred in some milk and promptly ignored Angie's comment. "Is it her link to Brooke and that whole sordid mess that makes you uncomfortable?"

"No, Ma. It wasn't Vic's fault that any of that happened."

"All right, then what?"

I have a shrink, she wanted to say, but didn't. Families were funny. There was that bond of unconditional love, of shared experiences, but for Angie anyway, confiding very personal things to her family didn't come easy. It was all part of not letting people in, she supposed, and bit the inside of her cheek. Melanie told her to start with small steps. Maybe this was one of them.

"It's just…well, you and Dad have always had a good relationship. And even Nicky seems to have managed it." Nick, who used to chase the neighborhood girls with a freshly caught snake or frog dangling from his hand and who once got grounded for a month because he'd pranked a girl into believing his best friend had a crush on her. How the hell did Nick end up with someone as awesome as Claire?

"And you don't think you can."

Angie's gaze drifted to the snow-covered vineyards outside. Her next day off, she'd drag out her snowshoes and do a circuit around the property. "I don't know. It seems not, up to this point."

"Look, I'm going to say this to you once." Suzanne's voice hardened into a tone Angie remembered well from childhood, like the time she and Nick had wrestled so intensely that they'd broken a chair. "You can do anything you set your mind to. We've always raised you two that way. And that includes a loving relationship, if that's what you want. So stop acting like it's something that's just going to drop into your lap out of a clear blue sky. Like it's winning the lottery or something. Love happens to people who go for that brass ring and grab onto to it for all they're worth."

Angie's spirits plummeted further. "I don't know what to do." *And I'm not sure I'd recognize this brass ring she's talking about.*

"First thing is, you find a good woman. Maybe you already have. Then you take a chance, you surrender yourself. And lastly, you hang on like hell and don't let go."

Angie shook her head, unable to subscribe to such a simplistic view. "That's all there is to it, huh?"

"Yes. It's easy, the simplest thing at first. And then it's the hardest thing ever. You've got to fight for what you want, Ange, and then you've got to fight like hell to keep it. I'd have put money on Nicky as the quitter in this family, not you."

Her mother's words stung, but were by no means a knockout blow. "Who says I'm quitting anything?"

CHAPTER EIGHTEEN

Vic had set about the task of cooking a turkey like she was on the path of discovering a cure for a rare disease. She consulted a handful of cookbooks and about twenty foodie websites (and placed an emergency phone call to Olivia) before settling on a method that included garlic, olive oil, and fresh sprigs of rosemary and thyme. By the time Angie showed up with a bouquet of flowers, two chilled bottles of chardonnay and a wrapped box, Vic had to admit the house smelled divine.

"Smells wonderful in here," Angie said in the kitchen, breathing in deeply before kissing her on the lips. "You smell wonderful too." She nuzzled Vic's neck.

"You mean I smell like a turkey."

"Well, it's true you do smell good enough to eat."

The glint in Angie's eyes made something melt inside Vic. "I think I'd smell much better after a quick shower. Why don't you start a fire and find some music to play? I'll be down in ten minutes."

"All right, but at ten minutes and one second, I'm coming up to find you if you're not down."

Vic kissed Angie. A deep, sizzling kiss full of the kind of promise she wasn't entirely sure she meant. "Don't tempt me," she mumbled before racing off. She loved it when they flirted, loved how it set her heart thumping in her chest and, most often, the accompanying pulse between her legs.

But the thought of their words turning into action both scared the hell out of her and set her blood on fire. Karen had been her only lover in more than a decade, and sex between them the last couple of years had grown predictable, bromidic, increasingly rare. She feared she would disappoint Angie in the bedroom (if it ever came to that). The last time she'd gone through all the drama of dating and should they/shouldn't they have sex, she'd had no baggage, nothing to stop her from diving headlong into an affair and nothing to cause her to fear sex. Now she felt like a virgin and a dried-up old prune at the same time. *It's just stupid, baseless fear*s, she tried to tell herself by way of expelling the pressure, the doubts. The times she let her mind wander without reservation, she could imagine Angie's mouth on her breasts, Angie's fingers dancing over her, inside her, and in those moments, she wanted nothing more.

By the time she returned downstairs, a glass of chardonnay was waiting for her and Christmas jazz music burbled softly from the stereo. Rosemary Clooney at the moment.

"I didn't know if you owned any Christmas CDs," Angie said. "So I brought a couple of mixes I made up. Hope you don't mind."

"You've thought of everything, haven't you?" She couldn't remember the last time a woman had spoiled her this way.

Angie pulled Vic down to the sofa with her. Sitting so close, sipping wine... It felt like something they'd done a thousand times before. "What I haven't thought of, I'm counting on my imagination to figure out."

Angie leaned close and kissed her, slow and deep, a hand resting lightly on her thigh, the other arm loosely circling her shoulders.

"I'm very interested," Vic said as Angie's lips moved to her throat, "in what your imagination is rustling up."

"Are you now?"

Angie's lips trailed along Vic's jaw, and Vic's eyelids fluttered shut. The touch of Angie's lips, of fingers that had moved up another inch along her thigh, heated her from the inside. She'd not expected to become this aroused, this hollowed out with desire, so quickly. If she didn't slam on the brakes and soon, her last shred of resistance would be gone.

Roughly, she whispered, "Ange, you don't know what you're doing to me."

"But I haven't even told you what I want to do to you. Let's see." Her tongue, wet and warm, tickled Vic's earlobe. "I'd unbutton your blouse. Slowly. And I'd lick where each button exposed skin."

"Dear God," Vic breathed.

"I'd put my hands on your waist, feel the soft skin of your abdomen." Her mouth moved to Vic's other ear. "With my fingertips, I'd trace your nipples through your bra, feel them harden beneath my thumbs."

"Please, you have to stop." Vic pulled away slightly as heat rolled through her body. Her breath came short and quick, and she feared she'd actually come if Angie said one more thing or moved her hand up her leg one more inch. "The…the turkey, I need to check on it. It…I don't want it to burn."

A smile, smug with victory. "Let me help."

"No!" Her breath still ragged, Vic jumped up and held up a hand to keep Angie from getting up and following her. She knew exactly the kind of help Angie was proposing—backing her against the stove and kissing her senseless. "Stay there and enjoy your wine. I'll be back in a minute. Maybe, um, you could add another log to the fire."

"All right. And Vic?"

"Yes?"

"You're awfully cute when you're nervous."

* * *

The turkey, mashed potatoes, gravy, and all the trimmings, was almost as good as Angie's mother's, and that was saying a lot. She raised her glass of wine to salute Vic. "To the chef. I didn't know you were such a good cook. Dinner was absolutely incredible."

"I'm not really, but thank you. I researched it and simply followed a good recipe."

"Well, however you did it, it was amazing. You're amazing."

Vic blushed; she was so adorable when she did. Angie knew that her attraction to her, her admiration for her, the vividness and force of falling in love with this woman, should be making her nervous. It was all happening so fast, so unexpectedly. Instead all she felt was strangely calm. Vic was someone worth fighting for, that much couldn't be clearer. The trick was figuring out how to fight her own insecurities, to fight the feeling that she didn't deserve someone as good as Vic. That she didn't deserve this kind of happiness. She knew how to romance a woman, but she had yet to figure out how to actually abandon herself to one.

"I'm glad it pleased you. Tea? Coffee? Or more wine?"

"More wine please. And more you." There was that blush again that shot a streak of arousal right down to Angie's toes. "Come on," she said, rising from the table. "Let's go into the living room. I have a present for you."

"All right. But I have one for you too. I'll meet you there."

When Vic returned she was carrying a rather large box and a heavy one at that, judging by the way she struggled with it. She set it down with a thump on the coffee table.

"You first," Angie said, handing the much smaller wrapped gift to Vic. She felt suddenly inadequate about it; it was so much smaller than whatever Vic had bought her.

"All right." Delicately, Vic pulled the paper away. When she saw what was inside, her eyes grew wide and her smile nearly swallowed her face. "Wow. *To Kill A Mockingbird*." She flipped to the inside page of the book. "Oh my God, it's a first edition. Angie, you shouldn't have."

"Yes, I should have. Do you like it?"

"Do I like it? It's my favorite book ever. And you remembered that it was, which means even more to me."

Her eyes brimmed with moisture, but she sprang quickly up from the sofa to put the book onto the built-in shelf beside the fireplace, displaying it by leaving its cover facing forward.

"It never occurred to me to try to find a first edition of it. Wait. That antique shop in Charlevoix?"

"Yup. That's why I sent you away, so I could buy it and sneak it into my knapsack in the car."

Vic laughed. "That's some store. Your gift is from there too."

"You mean this big box? How did you manage that without me seeing it?"

"When you went for a walk down the street, I saw you duck into that outdoor clothing store, so I quickly stashed it in the trunk."

"Now I'm dying to know what it is."

"Go for it."

Angie tore at the paper rather indelicately. It was some kind of hard, black case.

"There's a latch on it," Vic said. "Open it."

Angie did and slowly raised the lid. It was a typewriter. A very black, very old portable typewriter that, despite its age, somehow managed to gleam and look perfect. The keys were small and round and made of glass. Angie had only seen such a thing in magazines and old movies.

"Holy shit, Vic. This thing is amazing!" She ran her hands over it. It was smooth, delicate, and yet indestructible. She lightly pressed a key, then another one. "The keys even work! How old is it?"

"They assured me it works perfectly. It's a 1937 Underwood. It's what every writer needs in her office as a muse."

"It's beautiful, Vic." It was the stuff of legends, or at least, the tool of legendary writers such as Hemingway and Fitzgerald, Margaret Mitchell and Patricia Highsmith. It was humbling to think they wrote entire novels on these contraptions. "I don't know that I deserve this. I'm not really a writer yet."

Vic touched her hand. "Nonsense. Published or not, you're a writer, my dear."

Tears pricked the back of Angie's eyes. God, she was becoming such a crybaby lately. "I'm going to write a story on this thing, even if it takes me a month to type it out." She thought about the one she was currently writing, about a mother who tries to overcome the guilt of seeing her young child hit by a car. It was material that had come directly from her job, a job that injected her into peoples' lives at some of the most difficult and horrifying times. Venting that emotion onto a page felt gloriously liberating—a vindication of sorts.

"Good. That gives me a really nice image to visualize. Wait. You're not going to do it with a cigarette hanging out of your mouth and a glass of scotch beside you, are you?"

"I don't know. If I do, will it make me a famous writer?"

"I don't think it works that way."

"Come here."

Vic nestled into her shoulder, her presence there feeling so right, so perfect. The air crackled with something at once untroubled and turbulent, peaceful yet incendiary—layers unseen but felt. The smallest fissure had begun opening in her heart, Angie could tell. She was letting this woman in, and it felt…strange yet exquisite. Perhaps it was the perfectness of it that was the strange part, because it had never felt this right, this complete, this *easy* with another woman before.

"Vic?" she said softly as the opening scene of *It's a Wonderful Life* began playing on the television. "Do you mind if I just hold you like this a while before I go?"

Vic turned her face to her. "I'd like nothing better."

CHAPTER NINETEEN

Vic couldn't remember a busier Christmas holiday, between working so many hours and then squeezing in dates with Angie. Mostly it was just a quick meal sandwiched between one or the other's shifts. But now it was New Year's Eve, and finally they were both off for the night. Olivia and her partner, Beth, had organized a private party at a golf course on the outskirts of town. It was invitation only, mostly people from the hospital and from the museum, where Beth worked. It was a mixed group of men and women, gay and straight, and the vibe was friendly and relaxed.

A buffet table featured everything from shrimp and cheese to fruit kebobs, while the cash bar served six different wines, four kinds of beer, two ciders, and ran the gamut of cocktails. No one was feeling any pain by the time the music started.

"Is your dance card free?" Angie said to her, holding out her hand. A slow song was playing: "If You Leave Me Now" by Chicago.

"Boy, that's an oldie," Vic said, stepping into Angie's arms. She liked how strong they felt around her.

"I didn't mean to pick something so depressing."

"I've never really listened to the words before, but you're right. It is depressing!"

Angie's arms stiffened a little. "You know something? I'm always scared that when anything good comes along, I'm going to lose it. So maybe the song's appropriate."

"I know what you mean. I never worried much about loss before. I was young when my mom and I became estranged, and when you're young, you bounce back. You figure there's lots more tomorrows, lots more victories on the horizon, that you can conquer anything. Now I know different." More collateral damage from their exes. It was like finding debris from a terrible storm weeks or months afterward. And suddenly, Vic didn't want to talk about it. Not tonight. "Liv and Beth sure know how to throw a party, don't they?"

"They do. Everyone's having a good time. But if I'm honest, I can't wait to get you alone."

They'd not spent any time alone since Christmas Eve, in private. "It's a bit early to leave." It wasn't even close to the midnight countdown yet, but Angie was right. Time alone seemed suddenly to trump everything else, and a small glow began to throb from deep in her stomach. "I did happen to notice the coatroom is, um, pretty isolated."

Angie growled softly in her ear. "Let's go. If I don't kiss you, I'm going to die."

The coats smelled faintly of aftershave, perfume, and cigarette smoke. Against a Canada Goose parka, Angie cupped her face gently and placed her mouth against hers in a kiss that Vic could only describe as tender. Angie had the softest lips, a mouth of velvet that Vic couldn't get enough of. Their kissing had a nourishing effect on her, a restoration of some kind of life force in her that too often trickled out after a long or difficult shift at work or if she let in reminders of her failed marriage.

"God, you feel good," Angie said, sliding her hands up Vic's side.

"So do you." Vic smiled against Angie's lips, slid her own fingers along Angie's biceps. She was wearing a crisp white tuxedo shirt that showed off her arms and shoulders. It would be so easy to demand more; she was fairly certain Angie would comply if she wanted to take things to the next level right here, right now or later tonight, back at Vic's house. But something held her back. Not a lack of attraction, that certainly wasn't it. She respected Angie, loved talking to her and spending time with her. Her heart lifted every time she thought of her or saw her. But dammit, Karen's ghost still sometimes stalked the halls of her heart. Which she hated. And which seemed worse now that Karen had been texting her almost every day for the last two weeks, asking to see her. So far, Vic had ignored her, but eventually she was going to have to acknowledge the texts, since there was no indication Karen was going to let up.

"You okay?" Angie said, concern in her eyes.

Maybe she should sleep with Angie. She wanted to, she was wet even now, and maybe doing so would banish Karen, or Karen's ghost, from her life once and for all. "Yes. I'm good." She threaded her fingers into Angie's, guided her hand down to the hem of her own skirt, then to the inside of her bare thigh.

"Oh, Jesus." Angie's voice cracked.

Vic's skin felt hot to the touch; it was burning up. Her head was thrown back, her throat exposed, and Angie nibbled it gently, eliciting a low moan that sent a pleasurable shiver up her spine. She was inches away from touching the most intimate part of Vic, of cupping her, slipping inside her underwear. Angie wanted to. Her racing heart urged her on and so did the hardening of her clit.

"Oh God," Vic moaned, slowly yet urgently tugging Angie's hand higher until her fingertips made contact with moist cotton. Then Vic was mashing Angie's hand against her, back and forth, hard, and God, she was so wet and soft and…

A few more seconds, Angie realized, and there'd be no stopping. They'd end up on a pile of coats, muffling their cries, rubbing and grinding and thrusting until they both came.

She stilled her hand against Vic's heat, kissed her hard on the mouth and, against her better judgment, said, "We can't, Vic. Not here. Not like this." She collected her breath, waited for the rushing in her ears to subside. "When I make love to you, I want it to be in a bed. And I want it to be all night long because I want to take my time with you and I want you to come about fourteen times."

Vic slammed her eyes shut, sighed roughly as she gathered herself. Then she chuckled quietly. "God, Angie. You're right. This isn't exactly romantic, is it?"

"Well, now that you mention it…"

"I got carried away. I'm sorry."

"I like when you get carried away, sweetheart. Just not here."

They kissed again and then Vic rearranged herself, smoothed out her skirt and blouse to remove all evidence of their make-out session.

"Do you think anyone noticed we've been gone?"

"Do we care?" Angie led the way back to the ballroom and plucked two glasses of champagne from a passing server's tray. Vic had cabbed it, and Angie had caught a ride with Liv and Beth. She was staying overnight at the couple's to keep the pressure off Vic from inviting her home for the night.

"Nope. But I'm not walking funny, am I?"

Angie squeezed her hand. "No, but you were pretty, um, excited."

"I was—am still. And yes, it's all your fault, you."

"Well, so you know, I was pretty we—"

"Oh, you two!" Liv slung an arm around each of their shoulders. "Don't you look so cute together. It looks good on you both."

A man walking past them stopped, quirked his head in their direction. He looked vaguely familiar, and Angie ran a list of names and faces through her mind. He was giving her and Vic the once-over before settling a sloppy, champagne saturated smile on them. "Sorry for interjecting, but Olivia's right, it does suit you both."

Aw shit. Michael something. One of the junior lawyers at Brooke's firm. Coolly, Angie said, "Excuse me?"

He continued smiling, but not with his eyes. "I should almost take a picture. For Brooke."

"Look, Michael, I—"

"Don't worry. She's not exactly my pal. In fact, I'd kind of enjoy seeing the look on her face. Especially now that she and Karen have broken up."

With force, Liv steered them away from him, but something was happening with Vic. She stumbled once. Her shoulders drooped. When Angie cupped her elbow, she flinched.

"Darling," Angie said as her chest tightened. "Are you all right? Vic?"

"I…Yes, I'm fine. I just…didn't expect to hear that. I mean, I didn't know."

"I didn't either."

Liv smiled nervously at them. "Look, the countdown's only a couple of minutes away. Come on, I'll grab you each a noisemaker. How are your drinks?"

Vic was staring at the floor and Angie was staring at Vic.

"Um, fine," Angie said. "We're fine."

Liv disappeared and Vic continued to visibly retreat into herself. *Great!*

"Vic," Angie said, converting her personal desperation into anger. "Brooke and Karen have nothing to do with us. This—whatever they're doing or not doing—has no effect on—"

"It's okay." Vic slowly raised her eyes to Angie's face. Cool, guarded eyes that gave Angie a sinking, wretched feeling. "Whatever. It's totally fine."

It absolutely wasn't. Vic was somewhere else, and when midnight arrived and the crowd erupted around them, they kissed quickly, perfunctorily, and it pierced Angie's suddenly broken heart. It came as no surprise moments later when Vic announced that she had a headache and was going to catch a cab.

"Fuck," Angie said under her breath. *Fucking Karen and Brooke.*

CHAPTER TWENTY

Vic hadn't meant to freak out the way she had on New Year's Eve after hearing about Karen and Brooke breaking up. Things had clicked into place, that's all. Like Karen's desperate texts, for one. Her own increasing feelings of anxiety, for another. As her relationship with Angie continued to deepen, a tiny kernel of panic paralyzed her, kept her from taking the next step. Now she understood that kernel was Karen. Karen who was now single, it seemed. Karen who desperately wanted to talk to her. Karen who couldn't quite get the hell out of her life.

Karen was seated at a booth in the restaurant when Vic arrived. Finally answering her latest text, Vic agreed to meet with her. Neutral territory seemed best, because she didn't want a scene and she wanted to be able to get up and leave whenever she felt like it.

"Don't get up," she said to Karen, who'd begun to rise. She looked tired, thinner, as though worry had taken a carving chisel to her.

"Will you be ordering lunch?" the server asked.

Vic noticed the mug of coffee Karen clutched like a lifeline. "I'll just have what she's having." Coffee was a good sign; it might mean this wouldn't be a long meeting. She shook off her coat and stuffed it beside her.

"You don't look well," Vic said carefully.

"I guess you heard about Brooke and me."

"I did. Is that why you wanted to see me?"

Karen's eyebrow twitched. "You're imagining that I can't be single for five minutes and that I'm dying to get back together?"

Vic shrugged. She didn't have time for games. "Why did you want to see me?"

Karen hedged, stirred her coffee for an interminable amount of time. "We were married, Vic. We were together a long time. I...I miss that."

The server deposited Vic's coffee in front of her, and she was glad for the momentary interruption. The timeout did nothing, however, to hold back Vic's catty retort once they were alone again. "You didn't seem to miss it when you took up with Brooke. Forgive me, but the timing of your missing me seems rather suspect."

"Vic..."

"So who ended it, you or Brooke?"

"Does it matter?"

"Yes."

"I did."

Vic wasn't sure if she should believe her. In any case, it wasn't her business and she didn't really care why they were over or how it had transpired.

"Anyway," Karen continued, "it was a mistake. Brooke. And I want to come back home."

Vic silently sipped her coffee, trying to remain calm.

"I'm sorry, Vic. I'm so, so sorry for all the stuff that happened." A tear, perfectly timed, spilled down Karen's cheek.

Stuff? Ripping my heart out, refusing to talk to me, leaving our home, our marriage? That stuff? "There is no home to come back to," she ground out. "There is only *my* home now. And you have your settlement from me."

"Please don't keep punishing me," Karen whispered urgently. She had the look perfected, the one that was supposed to hit all Vic's emotional buttons. Or rather, Vic's forgiveness buttons. The quiet tears, the slight frown between her eyes, the downturned mouth, the defeated shoulders. "I love you, Vic. I always have."

"No, you didn't always love me. You told me that night in the hospital you weren't in love with me anymore. That you were in love with Brooke."

"I never stopped loving you. And I never meant to hurt you. I just…went a little crazy. Maybe it was a midlife crisis, I don't know. But you have to—"

"I don't have to do anything, Karen. I don't have to forgive you, and I certainly don't have to take you back." *Jesus*! Did she really think it was that simple? Karen had never been a stupid person, and yet here she was, acting like absolution came in the form of a nod or a kiss or a few simple words.

"You're right. You don't. I'm sorry."

Vic swallowed a large gulp of coffee and set her mug down. Funny thing was, when Karen left her she was hurt, completely demolished, but not especially angry. Not, certainly, the way Angie had been angry. But now, finally, she was damned pissed off. From her wallet she fished out a five-dollar bill and tossed it on the table. "I can't talk to you about this right now." She rose and squeezed out of the booth. Karen did the same.

"Please don't shut the door on this," Karen said, desperate now. "Let's talk again. Please?"

Vic slammed her eyes shut, remembering the house search they'd made in Traverse City almost a year ago and settling on the grand old Victorian home. There was that winter vacation to Hawaii as a belated honeymoon a couple of years back, where they scooped up black sand to bring home and drank Mai Tais late into the nights. The ski trip to Vermont early in their relationship, when Vic had twisted her ankle so badly she thought she'd broken it and Karen had nursed her back to health. At lightning speed, so many memories, too many, kaleidoscoped through her mind. When she looked at Karen again, she saw the same thing in her eyes—their shared past. And it wasn't something that could be wiped away with a few words and certainly not over a cup of coffee.

"All right," she relented, not at all convinced it was the right thing to do. "We'll talk again. But not about getting back together." Now that she'd established that rule, maybe she could stop hating Karen.

* * *

It was a drug deal gone bad that had landed a nineteen-year-old college student in the back of Angie's rig with a stab wound to his chest. Not that he and his buddy admitted as much to her and Shatter and the two cops who pulled up to the scene a couple of minutes later, tires screeching and hands on their holsters, but it seemed like a good bet.

Ethan was the kid's name. He was still conscious, but his breathing was slowly growing shallow. "Hurts to take a deep breath," he mumbled to her as she put a line into him, thankful there were no potholes in the road at the point of insertion as the ambulance sped to the hospital. At the ER, she handed the kid off to Vic, who was all business. They had traded only a few texts, a rushed phone call in the week since their New Year's Eve date. Just busy, Vic had claimed. Distracted beyond reason, gone cold on her, was how Angie saw it. Something was clearly up with her, and it didn't take a genius to link it back to the news that Karen and Brooke were no longer a couple.

As far as Angie was concerned, Karen and Brooke's breakup was karma biting them in the ass. It served them right, and to her, the news changed nothing. But Vic possessed a different emotional makeup. She was sensitive, a thinker, a muller of things, maybe even a bit of a martyr. She was probably thinking this thing to death, because she certainly wasn't talking it to death. Angie had tried on the phone to bring it up, but Vic had quickly changed the subject. Case closed.

To Angie, one of the cops said, "Make sure you stick around so we can talk to you." She was bigger than Angie, an inch or two taller and brawnier by probably a dozen pounds, with skin the color of bronze. "We'll need a statement from you and your partner."

Angie stuck out her hand. "Angie Cullen. You new on the force?"

A nod, then a polite smile accompanied by a firm handshake. "Transferred up here from Grand Rapids. Shawna Malik. Since you guys got to the scene before us, we'd like to know what you saw, heard…you know."

"Absolutely. Kid's buddy called us before you guys got the call, sounds like."

"Yup. Thought they could get away with just calling the EMTs." She lowered her voice. "Random attack, my ass."

Vic was calling out orders, her voice tight, urgent, which told Angie the kid's injury—a small, single stab wound to the lower left part of his chest near his sternum—might be more serious than it looked. A small spray of blood squirted out of the pencil-sized hole with each heartbeat.

"Blood pressure's normal," Liv called out. "One-thirty systolic, one-ten heart rate."

"Call cardiothoracic surgery," Vic replied. "And give him two liters of saline, wide open. I want his blood typed and matched too." A quick glance from her confirmed that she feared the knife might have nicked or penetrated the kid's heart, that he could flatline or bleed out without much warning. Angie had begun to be able to read Vic's body language.

"Am I doing to die, Doc?" Ethan's eyes were stark and wide with the terrifying realization that things might not be going in his favor. "The guy just stabbed me for no reason. It missed my heart, right?"

He began to thrash a little. Shawna took a step closer, ready to intervene. "I can't believe it," he continued. "I got a hockey game next week. I…" His voice trailed off and his eyes fluttered shut.

Liv announced the obvious. "He's crashing."

Vic glanced at the clock. "Bring the ultrasound. Set up a thoracotomy. We need to crack his chest!"

Angie had witnessed the radical procedure four or five times before, all of them in the theater of war and never at this hospital's ER. But under Vic's command, it had the hallmarks of a routine procedure. With every barked order, every proficient move of her hands, she exuded the kind of confidence that steered all eyes onto her.

Quickly, she squirted ultrasound gel on Ethan's chest, moved the probe around while keeping her eyes on the portable machine's monitor. "Pericardium's been penetrated. Where the hell is cardiothoracic?"

Liv gave a helpless shrug. "They said they're on their way."

Vic nodded at Julie Whitaker, who stood across the treatment bed from her. "Intubate him while I gown up."

A nurse helped Vic into a full-length protective gown, tied it at the back for her. Next, she slid on a plastic face protector. Liv handed her a scalpel.

"Jesus," Shawna whispered roughly to Angie. "I'm outta here." She backed out and disappeared, but Angie wouldn't be pried from her spot. She wanted to see this.

Someone splashed disinfectant on the patient's chest, and Vic sliced between the two ribs over the heart. Rib spreaders were handed to her and she spread the boy's ribs until she could see his heart in its bloody sac. She sliced into the pericardium with scissors, watched as clots of blood popped out. She lengthened the incision and more clots came out, freeing the pressure from his heart, which suddenly began beating normally again. Over the bodies clustered around the table, Angie heard Julie's voice call for sedation so the kid didn't wake up. "Suction?" she said to Vic.

"Suction," Vic repeated. Through the glut of bodies, Angie could no longer see what was going on anymore, but she could picture it. "Nylon stitch on a needle driver, please."

The surgeon walked in, a petite woman with a deep voice and a head full of wavy gray hair. She nudged people aside. "Nice job, Dr. Turner. Everyone. I'll take him up for final repairs."

"All yours," Vic replied with a tight smile. Angie followed her out, striding to catch up as she discarded her mask and gown in a bin down the hall.

"With moves like that, the army would take you in a flash."

"No thanks. Civilian medicine has all the excitement I can handle."

"Vic? Can we talk? When you get off work?"

She pursed her lips, shook her head. "I don't know when I'll be off. Have you seen the waiting room?"

Angie hadn't. "What about tomorrow? It's your day off, right?"

"Sorry, can't. I've got a lot of things I need to do."

Angie's scalp prickled with heat. "I'm not someone you need to book an appointment with."

Vic's expression softened. "I know. I'm sorry. I'll call you."

She was off with long purposeful strides, leaving Angie wondering, again, what the hell she'd done wrong. And what she could possibly do to fix it.

CHAPTER TWENTY-ONE

Vic sat at one of the nursing station computers and signed off on another patient from the night. The day shift folks had come in almost an hour ago, and she was trying to leave them with an empty dry erase board. So far so good, except for a drunk sleeping it off and a mental patient currently being assessed by psychiatry.

Adrenaline from the stabbing case hours earlier had finally burned off, leaving an empty shell of exhaustion in its place.

"Breakfast?" Liv asked.

Vic shook her head. "Too tired. I'm going home straight to bed."

"I'm still keyed up from the stabbing. That was a nice save. And cracking his chest—that was some slick Chicago move, Dr. Turner!"

"I've done it once or twice there." She winked. Stabbings and shootings were as common in Chicago's emergency rooms as the sniffles were in Traverse City. "But yeah, it was the highlight of the month for me for sure."

"I checked on him a few minutes ago. They'll keep him in CICU a day or two, but it's looking like a full recovery."

"Good. Let's hope he makes better choices in the future. By the look on the cops' faces, I'm thinking he's in a little bit of trouble when he gets out of here."

"Well, nothing like the trouble he was in a few hours ago. Vic? Are you doing okay?"

"Sure. Aside from this crazy shift. Why?"

"Just wondering how you're feeling about the news."

"What news?" She was too tired for riddles.

Liv looked around to make sure nobody was listening and dropped her voice. "About Karen and Brooke."

"Sure, whatever. It's fine."

Liv stared at her. It was that look that said she didn't believe her.

Vic blinked. "All right. What?"

"You're not having second thoughts about her, are you?"

Exhaustion had a way of obliterating her cognitive abilities. "Second thoughts about what?"

"Reconciling." Something came to life in Liv's eyes. "Oh, good God. Don't tell me she's come crawling back to you."

"Liv, I don't want to talk about this. Not now and certainly not here."

"Fine, but please don't do anything rash. Or stupid. Like taking her back."

"I'm not doing anything. I've been talking to her, that's all." Vic punched a key to get to the next chart, feigning preoccupation. Explaining things to her best friend was pretty much impossible right now, mainly because she had yet to figure it all out herself. Of course she wasn't stupid enough to take Karen back, at least not right now. Not without the passing of a lot of time, some joint counseling, a rebuilding of trust, and God knew what else. As far as she was concerned, reconciling was an extremely remote possibility. But in the meantime, she wanted to be sure of where her heart stood before she went any further with Karen or Angie.

Liv's face clenched; she was in full snark mode. "Well, just be careful with her. Because if she hurts you again, I swear I'll kick her ass all the way back to Chicago."

"Don't worry, I'm a big girl. I promise I can take care of myself. And if I can't, I know where to find you."

Later, as Vic crawled between the flannel sheets on her king bed, it was Angie who trickled into her thoughts, not Karen. And it was like a warm blanket around her, the vision of Angie smiling at her, reaching out to place her arms around her, pulling her into her. *Safe, that's what I feel with Angie.* Which was something she no longer felt with Karen and hadn't since that night in late August when Karen had pulled the rug out from under her, had annihilated their marriage. Safe was something she thought she'd never find again.

And yet. And yet…

She'd never failed at anything in her life, never quit either. Not even when her mother threw her out and she had to get bank loans and part-time jobs and couch surf for months to get through medical school. When something was hard or seemed impossible, well, that was fuel to her. It juiced her, propelled her on, appreciating that she was triumphing against the odds. She was the marathon runner who limped her way to the finish line, no matter what had happened to her along the route. Nothing in her life was ever over until she was good and ready to decide it was over.

Dammit. Why can't I fucking let go?

* * *

Bleary-eyed after a sleepless night, Angie could come up with no better plan than the one she'd thought of well before the sun rose this morning. She needed to know where she stood with Vic, needed to know what the hell was going on, because these sleep-deprived nights were killing her. Grouchy at work, feeling like her decision-making and thought processes were a second or two behind the rest of the world. It had to stop. She'd go get a nice bouquet of flowers, surprise Vic, who wasn't working today. They could talk in person, away from the chaos of the hospital, put an end to the frustrating texts and phone calls that had been going exactly nowhere.

I want to be her girlfriend, Angie thought as she maneuvered her SUV around a bank of drifting snow that had crept onto the roadway. And she would tell that to Vic. She wanted them to date for real, to be a couple, to commit to the idea that they were truly starting over. With each other. Because the truth of it was, she'd never felt this connected to a love interest before. Not Brooke. Not the handful of women she'd dated before Brooke. No. Vic, with her shared love of books, with her mischievous dimples and her serious eyes, with her impossibly soft lips and the layer of vulnerability she kept carefully hidden behind the competent, controlled exterior, had crept into Angie's heart. Melted it, more like.

"Girlfriend," she said out loud, liking the way it rolled off her tongue and filled the interior of her vehicle as she practiced saying it out loud. She rolled down the window a couple of inches, let the cool air invigorate her. She thought of seeing Vic's face as she opened the door, and her breath caught in a pleasant, revitalizing way.

Noticing a strange car in Vic's driveway, Angie parked on the street. If Vic had company, she'd hand her the flowers and make plans to see her later. Not the ideal scenario, but she hadn't called or texted ahead.

Clutching the flowers, she knocked on the heavy wooden door, stamped her feet on the rubber welcome mat to dislodge the snow from them. The door creaked open and Angie raised her eyes. Karen Turner stood looking at her with piercing eyes full of curiosity and judgment. For a moment there was only the sound of a passing car, until finally, Angie, verbally tripping over herself, asked if Vic was home.

Karen's gaze drifted to the flowers that were now wilting from the cold, then back to Angie, where they seemed to do a quick calculation. "She's in the shower."

The shower? The *shower*? Worse was the way Karen had said it, with cool detachment like there was nothing unusual about Vic taking a shower while Karen was in her house.

Angie backed away, her heart in her throat. Time seemed to thicken, and the meaning of what she was seeing and hearing traveled at a painstaking pace. Vic was in the shower while Karen was answering her door like she belonged there, like everything was as it should be. Had she stayed the night? It sure looked like it. And did it mean she and Vic were back together without Vic having the guts to tell her, for fuck sakes?

She dropped the flowers on the stoop and stumbled back to her car, blinded by her own tears. Behind the wheel she decided to think about something else. The oil change her car needed, the latest movie showing at the local cinema, the new releases on this week's list of bestselling books.

Shit. It was no use. She and Vic were done. Over before they'd ever really gotten started. The tears continued to stream down her face as it occurred to her that she hadn't cried like this when Brooke left her. Hadn't felt this alone, this abandoned.

CHAPTER TWENTY-TWO

"What do you mean Angie was here?" Vic could hear the desperation in her own voice.

Karen held the droopy, chilled flowers at a distance, as if they contained some icky disease. "She asked for you and brought these pathetic things."

Vic grabbed the flowers from Karen's hand. "What did you tell her?"

"The truth. That you were in the shower."

Great. Vic painted the scene in her mind, knew the thoughts that must have ripped through Angie's mind. It wasn't good.

"I need you to go home, Karen. Now."

"But I thought I'd hang around and we'd have breakfast or something."

She handed Karen her coat. Karen had come by to return a couple of books of Vic's that she'd taken by mistake when she moved out. And then when she'd spied a new dining room light still in its box, she'd offered to install it while Vic showered. Karen was handy at fixing things, and, as it turned out, a little too eager to help out around the house. Vic should have hustled her out before she dove into installing that stupid light. "And thanks for putting in the light, though you shouldn't have." That was an understatement.

Karen was halfway out the door when she turned around. "Is it true you and Angie are dating? I mean, I'd heard something, but I thought it was some kind of joke."

"It's not a joke. And you're not helping yourself right now."

"What'd I do?"

"Nothing. Goodbye, Karen."

Vic ushered Karen the rest of the way out the door, then jumped into her car, hoping to track Angie down at her family's farm.

"Is she here?" she said to Claire at the door, her heart pounding a mile a minute as the sinking feeling in her stomach only intensified. Angie would definitely have misread the situation with Karen. And knowing Angie the way she did, she knew Angie would be upset. Hurt. Thinking the worst. What was the worst-case scenario anyway? Claire handed her a pair of snowshoes.

"Sorry, what are these for?"

Claire smiled. "She's out on her snowshoes in the back vineyard. You can catch her if you're in shape. Here, I'll point the way."

Vic was a city girl. She was in decent shape, but she'd never been on snowshoes before. "Hmm. Going to be a little hard to catch her if I'm on my ass."

"Nah, it's easy. If you can walk, you can snowshoe. At least in these modern ones."

After Claire helped strap her in, Vic set off in Angie's tracks, having no idea what she was going to say to her when she found her. She stumbled, but recovered before doing a complete face plant. It might not be an issue if she ended up buried in some snowbank, not to be unearthed until spring. She had a feeling that whatever explanation she might try to give, Angie wasn't going to buy it.

"Hey!" she called out, catching a glimpse of Angie's dark blue parka partway down a row of vines, which looked like stiff, brown fingers strung up on wire fence lines against the backdrop of snow.

Angie spun around, a look of grim surprise on her face. But she waited for Vic.

"What are you doing here?"

Vic took a moment to collect her breath. Apparently she wasn't in as good a shape as she hoped. "I heard you were at my house a little while ago."

"*Karen* tell you that?"

Angie's tone spoke volumes. "She did."

"It seems you were too busy to come to the door."

Vic closed her eyes, the cold making them sting. And the hurt Angie seemed bent on dishing out as well. When she opened them again, Angie's eyes remained unforgiving. "Yes. I was in the shower."

"So she said."

God, even in her misery Angie looked adorable, the fur trim of her parka's hood framing her handsome face. Her brown eyes seemed much lighter in the snow and the sunshine, almost gold.

"I was…" Vic swallowed. "She came over to—"

"Are you sleeping with her, Vic?"

"What? No!"

"Then what are you doing with her? Because I'd really like to know."

"I'm not doing anything with her. We're just, I don't know, not enemies anymore."

"Then why can't I get you to spend time with me? Why have you gone cold on me? And don't tell me you're busy and that I'm overreacting."

How could she possibly explain things in a way Angie would understand right now? Or at least, in a way that wouldn't make her so angry? "Look. Karen and I are trying to be friends. Maybe. And I didn't think you'd understand, so I kind of didn't tell you."

"You're right. I don't understand."

"I don't want to fight with you, Ange. But I do want some kind of closure with Karen. If it's over for good between her and I and our divorce is to be finalized, then I need to know it's over on *my* terms and not hers. Can you understand that? *I* need to be the one who says it's over."

"You know what I think?"

"Do I have a choice?"

"I think you want to see if there's anything salvageable between the two of you while keeping me on a string as your backup plan. Until you figure things out."

Vic felt her eyes widen at the accusation. It was a horrible thing to say. "That's not true."

"Isn't it? Then tell me this. What is it that you want?"

Vic bit her bottom lip to keep it from trembling. Angie had landed a direct hit. Asked her a question she didn't—couldn't—quite answer. "I'm not sure. Time, I guess. Time to get my head together, to know for sure that—"

"Then I'll save you some trouble." Angie's tone was a guillotine poised to sever things. "How about I don't want to see you. How about I don't want to talk to you until you've figured out *exactly* what you want. Because I don't want to be part of a threesome. And I'm not going to expend my emotional energy wondering if you're with her, if you're going to get back together with her."

Angie watched Vic stomp off in her oversized snowshoes, occasionally swiping with the sleeve of her coat at what Angie guessed were tears, which only pierced her already broken heart. *What have I done?* she thought. And yet she'd been given no choice. If there was room for Karen in Vic's life, then there was no room for her. And no matter how much Vic tried to excuse and defuse, the sinking feeling in Angie's stomach only grew heavier. Letting an ex back into the picture was almost never good news.

She waited until she was sure Vic would be gone, taking the long way back to the house. The vines looked like they were wintering rather well. They'd been cut back in the fall, and she saw no sign of any buckling or breaking. There were several animal tracks in the snow. Fox probably. A rabbit for sure. Other ones she guessed belonged to a porcupine.

Claire was waiting for her inside when she disengaged her snowshoes and hung them up in the mudroom.

"Coffee's on," she said.

"I think I'll just—"

"Come and sit with me. I've got a fire going."

"Where is everybody?"

"Nick and your parents went into town for supplies." Claire thrust a mug of steaming coffee in Angie's hands and led the way to the great room, where a fire leapt and crackled in the stone fireplace. "How'd your snowshoeing go?"

"Fine." Angie sat down on the plush sofa and raised her socked feet to the coffee table.

"Liar." Claire sat beside her and did the same. The family home was comfortable and meant to be lived in. "Vic looked upset when she left."

"Spying on us?"

"Of course. Who else is going to make sure you don't screw things up with her?"

Angie bit back a rude retort. "Who says anybody is screwing anything up? And for that matter, who said anything about her and me being a couple?"

"We'd all have to be blind and stupid not to figure that out. And we're neither of those things."

Jesus. Was there such as thing as families that didn't snoop and interfere and bug constantly? Well, Vic's for one, but that wasn't a family. That was the absence of family. "It's fine. We're having a timeout because, I don't know, we can't agree on things."

"I see. It's become too hard, so that's it? Done?"

Claire and her goddamned judgy interference. Her mother was every bit as bad. Her dad too. Only Nick walked around the place like he didn't much give a shit about her personal life, but that was mostly because he was too busy thinking about those baco vines that weren't growing as well as they'd expected or the latest shipment of labels that had contained a misspelling and had to be sent back. Pinot spelled without the t. *Who does that?*

"I...Look. Her ex, Karen, seems to have wormed her way back into the picture."

"She and Brooke broke up?"

Angie nodded. "You don't get off the farm much, do you?"

"Apparently not. And so what makes you think Karen is a threat?"

She explained how she'd showed up unannounced at Vic's, only to be met at the door by Karen. "Plus Vic told me they're trying to become friends. That she wants answers from Karen. *Closure.*"

"Well, they were married, after all."

"Exactly my point. How the hell can I compete with that?" She couldn't. She didn't have shared memories with Vic. Not the way Vic and Karen had. She could easily imagine them reading the newspaper together on lazy weekend mornings, shouting out headlines to one another, talking in a verbal shorthand, finishing one another's sentences. All married people had those blurred lines, the encroaching of one into the other, possessing those solid suburban bonds of marriage that she'd been stupid to think she could supplant or erase.

"Did Vic say that's what she wants? To get back together with Karen?"

"Not exactly, but she hasn't denied it either. She said she wants time to figure things out. So I'm giving it to her."

"Well, it seems to me like you're giving up."

Angie thought about that. She used to disdain giving up, thought very little of people who quit things. But some of that stubborn persistence had left her recently. Something in her—a hardened wisdom maybe?—had decided that fighting, persevering, sometimes came with too great a cost. Yeah. She'd learned a thing or two over the years, and especially over the last few months. She sipped her coffee and stared at the flames in the grate. "It's not worth fighting when you're already beat."

CHAPTER TWENTY-THREE

A man waiting for medical clearance to enter a detox facility was picking fights in the waiting room. A code had been called, alerting the nearest doctor as well as hospital security to attend. Vic saw that the patients in the waiting room had moved away from the man while continuing to watch him with their peripheral vision. Like avoiding the dead animal pancaked on the road, not wanting to get near it, but compelled to look. He was short and stocky, his neck tattooed, his hair dirty and stringy.

Two security guards arrived, ordered him to calm down even as he pulled his belt from his pants and began swinging it around his head like a lasso. "Come on," he yelled at them, his eyes including Vic in the fun. "I dare ya!"

"Time to go outside, mister," one of the security guards said, his right hand resting on his baton, the other on the canister of pepper spray attached to his belt.

Great, Vic thought, *exactly what we don't need on a Friday afternoon around here is a cloud of pepper spray making everybody sick*. She wrote a note on the chart in her hands: "Intoxicated but alert. No apparent injury." She nodded at the security guards, her signal that the man wasn't injured and needed to be escorted out. *Come back when you're sober, buddy.*

Room Five was her next stop. A woman with a bloody eardrum, purple and swollen, the man who'd done it pacing out in the hall.

"Let me call the police," Vic said to the woman. "Or at least a women's shelter."

"No."

"He'll say he loves you, but he doesn't. He'll do it again. And next time it could be worse. It's not safe for you. Let me call our security guards to take him—"

"No. Will I hear in it again, Doctor?"

Vic sighed and retrieved the silver otoscope from a pocket of her lab coat. "I don't know." Every month she saw at least one woman in this situation. In Chicago, it was every day.

Next was a lumber mill worker whose saw had slipped, penetrating his thigh with a gash that required forty stitches. After that it was a migraine, then a case of probable pneumonia.

Vic loved the fact that with emergency medicine, you never knew what was arriving in the next ambulance or waiting in the next treatment room. There was the adrenaline of saving a life, the satisfaction of making a quick but accurate diagnosis under less than ideal circumstances. Emergency medicine offered little puzzles to be solved every hour, sometimes every minute. But this window into humanity also came with tears, screaming, piss and shit and vomit and blood. The need for peace, for escape, was why she sailed and played tennis in her spare time. It was also why she used to enjoy having a companion to come home to, to share a quiet drink with, to watch a comedy together on the television or quietly read together. She missed that.

When her shift ended, forty-five minutes later than it should have, Karen was waiting for her in the staff parking lot.

"Dinner?" Karen asked, and it took a moment for the surprise at seeing her to register with Vic.

"All right." She led the way across the street to the little diner with the vinyl and Formica booths and the ubiquitous smell of cooking oil. Vintage Lionel Richie made up the background music. The place, she guessed, hadn't changed in forty or fifty years, which felt exactly right. She didn't want Karen thinking dinner with her was special or took a special effort.

"Tell me something," she said to Karen once they'd ordered their dinner (meat loaf for Vic, battered fish for Karen). "When did you decide you weren't happy with me? Was it after we moved here?"

"Before, I think. Moving here would change things, I thought. Hoped."

"And it didn't?"

"No. It didn't."

It kept eating at Vic that if Karen hadn't been happy with her before, what made her think she could be again? She cleared her throat against her nervousness. It was never easy listening to what someone didn't like or love about you. "And so what made you not love me anymore? What was it about me that—"

"Oh, Vic. It was never you."

"Pardon?"

There was the glisten of unshed tears in her eyes when Karen blinked. "It was *me*. I wasn't happy with me. And when you no longer filled that space I needed, I looked elsewhere. I'm getting counseling now. I'm working on myself. Finally."

Vic used the time it took the server to deliver their food to think. It wasn't unusual that people looked to others to fill the void of unhappiness in their lives. Karen had fooled her, though. Karen had always seemed to have that cheerful gear she could slip into when she needed to. Distracted sometimes, yes, but she never yelled or acted particularly miserable in all the years they were together. She was a woman in control, always in control. Until she wasn't, Vic supposed.

"The thing is, Karen," she said while picking with her fork at the meat loaf. "I *was* happy with you. With us. Back when we were together. The last few months have been…difficult."

"And what about now?" Karen leaned closer, hope cresting in her smile.

Oh, she knew what Karen wanted her to say. But she couldn't, because she could not lie. "No. I'm not happy. With you. And I don't know if I ever can be again."

Karen's face dropped. "All right. I deserve that. But I'm talking about down the road. After some time has passed."

"I can't know how I'm going to feel two weeks or a month or six months from now. I can only know how I feel right now."

"Fair enough." Karen speared a piece of fish, chewed it thoughtfully. "What is it that you think you want?"

God! Everyone wanted to know what she wanted. Big picture, wanted. Not what she wanted to read next or eat next, but what she wanted for her life. *Who* she wanted in her life and in what capacity and for how long. And they wanted the answer right this damned minute.

"You know what I want?" Vic finally said. "I want to *not* be asked what I want. I want to *not* be pressured, you know?"

Why couldn't she just be left alone in the here and now, wanting nothing? Was that not allowed?

"You're right. And I'm not trying to pressure you into anything."

"Actually you are."

"I don't mean to. Is Angie pressuring you too? To choose?"

Vic set her fork down. She'd barely eaten half her meal. "I'm not here to talk about Angie. In fact, I'm not hungry anymore." She signaled to the server. "I need to go home."

"Wait. Are you angry with me?"

No, Vic thought. *I'm angry with* me *for letting myself get pulled into all these directions.*

* * *

The call came over the radio as a three-car MVA, no serious injuries. When Angie and her partner arrived at the scene, all but two people, an elderly couple in the middle car, were out standing by their wrecked fenders and bumpers.

Angie opened the driver's door, Jackson the passenger door. "You all right, sir?" she said to the man, who looked to be in his late seventies or early eighties. His eyes were alert, his skin color looked fine.

"I'm fine. But I'm worried about my wife. Ethel darling? Are you okay?"

"Yes, it's just, my chest hurts a bit."

Probably from the seat belt, Angie guessed, but it was far too early to rule things out. "All right, let's get you both out of here so we can examine you better."

In the back of the rig, she put each of them on an oxygen cannula, because of their age, and placed cervical collars around their necks as a precaution.

"It was my fault," the old man said over and over. "I ran into the back of the car ahead of me and then the car behind me ran into us. I'm so sorry, Ethel. God, did I hurt you?"

"I'm not hurt, Tom, just bruised, I think. Dear," she said to Angie. "His heart isn't great, I'm worried this might have given him a jolt."

"Don't worry, I'll check him out." She and Jackson put them both on heart monitors. They both showed a normal sinus rhythm, though Tom's blood pressure was high.

"It always runs high," he said. "Don't worry about me."

"Sir, if you can lie down on the stretcher please. We're going to take you both to the hospital to get checked out."

Ethel sat on the bench beside her husband. They held hands the entire ride to Munson.

At the hospital, Julie and another resident caught the case. Angie conferred with them, assured the couple they were in good hands. Back in the ambulance, she wrote her run report on the portable computer, then went back in to check on Tom and Ethel.

"I'm worried about Tom," Ethel said to her in the treatment room. "We're supposed to go to an anniversary party for a friend tomorrow, but now I'm worried he won't be able to drive, since the crash was his fault."

"Can you catch a ride with someone else?"

"I don't know. Our kids all live out of state and most of our friends don't drive anymore."

"Don't worry, ma'am. If you give me your address and the time you need to leave, I'll make sure you get a ride." Between herself and Jackson they could swing it, especially since tomorrow was their day off. As long as it didn't interfere with her counseling session with Melanie Scott.

In the adjacent treatment room, Tom continued to blame himself for the crash. "Are you sure Ethel's going to be okay?"

"Yes, I'm quite sure, Mr. Compton."

"Are they gonna give her one of them x-rays?"

"I'm quite sure they will. She's in good hands. Try not to worry, okay?"

Angie retreated to the corridor, where a sudden flood of tears welled up in her throat. Would she ever have someone in her life so devoted to her? To share not only a long and intertwined life together, but a deep and devoted love, the way Tom and Ethel did? Who was she going to grow old with?

"You okay, Angie?" It was Julie, giving her a quizzical smile.

"Yes, fine." She straightened. "How's our elderly couple?"

"Oh, they're fine. Rattled but fine. I'll be releasing them shortly."

"Good. Thanks."

"Sure you're okay?"

By now, she figured the grapevine, once burbling with the news of her and Vic dating, had reversed itself with the news that they were no longer dating. Was that why Julie was looking at her like she didn't quite believe her?

"Absolutely," she said and pushed off the wall.

The next day, she told Melanie all about Tom and Ethel and how it made her feel seeing them together. "I'm picking them up in an hour to take them to a fiftieth anniversary come-and-go tea."

Melanie was silent for a long time, tapping her pencil against her notepad. Angie was used to these long, thoughtful silences, which usually preceded some kind of wise observation. Which then, more often than not, sent Angie down the road of further self-discovery. She'd been such a skeptic when she started all this. Now she looked forward to her sessions, although she wouldn't call them pleasant. They were damned rough sometimes. Like the ones where'd they'd spent discussing if Angie's joining the army was her way of rebelling against her always nurturing and sometimes smothering family and the predictable life she'd have with them, working and living on the farm. Well, half of that equation had certainly materialized.

"Angie, you've always been a fighter. You've spent a good chunk of your life fighting for others. In the military. On the streets as an EMT. But let me ask you this." Melanie leaned forward, her notepad closed on her lap. "When are you going to fight for *you*?"

"What do you mean?"

"Exactly what I said. You've been moping and crestfallen because a woman you've been interested in has pulled back from you and may be considering going back to her ex."

Angie had never divulged Vic's name to Melanie and had purposely kept the details vague. "What are you saying? That I shouldn't be upset about that? I think I'm falling in love with this woman. Christ, I can't stop thinking about her. About being with her."

"Then fight."

"No. I refuse to fight with her ex over her like she's the prize at the end of the battle. I won't do that."

"No, no." Melanie shook her head like a scolding schoolteacher. "Not fight for *her*, fight for *you*. If this is what you want, if she's the one, then don't give up. But do it for you. You owe it to your heart to try, and it might be the toughest thing you've ever had to do, but that's no reason to give up."

Why had she given up on Vic so quickly? She wasn't afraid of difficult journeys, so that wasn't it.

"What are you afraid of?" Melanie persisted.

"I don't know. Getting hurt, I guess." *Losing*. She was afraid of losing.

"So you get hurt. So what. And here I thought you were this tough soldier girl, a hardened EMT."

"All right, Melanie. You're trying to goad me. Just say what you want to say."

"Two words. Fear and pride. Those are the two things that are making you run away from this person with your tail between your legs. And I think you're better than that. I think you're more of a woman than that." A smile flickered at the corners of her mouth. "You going to prove me right or what?"

CHAPTER TWENTY-FOUR

"Guess who's in the waiting room?" Liv could hardly contain herself.

"Please tell me it's Wonder Woman. Or Batwoman. Or some sexy superhero who can throw me under her cape and whisk me away," Vic replied, not entirely joking. She was working a hybrid noon to midnight shift, and with only an hour to go, she'd begun counting the minutes until she could flop on her couch with a glass of wine and the new Lisa McInerney novel. Man, that woman could write about the gritty, noir side of Ireland like nobody's business. Reading the noir and grit of a country other than her own was exactly the distraction Vic could use right now.

"Actually, she's pretty close to a superhero. But then, so are you."

On the computer, Vic called up the chart belonging to a teenager with appendicitis. "What are you rattling on about?"

Liv rolled her eyes playfully. "It's Angie."

"In the waiting room? Is she hurt? Or sick?"

She'd only encountered Angie at the hospital once in the past week and that was at a distance. She was transporting a construction worker who'd fallen from the third floor to the second floor in the new home he was helping build, while Vic was treating a pregnant woman down the hall. They pretended they hadn't seen one another. Vic knew she should sit Angie down and make her listen, but she was full up to her neck with trying to make other people understand things, with trying to placate and explain and coax and mediate and explain herself. She needed a break from drama. From women. But now her heart gave a little squeeze, because as much as she told herself she needed this respite from the entanglement of a relationship, she missed Angie. Terribly. Three times she'd nearly texted her about the McInerney novel. And just this morning she was awakened by a dream where they were kissing in the deep end of a warm swimming pool surrounded by palm trees and blue skies. It was exactly the kind of dream she wanted to sink back into, and did, until her snooze button went off for a second time. Thread by thread, Angie had woven her way into Vic's heart, whether she wanted to admit it or not. There was no possible way to expunge from her heart what had already set down roots there. Angie wasn't going anywhere from her heart, at least not anytime soon. *I was so stupid to think otherwise.*

"She's fine," Liv said. "She told me she's waiting until your shift is done, that she wants to talk to you. So there. I think she *has* come to whisk you away under her cape."

Vic had confessed to Liv that Angie didn't want to see her anymore, on account of Karen's reemergence into her life. She couldn't entirely blame Angie for losing patience. But still. It hurt that she had taken such a hard line with her, that she refused to give her the time she needed to sort out her thoughts, her heart, as she had requested. Angie was so damned black and white. Infuriatingly so. But Vic wouldn't be pushed into something she wasn't ready for. *I can be stubborn too, dammit.*

"I'm not sure I'll even be done on time. Maybe I should go tell her not to wait."

"She knows. And she says it's important."

"I'm disappointed in you, Liv."

"What? Why?"

"You seem to be losing your powers of persuasion. You didn't extract from her what she wants to talk to me about?"

"Well, I did try my best, of course. But she's a tough nut to crack when she wants to be."

"Tell me about it."

Vic heard the commotion before the code crackled urgently over the intercom. Something was happening in the waiting room. The code meant security and an ER doctor should attend.

"Come on," Vic said to Liv and rushed through the double doors leading to the waiting room. Julie followed a few steps behind them.

Chairs were scattered like matchsticks. A handful of patients clustered together in the far corner, their faces as blanched as the walls. In the nearest corner stood a giant of a man, at least six-foot-six and well over two hundred and fifty pounds, brandishing a knife in a hand that was the size of a dinner plate. His camo pants and white T-shirt hung baggy and were dingy with dirt and sweat. His face looked like a mask of rage and delirium. Vic's gaze swung to the gentling voice that told the man it was okay.

"Oh God, Angie, no," Vic muttered below her breath. Calm, erect, hands at her sides, her voice low and steady, Angie emerged from the cluster of frightened people.

"Let's talk about this," Angie said to the man. "I'm an EMT and I'm here to help."

"No. I want a doctor." His chest, Vic noticed, rose and fell rapidly. Pulse must be sky high. "I need some pills. For my...my heart and stuff."

"The doctors can't help you when you're in this state. I want you to calm down, all right? Then we can figure out what you need."

His head, the size of a cinder block, shook back and forth. "There's Taliban fighters over there. Behind that desk, see them?"

Oh shit, Vic thought. A former soldier going all PTSD in front of them. "Liv," she whispered quietly. "Back up real slow and go call the police, okay? Make sure you tell them he's got a weapon and there are potential hostages in here. And make sure they know he's a former soldier."

Most law enforcement had training for dealing with PTSD cases, thanks to all the returning soldiers from Iraq and Afghanistan over the past decade and a half. But Angie wasn't a cop, and though she had been a soldier, she wasn't armed, wasn't equipped for this kind of volatile situation. *Angie*, she pleaded in her mind, *you need to get the hell away from this guy. Please*!

But Angie took a step closer to him.

"I can't let them get to my platoon," he said, his eyes flashing from Angie to a spot behind her.

"I won't let them...Corporal? Or Sergeant?"

"Corporal McIver."

"I'm a Sixty-Eight Whiskey," Angie said, using the army lingo for combat medic. "Sergeant Cullen."

"Haven't seen you around here before, Sarge."

"I'm an F6." A flight medic. "Maybe that's why. But I've been around."

The trembling hand that clutched the knife stilled and the man's breathing slowed ever so slightly. "You cover me while I get a doctor?"

"Yes, I'll cover you. But the doctors can't help until you put the knife down, okay? Nobody here's going to hurt you, Corporal."

Stateside, Angie had seen plenty of soldiers with PTSD, but nothing quite like this. She herself had had a few flashbacks, occasional nightmares over the years, but this guy was reliving something; he thought he was actually there, in the theater of war. She tried to catch Vic's eyes. If security or the cops came busting in, things could get real bad. The sight of a gun or a uniform could tip this McIver guy completely over the edge.

"You!" the man said, pointing toward Vic and Julie with his free hand. "You a doctor?"

Vic bravely nodded, but Julie froze up.

"Doc, I need something for my heart. It's beating so fast it's going to explode."

"All right, sir," Vic said. "I'm going to ask my colleague here to go get something to help calm you down." She turned and whispered to Julie. It was at that moment that two security guards roared through the double doors, their Tasers drawn.

"No!" Angie yelled. "Hold on!"

McIver took a lunging step toward Vic, then pivoted toward Angie, grabbing her by the wrist as a Taser dart hit him the chest. He wheeled around, staggered, dragging Angie with him. The hand holding the knife flailed wildly as they crumpled to the floor, his body dead weight on her, the shock of the Taser doing its job and incapacitating him. But a sharp pain lanced through Angie's upper abdomen. She wrenched herself out from under him, the pain in her side a hot poker. She inched her hand down to where it hurt. It came back sticky with blood. *Shit.*

The security guards were all over the fallen McIver, handcuffing him, but he was lying on the floor like a fallen tree—motionless, semi-conscious, gasping for air. Shocking someone in agitated delirium wasn't usually a good idea; people died from it every year.

Julie was at McIver's side with her stethoscope and barking orders for a stretcher. Before Angie could crawl away much further, Vic was on her hands and knees, bending over her, her face a map of worry lines.

"Angie, are you hurt? You're gray."

"I…I think maybe."

Vic's eyes traveled the length of her body, settling on what Angie could now see was a bloody patch on her shirt.

"All right, lie back and don't move. Liv! Somebody! I need a stretcher over here too."

"Vic, wait—"

"Angie, this could be serious. I think he got with you with the knife. And I know he didn't mean to, I saw it all go down, but I don't want you to talk right now. We're going to get you into a treatment room and take a look at you, okay?"

Angie jerked a thumb toward the man who'd hurt her. He was being hauled onto a stretcher, completely unconscious now. "I think he needs help first."

"Julie's got him. I'm not letting you out of my sight."

Words deserted her, so she smiled instead. The pain was beginning to flood her senses, fog up her mind. For an instant she was back in Afghanistan, crawling out of the troop carrier she'd been in after it rolled over. The vehicle ahead, a Humvee, had run over a buried mine, and Angie's vehicle couldn't avoid the mess in time, glancing off the burning heap and into a ditch beside the road. There was the stink of burning metal, spilled diesel fuel, burning flesh and hair too. Even now the memory of it seared her nostrils, making her want to gag.

"Angie? Angie, stay with me, sweetheart." *Vic.* Her voice was calm, measured, but Angie could hear the worry beneath the veneer.

She cried out as hands slid her onto a hard plastic board, which was then placed on a stretcher. It reminded her of the pain from the broken wrist she'd suffered in the rollover. Nothing, however, that compared to what had befallen some of her fellow soldiers. She'd managed to apply a tourniquet to a soldier's leg with her good wrist; a hunk of shrapnel the size of a hammer stuck out of his thigh. She sprinkled clotting powder on the gaping chest wound of another. Jesus, it was awful. A third soldier, blackened from fire, hung half out of the driver's door of the burned wreck, his eyes still open, frozen in a look of terror.

Someone had hold of her hand as she was being wheeled down the hall. It was Vic. She squeezed it to let her know how much the simple act comforted her.

"Vic."

"Shh, don't talk right now. I need you to save your energy. And I need you to stay calm. Can you do that for me?"

Angie nodded. *But there are things I need to tell you,* she shouted in her head. The reason she'd come here to wait for Vic's shift to end was so she could tell her that she loved her, that she would wait until however long Vic needed to figure out her life. That she wouldn't pressure her in any way. She'd been planning to tell her how much she missed seeing her, talking to her, and, well, kissing her too. Kissing her, for sure. She'd been planning to say a lot of things.

"I'm sorry, Vic." She wasn't sure whether she'd spoken out loud or not.

CHAPTER TWENTY-FIVE

"Heart rate is one-twenty," Liv said of Angie. "Respiration is forty, blood pressure ninety over sixty."

Okay, okay. All good, Vic reassured herself. She took a long, steadying breath, startled by the shakiness in her knees. Angie had a penetrating stab wound to her upper left abdomen, right beneath her ribs. She'd treated these same injuries hundreds, maybe thousands, of times. Piece of cake. *And yet…and yet.* Her head spun because it was Angie Cullen lying semiconscious before her—bleeding, pale, sweating from the pain. *Her* Angie. The woman who'd come to mean more to her than she'd ever dreamed possible and in such a miraculously short period of time. Oh, how she'd tried to resist, throwing up roadblocks at every turn, discounting and excusing and denouncing and, as a last resort, ducking for cover. She'd driven Angie away with her stupid insecurities and fears, and for that, she wanted to smack herself. Of course reconciling with Karen was a terrible idea, so why the hell had she allowed Karen a foothold to fuck with her head? Why had she even entertained the idea that she might be confused about what she wanted? And worse, use it as an excuse to pull away from this woman? *Oh, Ange, what the hell have I done?*

"Vic?" Liv pinned her with her eyes. "Should I get someone else...?"

"No." It was all hands on deck with Julie and Jeff Greene trying to revive McIver in the next room. Vic was it, and she needed to pull herself together for Angie's sake. *I can't lose her. Not now.*

She took a couple of deep breaths to slow herself down, the way she'd trained herself to do in a crisis. Every command, every move, needed to come with calm deliberation. It was how she exerted her dominance over a situation that was often on the brink of sliding into chaos.

"Give her some O-2 and let's get an IV in her. Angie, can you hear me?"

Angie nodded weakly.

"Here's what we're going to do. We're going to get a chest x-ray, an abdominal CT scan, EKG, and blood gases. I've already alerted Surgery. I can't be sure yet of your injuries, but it's a penetrating stab wound in your upper left abdomen. A inch or two in, by the looks of it." She reached for Angie's hand and gave it a squeeze. "We've got you, okay?"

"This..." Angie winced in pain. "I never thought something...like this...would happen to me. Not stateside. Iraq...Afghanistan maybe." Her eyes looked more haunted than scared, and Vic could only imagine the tragedies Angie had witnessed, all of them so far away from home, while overseas. "Will you stay with me?"

Tears pricked the back of Vic's eyes. She leaned close and whispered roughly, "Baby, I'm not leaving your side. I promise you."

Twenty minutes later, Angie was on her way upstairs for surgery, Vic holding her hand as the bed was wheeled down the hallway and into the elevator. Angie's spleen had been lacerated. They'd try to repair it, but if they couldn't, there would need to be a splenectomy. Which meant she'd gotten off lucky. If the knife had nicked her intestines or a vital organ, Angie would be a world of trouble right now.

She had to let her go at the automatic doors leading into the surgical suites, and it was like a physical cleaving of something from her body. A hollowness crept into her gut as she stumbled down the stairwell back to the main level, tears blurring her vision. Angie would be okay. She was healthy, young, would tolerate surgery well. And if it came to a splenectomy, it was really no big deal. People lived long, healthy lives without one, so it wasn't that. It was…

Christ, she didn't know what it was, except she was scared, desperate for everything to be okay. How incredibly different this was from a typical patient, someone she'd treat in the ER before either shipping them home or off to Surgery, Cardiology, the Medical Floor, ICU…somewhere else. Once they were gone from her sphere of concern, it was onto the next patient without so much as a glance back. There was always someone else about to come through the door, and once her role was completed, that was it, out of sight out of mind. It was the only sane way to do her job, to be able to focus on the tasks at hand. But Angie… She didn't, couldn't, let her go. Screw the rest of the patients piling up in the waiting room. Angie was not just anyone. Angie was everything, and that, she realized, was something she'd been waiting for, wanting more than anything, and for a very long time.

"Hey," said Julie, intercepting her outside the stairwell door. "You okay?"

Vic leaned against the wall, holding herself like she might unravel. "Yeah. I'm good."

"You look a little green around the gills. Angie okay? I hear she went up to Surgery."

"She's okay. Spleen. What about McIver?"

Julie shook her head. "He didn't make it."

What a waste, Vic thought. All of it. A guy—a former soldier—dead. And he'd hurt Angie. *Goddammit.* For what? What had been the point of it all?

"Vic, go home. Or go wait for Angie to get out of surgery. The rest of us can cover the department, plus I've had Dr. Atkinson alerted that she might have to come in if things get busier."

"I appreciate it, but no need. I'm okay, I'll—"

"No. You're not. I know you outrank me, but I'm putting my foot down." There was a don't-fuck-with-me edge to Julie's voice that Vic appreciated. "And if you don't listen to me, you'll have Liv to answer to."

Vic snorted a laugh. "Well then. In that case, I'd be wise to take your advice, Dr. Whitaker. I know when I've been sufficiently ganged up upon."

"Smart woman." Julie patted her shoulder. "I'll be up to check on you and Angie later."

"Thanks." Vic turned to head up the stairs again before halting. "And Julie?"

"Yes?"

"When things settle down...I'd like to get to know you better. We haven't really had much of a chance yet to become friends, and I'd like to change that."

"Me too." Julie smiled. "I'd like that a lot."

* * *

Angie had no idea how much time had passed, but she sure as hell knew where she was. In the recovery room. In the hospital. Images flashed in her mind. The big ex-soldier with the panicked eyes and the knife in his hand, smelling sour, looking haunted. The security guards rushing in, the stumble, the blade catching her, the explosion of pain in her side. *Fuck.* Vic holding her hand, bending over her, talking quietly to her in the treatment room before the sedation kicked in and everything had gone black.

"How's the pain?" a nurse asked her. "Between one and ten."

"Um..." She squirmed a little to test herself, and the tiny move shot a bolt of pain through her side. "A four, I think. What have you got me on?"

"Fentanyl. Don't worry, we're going easy on it."

"Where's...what happened...in the OR?"

She was still groggy, but she remembered being wheeled up to surgery, Vic telling her something about her spleen being injured.

"The surgeon will be by to talk to you. Then you're being moved to a bed."

"What about Vi…Dr. Turner?"

"Ah, good, the patient is awake."

It was Vic, and a glow warmed Angie from the inside, spreading outward, like the sun warming everything in its path. The haze of pain, the uncertainty of what had happened to her, instantly vanished, because Vic was here. Smiling at her. Looking at her like everything was going to be okay.

"Hi, Dr. Turner," the nurse said. "I'll be right over here if either of you need me."

"Thank you, Jessie." Vic sat down on the vacated stool beside the bed and gingerly took Angie's hand—the one without the IV in it. "I'm so happy to see you awake." She stroked the back of Angie's hand softly.

"Oh, Vic. I'm so glad you're here. What the hell happened?"

"I just talked to Tim—Dr. Kennedy, your surgeon—out in the hall. He'll be in to chat with you in a few minutes. They had to repair your spleen, but he thinks it went well. He didn't have to do a splenectomy. They'll check in a week or two to see if it's functioning properly. If not, they might have to remove it at that point. And I talked to your mom."

"You did?" Her family would be sick with worry; she was surprised they weren't camped out in the hallway, trying to bust their way in.

"And yes, they're crazy with worry, but I think I convinced them to stay home and get some sleep and to visit you in the morning. But I basically had to tell them you were in a coma for the next few hours and wouldn't even know if they were here or not."

Angie started to laugh, but it hurt too much.

"How are you feeling, sweetheart? How's the pain?"

The blaze in Vic's eyes, the map of worry on her forehead, the urgent stroking of her hand, was almost too much for Angie to bear. A tear and then another rolled down her cheeks. *Shit.* She didn't want Vic to see her cry. She was a fucking ex-soldier, for Christ sake. What had happened to her sucked, but she wasn't mortally wounded, wasn't going to die. It was nothing compared with what she'd seen others have to deal with.

Vic reached up and thumbed the tears away. "Oh, Angie, I'm so sorry," she whispered, her voice breaking, her eyes glistening.

Angie pulled her hand away. She didn't want them both dissolving into tears. Instinctively she wanted to protect Vic. "I'm okay. I'm glad it wasn't worse."

"No. I hate what happened to you. I should have handled the situation differently. I should have made sure security was better apprised of what was going on instead of rushing in there like a house on fire. And then when—"

"Shh. Stop, okay? He was a ticking time bomb. And he wasn't going to go quietly." They were both experienced enough to know how volatile situations like these were, how unpredictable someone suffering a mental breakdown could be, how fast events moved.

Vic's gaze wandered as she retreated into her own private contemplation of the tragedy. Her face took on the hard and unforgiving expression of someone who wasn't about to stop blaming herself, no matter what Angie said.

"What happened to him? McIver?"

Vic shook her head.

"Shit."

"Look," Vic said. "I'm so sorry you were there, that you got caught up in it. Why were you there? In the waiting room?"

"I...I was waiting for you." *I'd wait until the end of time for you, Victoria Turner, only I never got the chance to tell you that.* "I...I was—"

The surgeon, a tall man garbed in scrubs, cleared his throat loudly as he strode past the empty recovery room beds to Angie's side, the bounce in his step giving no indication that it was the small hours of the morning. "Dr. Turner. Ms. Cullen." He smiled and pulled up an extra stool. "Let's have a chat, shall we?"

CHAPTER TWENTY-SIX

Vic had managed three hours of sleep in the staff lounge, enough to get by on, but she wasn't entirely firing on all cylinders as she took the elevator up to Angie's room on the surgical floor. Maybe she could blame her crazy idea on her exhaustion. She would if she had to, because she was taking a sizable gamble with it.

Angie's parents, her brother Nick and his wife Claire hadn't left her side all morning. Vic was envious of how close they were, of how much they doted on Angie and how Angie pretended she was indifferent to their attentiveness. But Vic knew Angie ate it up, and so she should. She was lucky to have such an involved, caring family who loved her unconditionally. People learned how to love and be loved from the people who surround them in life. In Vic's case, she'd learned love only because it was the polar opposite of what she'd been taught. It was like figuring out beauty when all you saw was ugliness.

"Vic, honey," said Suzanne, pointing to an empty chair. "Did you get some sleep?"

"A little."

Claire smiled warmly at her, and Vic decided she would like to get to know her better. She could be a good friend. In fact, all of the Cullens could be good friends. Vic had never felt so comfortable with a pack of strangers.

"We're here for the day if you want to go home," Claire said helpfully.

Vic ignored the vacant seat and continued to stand. "I will a little later, thank you." She caught Angie's curious eyes and held them for a moment, aware that she'd struck the pose of someone about to make an announcement. Which she was.

"Is everything all right?" Roger Cullen asked.

"Sorry, yes. I want to propose something. To Angie mostly, but I guess it really concerns all of you."

She felt more than saw the puzzled surprise in Angie's gaze. She had to suppress a giggle. Perhaps the word *propose* was a slight misnomer.

"I was thinking that, with all of your permissions, Angie could move in with me for a couple of weeks. While she recovers. I have some time off from work owed to me, so it would be no problem to take a couple of weeks off, whatever Angie needs."

"Oh!" Suzanne's hand flew to her mouth. "Oh dear, dear Vic. That's so kind of you. But we've got this covered. Angie is in good hands with us. In fact, one of us can be by her side the entire time. Right, gang? We can look after her in shifts."

"Absolutely," said Roger. "We wouldn't have it any other way."

"Anything for my big sister," Nick said, more emotional than Vic had ever seen him.

Only Claire remained silent, watching Angie and then Vic, back and forth as though she were watching a tennis match. She smiled. "I think it's a fabulous idea."

The other three Cullens exploded in simultaneous disagreement, clearly insulted that Claire would side with Vic. Insulted by the whole idea that Angie, in her time of need, might leave the protective nest.

Vic held up her hand to quiet the room. "I'm sorry, Roger, Suzanne, Nick. I don't mean to cause family drama." She glanced at Angie, who had smartly decided to remain mute. "I only suggest it because I know you all have endless things to do on the farm. And I'm well qualified to look after her if there are any complications. And in fact if there are complications, my house is only a couple of miles from the hospital, where we can get her immediate help. Out on the farm, you're at least twenty minutes away, and with it being winter, weather could be an issue if she needed help."

"Well," Suzanne said, crossing her arms over her chest and giving Vic an inscrutable look. "I don't like it. I don't like the idea that my baby girl is sick and not at home under my watch."

"Ditto," Roger said. "Although it's kind of you to offer, really, we do appreciate it. But our daughter belongs at home right now."

Nick looked from his parents to Claire, clearly caught in the middle. "Um…"

"Hey," said Angie, waving her hand. "What about me? Do I get a say in this?"

All eyes in the room swung to Angie. Vic swallowed. *Please say yes*, she silently begged. She was trying to do Angie a favor, offer her an out from what was sure to be smothering attention on the farm. But she had her own selfish reasons too. She wanted to make up for lost time with Angie. Wanted to prove to Angie her devotion, her loyalty. Wanted to prove that Karen was, once and for all, her past and that she was ready to acknowledge where her heart stood. It was important to show Angie these things rather than to just tell her.

"I suppose Vic makes a good argument," Angie said mildly, as though Vic had proposed something as mundane as taking her for a car ride. "We could try it for a week. I'm sure I'll be back on my feet by then and able to look after myself."

Suzanne looked devastated.

"Mom, it's not like you can't visit. And besides, I'm going to get my own place again at some point. I just haven't found a house yet that I want to buy, but it's going to happen one of these days and probably sooner rather than later."

Roger emitted a defeated sigh. "If it's what you want, honey. I know we can be overprotective at times. But those years you were in Afghanistan and Iraq…you have no idea how much we worried about you. How out of our control it all felt to us. It was very hard on us."

Nick rolled his eyes. "Boy, you got that right. They drove me nuts with their worrying."

"We'd have been equally nuts if it'd been you over there, young man," Suzanne scolded.

Claire stood and motioned with her hand like she was herding a bunch of school kids in the schoolyard. "It's settled then. Mom, Dad, Nick, let's go get a sandwich and a coffee and let Vic and Ange work out the details."

"Thank you," Vic mouthed to Claire as the group passed, earning a wink in response.

"I don't know whether to kiss you or to be really pissed off at you," Angie said as soon as they were alone.

Vic pulled up a chair and laughed. "Well, I know which one I'd pick."

"Do you now?"

"Well, it's a bit of a toss-up, but yes, I do."

The mischievous glint in Vic's eyes was a joyful revelation, because it was like old times between them, flirting up a storm. But it wasn't all fun and games. She knew enough not to read too much into things right now—things that might not really be there, such as Vic feeling something for her beyond friendship or professional loyalty. "I appreciate the offer, Vic, I know what you're trying to do, but it's really not ne—"

"Whoa, wait a sec. I didn't make the offer just to be nice or to get your family off your back for a while."

"Is it guilt? Are you still beating yourself up about what happened to me? Because if you are, that's—"

"No, it's not that. I..."

Angie couldn't read what lay behind Vic's hesitation. Was she having second thoughts? Was she about to tell her something incontrovertibly painful and final, perhaps that she and Karen were getting back together again? Or were already back together? The thought made Angie instantly nauseous. *Please, anything but that.*

"Look," Vic continued. "I want to help you. In spite of us going off the rails the way we did, I care about you, Angie. That's never changed. And I want to be here for you. Let me do this. Please."

"I don't know what to say, Vic." Would it be uncomfortable, the two of them shacked up alone together? Christ, what if Karen was going to be there too? If so, it'd be the fastest goddamned post-op recovery in the history of the world.

"Say yes."

"Hmm, and if I don't?"

Vic eyeballed the IV bag hanging over Angie's bed. "Let's see. I could easily substitute your pain drip with saline solution."

"You wouldn't!"

"Oh, I would!"

Angie sighed dramatically. Whatever else was or wasn't going on between them, Vic made her smile. And while moving in with her for a week might not be the smartest decision she'd ever made, it beat the hell out of having her parents hovering at her side every minute. "All right. Deal."

"Good girl. Now the first order of business is to start reading this lesbian romance novel together."

"What?"

From her lab coat pocket, Vic withdrew a paperback novel, its cover featuring a hot-looking woman in a cowboy hat and checked shirt with cleavage as deep as the Grand Canyon. "We're going to read this together. I figured something not too heavy while you're all doped up."

"Is there sex in it?"

"Oh, I'm sure there is."

"Well then, what are you waiting for?"

Vic laughed. "Indeed." She slipped her reading glasses on and thumbed open the book. It occurred to Angie that there was nothing sexier than a woman reading, especially while wearing reading glasses. "All right, chapter one. Geraldine Strombecker pulled on her leather cowboy boots and—"

"What? Wait! Geraldine? And Strombecker? Are you kidding me? What kind of name is that for a romance novel?"

Vic laughed until she was doubled over and clutching her sides. "I'm kidding, I'm kidding. Oh my God, the look on your face."

With her good side, Angie reached behind her and tossed her pillow at Vic. God, even if it hurt like hell, it felt good to laugh with Vic again. Tears began to collect in her throat at the realization that there was nobody she'd rather be with than the woman who sat at her side, clutching a paperback novel with one hand and wiping away tears of mirth with the other.

Vic carefully replaced the pillow behind her head, fluffing it first, and flipped open the novel again. Angie closed her eyes, lost herself in the rhythm and melodic cadence of Vic's voice. She could listen to Vic, sink into those gray-green eyes, all day. And as she floated on the slow, loose ripples of pain medication and let the river of Vic's voice carry her away, it occurred to Angie that at this moment, she'd say yes to anything Vic might ask her. She wanted, in fact, to stay in this moment forever.

CHAPTER TWENTY-SEVEN

There was no shortage of offers to help settle Angie in at Vic's house two days later. Angie's firefighter buddy Vince, her brother Nick, and her EMT partner Jackson tried to carry her into the house until Angie finally barked at them to let her walk. Which she did, slowly. She wanted to visit with them in the great room or "parlor" as she sometimes called it (and usually in a teasing voice thick with an English accent), but Vic forced her by threat of barring future visitors to settle into bed upstairs in her own room, which was right next to the main bathroom and a short few steps away from Vic's room.

Vic had just successfully chased away the three men when Liv and Julie showed up. Tagging along with them was the brawny new cop in town, Shawna Malik. In a pullover sweater and jeans, she looked less bulky than in her uniform and protective vest. *But still*, Vic thought, *I wouldn't want to mess with her.*

"Thirty minutes," Vic said in her harshest tone, leveling them with a stare she hoped looked sufficiently threatening. "She needs to rest. Which the three of you should know."

Liv gave her a crisp salute, Julie smiled knowingly and Shawna cut her an apologetic look, spreading her hands as if to say she was simply along for the ride.

The three told Angie jokes and the latest gossip around the hospital. And while Angie eagerly devoured the company and the attention, she exhausted quickly. Vic had begun to notice the smallest signs of anything that looked off with her—her skin color, her breathing, the alertness in her eyes, the strength of her voice. And Angie, she could tell, was growing more weary by the minute.

Exactly twenty-eight minutes after the three women had tromped upstairs to see Angie, Vic shooed them away, promising them they could visit again tomorrow.

"But you're cutting our visit short by two minutes," Liv complained.

"Out. I'm not letting you kill my patient with kindness."

"Spoilsport. You're not this mean around the hospital."

"Yes, she is," Julie said, smiling to show she didn't mean it.

"Bring chocolate next time," Angie called after them. "And lesbian romance novels for Vic to read to me."

That earned a howl of laughter and a round of promises as the three noisily departed.

"Well, Vic. You've got the role of jail warden down pat," Liv said on a laugh. "Just don't take advantage of your cute prisoner."

Vic grinned. "Wouldn't dream of it."

"Am I missing something," Angie said to her when they were alone, "or am I sensing sparks between Shawna and Julie?"

Vic sat down on the edge of the bed. It was a double, so there was plenty of room. "I noticed it too. Did you see the little looks they were giving each other?"

"Yes. And the secret smiles when they thought nobody was looking. Do you think Liv knows?"

"No. If she did, she'd have already blabbed about it."

"Ooh, we know something that Liv doesn't? Better write down the date and time."

"Oh, my God, that *is* a momentous occasion. She usually sniffs out romances like a hound dog trailing a scent."

"What about you?" Angie's voice dropped an octave, managing to sound sexy even in her weakened state. "How do you feel about romances?"

Vic expected to see a teasing glint in Angie's eyes. Instead, the soulfulness she saw there nearly broke her in half. What she really wanted to do was lie beside her, stroke her arm, her shoulder, her neck, her cheek, and then whisper words of affection and promise. But it wasn't the time or the place. Perhaps, she reasoned in her mind, her reticence was because she couldn't quite get out of doctor mode with Angie. *Or, hell, maybe I'm just a coward.* And she took the coward's way out by turning her response into a joke. "Oh, I'm all for them. That's why I'm reading to you from a romance novel."

"I'm serious, Vic."

Vic took Angie's hand, stroked the back of her thumb softly and evenly, the way she might reassure a child. "This isn't the time to talk. You need to get better first, okay?"

"But I am better, aren't I?"

"Yes. You're definitely getting better, but you need to go slow with this, build up your strength again."

"But Vic, I—"

"Shh. There'll be time later, I promise." Vic leaned over and touched her lips to Angie's forehead. Her skin felt warm, slightly clammy. "Are you feeling all right? You seem a little warm."

"I'm fine." Her tone said she was disappointed and in a mood to sulk.

"You're probably worn out from being moved here. Not to mention the parade of visitors."

"I'm fine. I promise."

Vic stood. "I'm going to let you rest now. And I'll be right downstairs if you need me, okay? I'll be back up to check on you in an hour or so."

"Wait. Read to me first?"

The pleading in Angie's eyes shot straight into Vic's heart. Saying no to this woman took a colossal amount of willpower, and Vic had no real desire to resist. If Angie asked her to hold her, she would do it. If she asked her to kiss her, she wouldn't dream of saying no. She was gone, a sucker for this woman, whether it made sense or not.

She plucked the book off the nightstand and sat back down again. "Okay, sport. One chapter. And then you're going to have a nap."

Angie batted her eyelashes playfully. "Yes, Dr. Turner."

* * *

Sex. Good sex. No, great sex.

Hands everywhere, dancing over skin, skimming breasts, brushing shoulders, tickling thighs. Lips playing over nipples, then sucking gently. A mouth that was warm and wet and soft and oh, so skilled! A mouth that was everywhere at once.

Angie thrashed her head from side to side, her pillow damp. It was as though stones held her eyelids down. She gave up trying to open them, sank back into the fog in her mind that swallowed everything. Everything, that is, but thoughts (memories?) of sex. Heart-stopping, mind-numbing, bone-shattering sex. It was that book Vic had been reading to her, the characters, in her mind, were making wild love. No, wait. It was Vic. Vic had come in here and made love to her. Yes, maybe that was it. She was wet down there, aroused, hardened into a desperate yearning. She wanted Vic. Where was she? She tried to call out, uncertain whether her voice was working. Her jaw felt thick, stiff.

A hand, cool and soft, touched her forehead, her cheek. Again Angie tried to open her eyes, succeeding this time in opening them partway. It was Vic, her mouth tight with concern.

"Angie, you're burning up, love. How are you feeling?"

"Sex," Angie mumbled, the word rolling around in her mouth before spilling out. "Did we…"

"You're not making sense. You have a fever. Are you in pain?"

"You…we…were good together, Vic. You were so…hot… you were…I wanted…"

Her voice firmer this time, Vic said, "Angie, are you in pain? Does it hurt anywhere?"

"My...my side." *Jesus!* A red-hot poker jabbed her repeatedly, right where she'd had that damned spleen repair. She clenched her teeth against the pain, sobered by it, defeated by it.

"I'm getting a thermometer and a cold cloth. Be right back."

"Don't go," Angie tried to say, but managed nothing more than a grunt.

Vic returned and inserted a thermometer in her mouth, draped a cool cloth over her forehead. Angie mumbled.

"Don't talk until I get a reading, okay?"

Vic's voice was strained, her smile doing nothing to mask her concern. This wasn't good, everything about Vic said. When she extracted the thermometer, her brows pinched fiercely together.

"I'm going to have a look at your incision, okay?" Gently Vic pulled Angie's baggie T-shirt up, touched the skin around her incision with hands that were methodical, clinical, but a spark of arousal shot through Angie just the same. She missed being touched. She missed Vic. The Vic that wasn't a doctor.

"What?" Angie mumbled. "What's wrong?"

"I'm calling an ambulance." Vic was calm as she pulled her cellphone from her pocket.

"Why?"

Vic turned away to talk to an emergency dispatcher on the other end of the line.

"Five minutes," she said to Angie. "I think you might have an infection. I want a surgeon to look at it right away. Preferably Dr. Kennedy, if he's working. Or I'll have them call him in if he's not."

Vic was back on her cellphone again, calling the hospital's ER, ordering people about.

"Wait," Angie said after Vic finally put her phone away. Her posture was erect, stiff, as though every muscle in her body were on high alert. It was anything but comforting. "Am I going to be okay? You're...scaring me."

Vic took Angie's hand, kissed it and didn't let it go. Her face relaxed, her smile a lifeline Angie clung to. "I'm going to make sure you're okay. We'll get you on some IV antibiotics, do a scan, hopefully nothing more than clean out your incision."

"You don't...have to do this." Tears collected in Angie's throat, an obstruction she couldn't cough away.

"Do what, sweetie?"

"All...this. Looking after me. Being nice to me." *I don't want you being nice to me*, Angie thought. *I want you to love me, dammit.*

"I'm doing *all this*, as you put it, because I want to. And because I don't trust anyone else to look after you as well as I can."

"Vic, do you..." A siren wailed in the distance, growing closer. *Shit, they're using the fucking siren. I'm not dying for Christ's sake!*

"It's going to be fine," Vic said, but it was in that professional voice she used in the ER with patients or their loved ones, when the outcome wasn't at all a sure thing, but she didn't want to worry them needlessly. "I'll be with you every minute."

"That's not..." *I want to know if you love me.* "Karen. Are you and she...are you *with* her?"

Above any others, it was the answer she really wanted. Needed. She trusted that Vic would do her best to make sure this setback in her recovery—an infection, if that was what it was—would be dealt with. But if she was with Karen, if she *loved* Karen... Hell, she didn't know if she could handle that, if she could survive that.

"Ange, the ambulance. It's almost here."

"No." Angie squeezed Vic's hand harder. "Tell me. Please."

"Oh, sweetheart." Vic's face crumpled. "I'm not with Karen."

"But she...you..." It took too much effort to speak.

"No." Vic raised Angie's hand and kissed it, and when she spoke again her voice was strong, sure. "I'm not going back to Karen. Ever."

CHAPTER TWENTY-EIGHT

Claire gently took Vic by the elbow and guided her out of the surgical waiting room chair. Vic let her; she was wobbly from exhaustion and worry, but she was also sick of the helplessness of the situation. Angie had been in surgery for close to an hour now, and it could be another hour before Tim Kennedy came out to speak to her as well as Claire, Roger, Suzanne, and Nick. Before the surgery began, Tim told her he'd likely have to do a splenectomy, but that he wouldn't know for sure until he got in there. Vic had tried hard to manipulate her way into the operating room, but it wasn't exactly a secret around the hospital that the two women were somehow involved. Allowing a loved one, even a loved one who was an MD, into the operating theater was ethically frowned upon, not to mention a nightmare in practical terms. Vic herself didn't like family in the treatment room because emotions could easily get out of hand, making it difficult for the medical staff to do their jobs and all too often proving to be overwhelming for the patient.

"You look like you needed a break," Claire said in the elevator after pressing the button for the first floor where the cafeteria was located.

"Do I look as bad as I feel?" Vic wouldn't normally admit such a thing, especially to someone she hardly knew, but with Claire, she felt no judgment.

"Sort of. But you make a lovely basket case, if it's any consolation."

Vic smiled for the first time today. "Thanks. I think."

Claire touched her hand briefly. "It's okay. You're with family."

Family. With Karen she'd had a family. Until Karen had made her an orphan again. But with the Cullens, Vic could see how easily, how warmly and simply they could become her family. It was a progression that felt right, natural. It had since the first time she met them. "Thank you, Claire," she said against the sandpaper in her throat.

"Thank *you* for being there for Angie. That means the world to all of us."

Vic sipped the too-hot coffee because it helped cleanse the emotion from her throat. "I can see Angie means the world to all of you."

"She does. And *you* mean the world to her."

"I do?"

"Yes. You do. She's in love with you, you know. Even if she hasn't said it to you yet."

She couldn't argue with Claire, because Claire was right, and Vic knew it in the deepest recesses of her heart. She'd known it for weeks now, and Angie's love for her was precisely why there had been an emotional chasm between them the last little while. It wasn't about Karen, not really. What had scared Vic away was the truth that Angie loved her. She said simply, "I don't want to hurt her."

Claire looked at her with wide, searching eyes. "Are you afraid you're going to?"

"I was…am, yes."

"Because you're not sure if you love her?"

"No, it's not that. I think I was…am…afraid that I'll screw it up. That I'm no good at this."

"Because of your marriage ending?"

Vic nodded. She knew she wasn't to blame for Karen blowing up their marriage, but she also understood now that these things didn't happen without underlying reasons. Something led Karen to stray in the first place, even if that something was a neglected relationship on both their parts. They were both responsible for their marriage ending up on the trash heap.

"Do you mind if I ask you something else?"

"Of course not."

"As a doctor, did you ever screw up? Lose a patient because of something you did or didn't do?"

"Of course. It comes with the territory in this profession."

"Let me tell you something about myself that you might not know, Vic. Nick is actually my second husband."

"He is?" Angie hadn't said anything about it.

"Nick and I have been married for six years. But in my early twenties I was married for twenty-two months."

"What happened?"

"We were young and had no idea what we were getting into. First sexual partners and all that. We thought we were being so grown up getting married, that it was the thing to do." Claire rolled her eyes good-naturedly. "I knew pretty early on in the marriage that it wasn't going to last, that it was a mistake. Don't get me wrong, Brad wasn't a bad guy. We're still friends, actually. He plays hockey with Nick once a week."

Vic laughed. "That's rural life, I guess, huh?"

"Exactly. But here's the thing. I had to forgive myself for making a mistake. Brad did too. It's the flip side of giving yourself permission to take risks in the first place, but it's all part and parcel of the same thing."

"The thing is Claire," Vic said haltingly, "is that I'm not in my twenties anymore."

"Ah, so you think mistakes are solely for young people to make?"

Vic thought about the analogy Claire had made, and it uncorked something important. She'd always counseled young doctors that they would make mistakes, sometimes irreparable ones, but that it didn't make them bad doctors and it didn't mean they should stop doing their jobs. It was called life. And it was called not being perfect. "Point taken."

"Angie won't break, you know," Claire continued. "I think what's hurting her is not what you both may or may not do to one another in the future, but what's happening now. If you love her, you should tell her."

"I will," Vic said. But not yet. There were things she needed to take care of first, namely Karen. And she needed Angie to get her strength back and focus on her recovery. "When the time's right Claire, I promise I will."

Claire smiled at her. "Good. Because I can see in your eyes that you love her."

Vic blushed. "You can?"

"Absolutely. Now let's get back there and see if our girl is out of surgery yet."

* * *

If a truck had run over Angie, she wouldn't have felt worse. Her mouth was a desert, her side hurt like hell, and her entire body felt exhausted, heavy. An IV was connected in each arm, antibiotics and pain medication anchoring her to the bed. Not that she had the strength to get up even if she wanted to.

Vic's face came into view, and it was the loveliest face Angie had ever seen. Especially when Vic smiled. She didn't know if Vic knew it or not, but when she smiled that way, it was an angel's smile—warm, loving, comforting, beatific somehow. It made Angie's heart ache in the most pleasurable way. She did her best to smile back because every cell in her body wanted to, but it was a chore. "Wh—what happened?"

Vic's hand moved to Angie's forehead, then tenderly brushed her cheek. "You have an infection, sweetheart, but it's under control now. And Dr. Kennedy had to do a splenectomy. I'm sorry. But you're going to be okay. You're going to get better now. Finally."

"When? I don't remember…surgery."

"You were pretty out of it with your fever. We brought you in by ambulance last night and the surgery started at about seven this morning."

Angie swallowed painfully. "What time is it now?"

Vic checked her watch. "Just after nine in the evening. I sent your family home a couple of hours ago so they could have a proper meal."

"I've been out that long?"

"Yes, but you've been sedated and on some pretty heavy pain medication."

"When…can I get out of here?"

Vic's laughter sent a warm tingle through Angie. "You've only been here twenty-four hours and you want to go home already?"

"Yes." *As long as it's home with you.*

Vic pulled her chair closer. "Hopefully by tomorrow afternoon, and I'm afraid you're going to have to put up with me being your jail warden again."

"Good. I love your jail. I mean…your house."

"Do you remember much about last night? Before you came here?"

Angie shook her head. She remembered feeling hot and sick to her stomach and so incredibly tired. Sad too for some reason.

"You asked me if I was back with Karen. You were pretty adamant about it."

Angie tensed, her heart lurching at the answer Vic might provide. "Go on," she said, only half meaning it.

"I told you I'm not with Karen. And it's true. But things weren't entirely finished between us. Resolved, I mean, which is why the two of us have been having a few conversations lately. Earlier tonight, I met her downstairs in the cafeteria for dinner."

Dammit, why did it always feel like the other shoe was about to drop? Angie squeezed her eyes shut against what might be coming, felt Vic tenderly smooth her hair again, which started a slow ache in her chest.

Vic whispered, "Don't look so worried."

"Do I need to be?" She opened her eyes.

"No." That smile again that could undo Angie in a heartbeat. "I told her we couldn't ever be together again, that it was over. And not just because I couldn't ever trust her again, but because I don't love her anymore. I think I haven't loved her in quite awhile. I just...we got into a rut. Even when we decided to get legally married, we did it, I think, as some kind of Band-Aid to paper over what was missing from our relationship." Vic shrugged. "It took a crisis—her affair—for me to finally figure things out. To realize that our marriage wasn't worth trying to rescue."

"Wow." Angie's desire for revenge, to see Karen hurt, fell away. "I'm so sorry, honey. I'm sorry you were so unhappy for a long time. How did she take it?"

"Surprisingly well. She was actually quite gracious about it. When she and Brooke broke up, I think she was confused, lost more than anything, and didn't quite know where to turn. She's going to move back to Chicago. She's going to try to get her old job back."

"Good. And what about you? How do you feel?"

"Like a weight has been lifted. Like I might actually be on my way to finding my footing again. And I think I have some ideas on that front."

Angie smiled weakly. She was happy, thrilled at this turn of events. But something hollow, something that felt an awful lot like fear, shadowed her.

"We'll talk more when you're stronger."

A light kiss flitted across Angie's lips, and her blood thickened for a moment. Then the kiss was gone, the ghost of it lingering on her mouth.

"Sleep well," Vic whispered.

CHAPTER TWENTY-NINE

If there was one good thing so far about Angie's injury, it was the endless opportunities it provided for Vic to get to know the Cullens better. Angie had only been out of the hospital and tucked into Vic's house for four days now, but Angie's parents or Nick and Claire stopped in every day with casseroles, soups, and an abundance of entertaining conversation. Vic was in no hurry to return to work and had at least another week off, more if she needed it. She could get used to this, all of it—having someone around the house, welcoming regular visitors who were fun and warm and kind and, with gentle ease, made her feel like one of them.

Today was Angie's first day outside the house. Vic had driven them to the Cullen farmstead because Angie was getting bored and, though Vic would never admit it to another soul, she wanted to see if Angie was itching to move back home. The health crisis was over, Angie was recovering nicely, but Vic wasn't ready to let her go. Having Angie to take care of, to fuss over, to share conversation with, to read books to (she hadn't stopped the little habit they'd fallen into), to cook for (Angie was finally on solid food, though barely), made Vic feel useful, complete, in a way her job failed to do. Their connection warmed her soul, made her happy, dammit, in a way she hadn't been in years.

"So," Claire said with a lightness meant to mask the seriousness of her question. She and Vic were huddled in the Cullens' massive kitchen making tea for everyone. "How's life with your patient going? I mean, really going?"

"Good," Vic said, keeping her eyes on the boiling kettle. She knew exactly what Claire was trying to get at. "Nice. She's doing well and I'm enjoying the company."

"Just nice?" Claire chuckled, playfully bumping shoulders with Vic. The two women had become friends. "Not romantic yet?"

"Not romantic yet." Vic's grin dissolved as she thought of the cheerful but tidy routine she and Angie had fallen into. Angie's health was the first priority, and so Vic hadn't raised any further serious emotional topics with her. She wanted Angie strong and off the pain medication before they took any next steps. But it made her impatient sometimes, left her yearning for that emotional connection late at night when she was alone in her bed. She saw it in Angie's eyes too—the questions, the longing for something deeper. In an unspoken agreement, they both knew the time wasn't right yet to lay it all out there.

"Well, I don't know how much more time you're going to have Angie to yourself before Momma Bear carts her off and brings her back home. Suzanne's itching to have Angie back under her roof again. I swear she's jealous that you're the one who gets to do all the fussing and caretaking of our girl."

Shit, Vic thought. If that happened, she and Angie might never get time alone again. Or at least not for a few more weeks. Her sensible side told her that it would be okay, that no matter how many days or weeks passed right now, she and Angie wouldn't lose their special connection and that simmering desire for one another. But still, if she moved out of Vic's, it would put that much more distance between them.

Claire poured the kettle into a teapot practically the size of a microwave oven. "The good news is, Nick and I have an idea of something that might help keep Angie at your place indefinitely."

Vic's eyebrows jumped into her forehead. "Wow, really?"

"Yes, really. That girl needs to get her butt out of the parental nest. And soon, or she might never leave."

Just then Nick barged into the kitchen, and Claire and Vic began giggling conspiratorially.

"Speaking of never leaving the nest," Claire joked.

"What?" Nick said, looking adorably like Angie with his wide, startled eyes the color of warm fudge.

"Nothing, honey. You can help carry this tray into the great room in a minute. But not before you help me tell Vic about our idea to ensure Angie stays longer at her place."

Nick broke into a wide smile. "Oh, right. And it's a brilliant one, if I do say so myself."

Claire rolled her eyes as she placed freshly baked brownies and chocolate almond biscotti on a second, smaller tray. "You're just saying that because it was your idea. But I'm the one who's done all the legwork so far."

Vic butted in. "All right, you two, I'm dying of anticipation. Tell me about this great idea."

"A puppy," Nick said, grinning. "A yellow Lab. A breeder I know has a five-week-old litter."

"A puppy?" Vic liked dogs, though she'd never owned one, mostly because with her schoolwork, then her long hours of training and, lately, her shift work, a dog wasn't practical. Plus Karen had never wanted one. "How is a dog going to keep Angie from moving back here when I can no longer use the excuse of looking after her?"

Nick snatched a brownie off the tray, ignoring Claire's swat on his wrist and popping half of it into his mouth. "Easy," he said between chewing and swallowing. "Mom's allergic to dogs, so we've never been able to have one here. Not an indoor one. So Ange and her dog would have to get their own place."

"With the right personalities, dogs have amazing therapeutic qualities," Claire supplied. "I've done a lot of research the last couple of weeks. Many former soldiers swear by them, and PTSD therapy dogs are becoming a thing. Colleges are even using therapy dogs during exam time to help students deal with stress."

"I have actually heard of that." It boggled Vic's mind how little professors had cared about her stress levels when she was a student. They seemed to think that piling on more of it built character. And they were half right; it either built character or it destroyed it. "So this would be a sort of therapy dog for Angie?"

"Possibly," Claire said. "She's been through a lot, between her two tours with the army, now this attack at the hospital. I think it would be good for her. And Labs love the outdoors, just like Angie. It could be a companion for her, you know?"

"It wouldn't be a trained, licensed therapy dog," Nick added. "That takes time and a lot of red tape. But this litter's daddy is a trained therapy dog, and the mom is really good-natured too."

"Does Angie even like dogs?"

"Loves them," Nick said. "When she was a kid she kept bringing home strays and hoping Mom would change her mind. One day she even brought home the golden retriever that lived next to the school, claiming it was a runaway and she didn't know where it belonged."

Vic laughed. "A dognapper? Oh my!"

"The bigger question," Claire said pointedly, "is are *you* a dog lover, Vic? Would you be okay with taking in a puppy until Angie finds her own place?"

"If it'd be good for Angie, of course, I'm all for it. But what if I become attached to this little beast?" It was code for *I really don't want Angie and her dog to leave.*

"Visiting rights," Nick teased. "We'll draw up a custody agreement for you."

"All right," Vic laughed. "That eases my mind a bit."

Claire handed the heaviest tray containing the teapot and mugs to Nick and the lighter one with the snacks to Vic. "Now remember, this is a secret until next week. Can you bring Angie out to the breeder? We'll surprise her then, and let her pick out her puppy."

"You know, this is the most fun news I've heard in weeks. You give me the date, time, and address, and we'll be there."

Claire stood on her toes and kissed Vic on the cheek. "Thanks, Vic. I'm so happy Angie found you."

Me too, Vic thought, before amending it. *I'm so glad we found each other.*

* * *

Angie let Vic pick up the cardboard box from the front stoop, and a sigh of frustration escaped her. She hated others having to do everything for her, from helping her dress to making her meals. At least now she could manage her own showers.

"I know, champ," Vic said, reading her mind. "But no heavy lifting for another five weeks. Besides, I'm not a little weakling in need of some studly butch opening her doors and carrying things for her."

"No," Angie grumbled. "But apparently I am."

Vic shook her head, smiling, and set the box down on the foyer side table. She ripped open the tape binding it together and plucked out a note from inside. "Ooh, books from Julie and Shawna." She pulled one out, then another. "Lesbian romances! A whole pile of them. How fun!"

Angie was less than thrilled. All those things did lately was remind her that she and Vic had gotten exactly nowhere since New Year's Eve. Well, not nowhere exactly. They were warm toward one other, flirty even. Plus Vic had admitted she wasn't going back to Karen. But that was it. There had been nothing solid that she could bank any sort of future on. "Any cowgirl ones in there?"

Vic dug through the box. "Not a single one, sorry. But there seems to be one about aliens. Oh, and another one featuring lesbian vampires."

"Um, maybe you could put those ones on the bottom. Aren't there any sexy ones about a doctor and an EMT?"

"Actually, I think there are a couple of medical romance novels in here. But a hot doctor and a super sexy EMT? I think that one's waiting for you to write it."

Angie hadn't gone near her laptop since the attack. Not only did the energy for writing elude her at the moment, but so did the ability to concentrate for very long. Her pain medication was of the milder variety now, but this inability to concentrate was worrisome. It was partly why she had encouraged Vic to continue to read to her. That and because she loved listening to Vic's voice. It was a lethal combination of soothing and sexy.

"All right, one of these days maybe I'll try writing one."

"Promise?"

Angie nodded. She was tired again, exhausted from the afternoon spent at her family's. And while she loved getting out and seeing her family, she wanted nothing more than to climb back into bed and close her eyes.

"Come on, let's get you up to bed."

"Only if you'll join me." They often bantered in this manner, and while it was fun, Angie found herself wishing the words meant something. That, for once, they led to something more. Like making out. Like confessing their love for one another.

"That's an offer I can't refuse." Vic looked at her with those eyes that said she wanted to eat her up. Unfortunately, said desire never got any further than her eyes.

Vic scooched in bed beside Angie, leaving a few inches between them for decorum's sake. "Want me to read to you?"

"I think I'm too tired for that right now."

"Are you too tired to talk?"

"Depends what you have in mind?" Was this—finally—where they got to talk about the future?

"Your tours in Iraq and Afghanistan. Were you afraid of dying over there?"

"Not really. I mean, it was in the backs of our minds, for all of us, but you couldn't let it paralyze you. You had a job to do. Life had to go on."

"What about that night in the ER, when the attack happened?"

"No. I was more worried about you. And the others." She studied Vic, trying to understand why she was asking these questions. "What about you, were you afraid that night?"

"I was, yes. But not for me, for you. First when you got close to him to try to talk to him. And then when he grabbed you. I thought…" Vic's voice trailed off. When her eyes misted over, something sharp tugged at Angie's heart.

"Oh, sweetheart. Come here." Angie pulled her against her shoulder, circling an arm around her. "I'm so sorry. I don't want you to be afraid of anything, especially on my behalf." She kissed Vic's temple, basked in the peace, the tranquil elation of having Vic in her arms. She swore that she could stay like this forever, just the two of them wrapped in their own cocoon with the outside world nothing but a gauzy memory.

She felt Vic's lips on her neck, moving against her skin, tasting her, and Angie dipped her head to capture Vic's mouth with her own. The kiss was soft, yet heavy with meaning. And all at once it was like circles closing and puzzles clicking into place as Angie's world settled into an order she'd never known before. She deepened the kiss as arousal flamed slowly to life deep in her belly. And oh how she loved the way Vic was responding too, increasing the pressure with her mouth, pressing her body harder into Angie.

"Oh Vic," Angie murmured. "So much I want to say, to do to you…"

And with that the spell was broken. Vic eased back, stood and straightened her clothes, as if to erase all evidence of what had transpired.

"Vic…I won't break, you know. It's okay."

The soft click of the door closing was Vic's only response.

CHAPTER THIRTY

For the next couple of days Vic had been able to avoid getting snared into a discussion with Angie about the kiss. She knew Angie was dying to talk about it, but Vic kept her distance. There was laundry to do, the house to clean, groceries to buy, bills to pay, meals to cook, calls to return from friends and colleagues asking how Angie was doing. She wasn't quite at the point of admitting to herself she was afraid of where the conversation might take them. Would they be on the same page? Feel the same way? And most of all, was it too soon? Were they ready for the next step?

By evening, after a simple dinner of chicken and rice (Angie was still on a bland diet), Angie's fingers crept into Vic's hand at the small kitchen table, the dirty plates in front of them. Vic had been just about to rise and take them to the sink when Angie's hand tugged her back.

"Can we talk?" Angie said, the purposefulness in her eyes bringing Vic's heart to a standstill. "Please? In the parlor?"

"It always sounds so formal when you say 'parlor.' Like we should have chaperones or something."

Angie's grin was sexy and provocative. "Maybe we should. Oh, wait. Chaperones would be a very, very bad thing."

"Really?" Vic enjoyed playing along with these little games, although she knew it would not derail Angie from wanting to talk seriously. "That must mean you have something very bad in mind."

Angie stood and, still holding Vic's hand, led them to the front of the house. "Oh no, not bad. Something very, very good, actually."

They sat down together on the sofa, and without preamble, Angie reached out and tilted Vic's chin toward her. Her lips, soft and gentle, brushed Vic's, and the sensation reminded her of butterfly wings. She closed her eyes so that she could more deeply feel Angie's mouth on hers, feel the kiss that was tender yet bold, respectful yet framed with resolute insistence.

They fit so well together, their mouths moving in perfect synchronicity, and Vic couldn't help but wonder what sex with Angie would be like. There would be dominance, but it would alternate, she felt. First one on top, then the other. And each would be bold in taking and doing what she wanted, in demanding and claiming pleasure, in wringing everything physically and emotionally from the act. It would be thrilling but also lovely, exhilarating but fulfilling. It would be raw and complete, as though her body and mind would be occupied while she also did the occupying. She could almost feel now Angie's naked skin pressing the length of her, the hard muscles turning her on, making her crave more. She felt a blush work its way up her neck, relieved that Angie was too busy to notice it.

"I missed this," Angie murmured against her. "I've been dying to kiss you again since the other night."

Me too, Vic thought though she refused to give voice to it. She had to keep a lid on this. Angie was still sore, still recovering, plus she didn't want them getting ahead of themselves and letting sex define their relationship. But then Angie's hand began moving up her side, spanning her stomach, crawling up to the underside of her breasts, and all rational thought beat a hasty retreat.

"You're so sexy, Vic." Angie's mouth suckled the soft skin at the base of her throat, and her vocal chords instantly numbed at the pleasure.

"Angie…"

Then that exquisite mouth was kissing the underside of her jaw, began nibbling her earlobe, and dammit all, her resolve was soon burning off like a hot sun pulverizing a morning mist. Lips were on hers again, harder and hungrier this time, and Vic matched Angie's intensity with her own. It was only when Angie's hand cradled her breast, a thumb absently brushing her nipple, that Vic gasped and reared her head back, a moan of surprise and need escaping her. That one simple move had reached in and unraveled her.

"What…wait, Ange. What are you…we…doing?"

Angie's hand wasn't stopping its exploration. "I want you, Vic. I want you so much, I always have. And since you don't want to talk about us, I figured action was called for."

Vic reached down and stilled Angie's wandering hand. "But you're still weak. You're still recovering."

"I am, but I'm not dead. And I'd have to be dead not to want to do this to you."

There was so much raw need filling Angie's eyes, and Vic feared there was as much on display in her own eyes. They were two freight trains on a collision course, and, yes, she could slow it down, but she couldn't stop it. She knew that.

"Ange, I don't want to make love with you until we both know where we stand with each other. Until we're both ready to make the kind of commitment to one another that I need and that I suspect you need as well. I want us to be ready for this. Sure about it. And not just physically."

Angie sat back against the couch, letting her hand fall into her lap. "I went to the ER that night to tell you I'm in love with you, Vic. That I was stupid giving you ultimatums and not being patient with us. I was done with all that. I was ready to give you whatever time you needed."

Vic's breathing slowed. "Oh, honey. I didn't know."

"I thought…I thought you wanted Karen." Angie's face collapsed. "I was…am…willing to fight for you. That's what I wanted to tell you that night. That even if Wonder Woman walked in and flung herself into your arms, I'd beat her off, dammit."

Vic pulled Angie into her arms and held her, rocking her, massaging her back in delicate circles. "You don't have to fight. I'm here. And I dream of the same kind of future for us that you do."

"You do?"

"I do." They held each other's gaze, and Vic was shocked at the hesitation in Angie's eyes. "But you…" She inhaled a calming breath, told herself that it was okay, that Angie hadn't changed her mind. Their making out was evidence of that. "Talk to me, Ange."

"No. I mean, I do want it too, Vic. But…"

Angie began softly crying, and Vic had never felt so helpless, so unsure. The ground she thought was firm had turned suddenly to sand. "What is it, darling?"

"I'm…damaged. I…don't know if…I can do this. If I'm actually capable of any of this." Angie's voice went from halting to practically tripping over itself. "I want to, so much, you have no idea. But it might be too late for me, Vic. So much has happened to me, and I don't know if…"

"Ah, so you think you've surpassed your Best Before date? Is that it?"

Angie coughed away her tears. "Something like that."

"Well, it's true you've crammed a lot of things, some not very nice things, into your thirty-seven years. But that does *not* mean it's too late for you, Angela Cullen. It means you have some challenges, sure. We all do. But you deserve to be loved. Do you hear me? You deserve to be happy. We both do."

"You make it sound so easy."

"No, I don't, because it's not easy. But I hope I make it sound right and true and doable. Because you can do anything you set your mind to, including this. You know that, right?"

Angie looked at her and Vic could instantly see the clouds part in her eyes. The old Angie was back. "You have a lot of confidence in me."

"I do. And I'm right to."

"You're pretty special, do you know that? If someone like you can make me feel like I have a chance, then who am I to argue?"

Vic grinned. "Arguing with me is a very bad idea, in case you haven't figured that out yet."

"Hmm, I can see that."

"And I'll tell you something else." Vic's voice grew serious. "I haven't exactly waltzed through life without a few scars of my own, in case you haven't noticed. You're not the only one who's been damaged, my love."

"'My love'? Okay, wait, anything you said before that is gone because *my love* is all I can think about."

"I'm trying to be serious here," Vic scolded, but she was grinning.

Angie took her hands in hers. "I know. And you're right. We both carry around a lot of pain, don't we?"

"And doubt. And fear. And bravado and sometimes even denial to wallpaper over all that doubt and fear. I've come to realize these last few months that with age comes baggage. But so does wisdom."

"Wow. I picked myself a smart woman, didn't I?"

"You did. And so did I."

"So I guess the million-dollar question is, what are we going to do about this?"

"Indeed." Vic raised Angie's hand to her lips and kissed it. "I don't have all the answers, but I'll tell you this. I don't want to lose you. And I don't want to throw away a future for us. Because I'm willing to do whatever it takes for us to stumble through this thing together. Are you?"

Angie's smile nearly broke Vic's heart, because it wasn't quite confident, but it was a start. "I'm willing to as well. But Vic?"

"Yes?"

"I might lose my way once in a while. Screw up."

"Good, because I might too. What do you say we go slow. As in s-l-o-o-o-w slow. And see what happens?"

"Yes, okay, but…does the slow part mean there's still kissing involved?"

There was in her imploring eyes that joyful mix of curiosity and satisfaction that some part of Vic seemed to need like oxygen. "Oh, I think kissing is allowed."

"Touching?"

"I see we're into some hard negotiations now."

"Just trying to learn the rules." Angie shot Vic a sly wink that reignited her arousal.

"I think we'll know where the forbidden zones are when we come to them."

Angie snuggled closer, burying her head against Vic's neck, her breath warm and ruffling Vic's hair. "Oh good. That gives me lots of leverage to play with."

Vic welcomed this new lightness in her heart. She reached over and switched off the Tiffany lamp, throwing the room into darkness. Nestled together, they stared at the large double windows and the falling snow that was like glitter illuminating the darkness.

* * *

The dryness in Angie's throat, the slightly elevated heart rate, was not unexpected as she and Vic stepped into the waiting room for the ER. Angie knew quite a lot about PTSD, partly from her training as an army medic, but mostly from firsthand experience working in military hospitals. Especially at Walter Reed in Bethesda, where some of the worst cases were treated. Her thoughts drifted to McIver, the former soldier who'd inadvertently stabbed her just feet from where she stood now. He hadn't intended to harm her; she believed that. But he was sick, in need of serious treatment and was probably among hundreds, maybe thousands, of the walking wounded who continued to suffer after serving tours in war zones. War changed people. It was both that simple and that complicated.

Vic squeezed her hand. "You ready for this?"

Angie nodded, took a deep breath, held it. She'd been lucky. She had never suffered from anything more than mild depression and mild PTSD, but being here brought that night back again. Brought back how quickly things had happened. She hadn't been scared, not really, because foolishly or not, she thought she had some control over the situation. Scared came later, after she realized she'd been hurt, after seeing the uncharacteristic panic in Vic's face that she had tried—and failed—to contain.

Angie counted to ten, slowly. She wasn't always in control of her surroundings, far from it. But she was in control of her feelings. She could control how she felt about something, how she responded, and right now she felt safe. She felt okay. Sad, but okay.

"What about you?" she asked Vic, knowing it had to be tough for her too.

Vic nodded once, cleared her throat roughly. "Yes. I'm all right."

"I wish we could have helped him."

"So do I. But I'm not sure we were equipped here to do so. I'm not sure he could have been helped that night."

Yes, thought Angie. Thinking that way helped. The outcome was a tragedy but it wasn't necessarily avoidable.

"I'm so sorry you got hurt, sweetie."

"I'm just glad nobody else did."

Vic smiled something unreadable. "You would say that."

One by one, staff greeted them, welcomed them back, inquired about their well-being. They thanked Angie for trying to intervene that night, told them both they were anxious to see the two of them back at work.

Hand in hand, Angie and Vic stood in the spot where Angie lay wounded two weeks ago and where McIver drew one of his final breaths. There was no evidence anything had happened. Carpets had been scrubbed clean, broken furniture replaced. Life went on, filling in and erasing evidence of the things, the people, the events that had come before.

Angie looked at Vic, felt her heart expanding against her ribcage. Nothing was perfect. And nothing was going to last forever. But she wanted, like never before, to see where her life was going to take her, what it had in store for her. There was another chapter ahead, and another and another after that. She wanted desperately to open them all and to open them with the woman standing beside her.

"Can we go now?" she said quietly.

Vic arched an eyebrow. "You sure?"

"I've seen everything I need to see here. And I'm tired of looking backward."

Vic wrapped an arm around Angie's waist, simultaneously planting a kiss on her cheek. "Okay, let's go. Lunch is on me. And someplace nice."

"If I'd known that I would have suggested we leave long before this."

They walked back into the bright sun and the tinkling sound of snow melting. But as she took a look back at the double glass doors of the ER entrance, it occurred to Angie with a sinking feeling that she soon wouldn't have Vic all to herself for much longer.

"I guess you're going to need to go back to work soon."

"Yes. Unfortunately." Vic unlocked her car, opened the passenger door for Angie.

"When?"

"One more week, I'm afraid, is about all I can squeeze out of them for time off right now."

Angie swallowed, bereft at the idea of being alone, of having to leave Vic's house. "I guess that means I'll move back to my parents' place next week."

Vic belted herself in, started the car, shifted it into reverse. "I might have some ideas on that."

"What do you mean?"

Vic's smile said everything and nothing. "I don't think we need to make any rash decisions about that right now."

CHAPTER THIRTY-ONE

Vic halted mid-sentence on the page she was reading and felt Angie's eyes on her. Impatient eyes. They were reading a lesbian romance novel out loud together on the couch, taking turns, but now the book had arrived at a steamy scene and it made Vic nervous. Nervous because, as she quickly scanned a paragraph on the next page, she saw that it wasn't just steamy make-out stuff, but full-out, graphic, jaw-dropping sex.

"Cat got your tongue?" Angie said playfully.

"Nope. Sex has got my tongue all tied up in knots."

"Ooh, too chicken to read it out loud, are we?"

Vic handed her the book. Angie was up to reading pages on her own now, having progressed from a few sentences, then a few paragraphs, before becoming exhausted or losing her concentration. She was getting back to her old self, which was great, but the upcoming scene, Vic feared, might overload the sex-starved circuits in both of them. "Go ahead, if you're so brave. Be my guest. But I'll bet you five bucks you can't do it."

"Deal." Angie harrumphed and began reading the scene like it was no big deal.

"'Jane whimpered and her eyelids fluttered closed again. She could only nod her assent, and before she knew it, Alex was mercifully undoing her pants and sliding them down her legs. She arched back into the couch as Alex's lips tenderly and unhurriedly trailed down her stomach, her body so rigid now, she felt like a guitar string about to snap.'"

Angie read on, showing no emotion, not even a hint of discomfort. Vic, meanwhile, had begun to squirm lightly because she was turned on, dammit. Which was exactly what she was afraid would happen if they read the scene out loud. How could Angie be so stoic, so immune to the steam rising off the pages? Did she not feel *anything*?

"'Jane thought she could not possibly hold off any longer when Alex began to fulfill her promise. Her fingers drew the panties aside just enough to make room for her tongue, and when it found her, Jane felt herself dissolve to a new level of liquid pleasure. She pushed back hard into the soft couch as Alex's tongue lightly, but in quick, sure strokes, plundered and caressed her to the very edge of diabolically sweet, swirling, delicious orgasm.'"

With a flick of her wrist, Angie tossed the book to the floor, where it made a satisfying thump. "All right, that's it, I can't take this anymore. You win."

"Now that's the best five bucks I've ever won," Vic cooed.

"Lording it over me, huh?" Angie began tickling Vic, her fingers like an invading army over her stomach and up her sides, leaving a pleasurable, fiery trail wherever they went. Even through her cashmere sweater Vic could feel her skin burning at Angie's touch.

"W-wait, that's so not f-fair." Vic giggled and squirmed as Angie worked her way up her neck, which was one of her erogenous zones. It was sensitive as hell, and right now she could hardly breathe.

"You're right, I'm not being fair using my hands."

Angie's lips took the place of her fingers on Vic's neck, licking, nipping, kissing the area around her collarbone, the hollow at the base of her throat. Vic was slowly combusting, melting from the outside in, wanting, needing this woman's hands all over her, under her clothes and on her bare skin, inside her. Her head was back, her eyes pinched shut, her body taut and turned on and ready to burst and she could think of nothing else but Angie making love to her. Angie's mouth crept to hers, sucked on her bottom lip, and Vic whimpered for more. They'd been posturing, flirting, skirting ever closer to acting on their sexual attraction to one another these last few days. Touches lingered longer, looks took on new heat, words of affection turned into innuendo. They'd been playing with matches, and the trouble was not the matches but in the dry tinder their bodies had become.

"Ange...wait, honey." Oh God, it hurt to stop. Physically hurt. "This...we..."

"I don't want to stop. I want to make love to you, Vic."

Angie's eyes were dark, almost black, with longing. She kissed Vic again, tenderly and with feeling. Her hand rested just below the swell of Vic's breast while a thumb rubbed slow, tiny, mesmerizing circles.

"Slow," Vic mumbled, her breath coming out in short, sharp bursts. "We're supposed to be...going slow."

Yeah, sure. Tell that to the hard throbbing that had taken up residence between her legs. Whose stupid idea was that anyway? Oh, right, it had been hers.

"I can't even remember why we thought that was a good idea." Angie kissed her again, dancing her thumb higher until it made contact with Vic's nipple. Sweet, agonizing contact that made Vic's stomach do a slow, tantalizing roll. And then Angie was pulling off her sweater, and Vic let her because she knew resistance at this point was little more than some principle whose power and appeal was fast disintegrating.

"I think," Vic said between breaths, "it had something to do with us wanting to be sure."

"Oh, trust me, I'm sure I want to do this." Angie's fingers made short work of the buttons on Vic's cotton shirt. She parted the material, stared with unveiled wanting at Vic's breasts and the lacey black bra covering them.

"I think…" Could she even think right now? "…it had something to do with being sure about us. About a future together. About commitment."

Angie's eyes swung to Vic's. "I am sure, darling. Of all of it. I don't want to wait any more for you to understand that I want us to be together. I want a life with you, Vic. I want a future with you. And I want it to start right now, because waiting any longer is making me crazy."

It was too late to take back her declaration now, but Angie carefully watched Vic's eyes to gauge its effect, because those eyes were the most expressive, unguarded thing about Vic and they never lied. Seconds ago the gray in them had been flecked with green and gold in what Angie guessed—no, knew—was arousal. Now they transitioned to something slightly darker, something obsidian. She could see that Vic wanted to believe her, but wasn't sure if she could.

"Angie…are you sure?"

"Yes. And I'm sorry it sounds impulsive, but it's something I've been thinking about for a while. Weeks. It's how I feel, Vic, it's what I want and it isn't going to change. Which means the ball is in your court."

Vic made some space between them. Not an entire cushion's length, but a few inches anyway. And that was bad news. "It's just…You know what I worry about? I worry that we're both perfectionists. Overachievers. I worry we won't confront a problem if…no, when we have problems, down the road." She laughed, but there was no humor in it. "I tend to put my blinders on and pretend everything is fine while I go save the world, and you…you clam up or close yourself off so you can't be hurt. Angie…" She looked at her with a mix of fear and hope that was almost heartbreaking. "I don't want to screw things up again."

Shit shit shit. I've misread everything. I'm an idiot. Vic doesn't want anything more than what we've been doing, of course she doesn't. It's why she won't take that next step and sleep with me. It's why she won't—

"Honey," Vic said. "You look like you're about to have a panic attack. Are you okay?"

Angie's voice came out three octaves too high. "Define okay."

Vic reached a hand out and touched her cheek, and dammit, Angie couldn't help but close her eyes and sink into the feel of Vic's soft skin. She wanted to cry, and it took all her willpower not to.

"Oh, sweetie. What I'm trying to say is that if we do this, there are some things we need to do a better job with. Like, we need to accept that we're going to screw up sometimes. That we might even hurt one another, even though we're not trying to. That we're not going to be perfect, that we're not going to be a perfect union all the time. And we need to be okay with that. We need to not run away from things. Which means we need to talk about everything, all the time." Vic laughed away her tension. "That's some kind of list, isn't it?"

"Kinda, but I love lists." Angie smiled because she was pretty sure Vic had just given her—them—her blessing to try to make this work. "Are you saying what I think you're saying?"

Vic leaned closer. Angie inhaled the scent of her citrus shampoo, the laundry detergent that smelled like sunshine. "I want to try to build a life with you. Do you think we can do that? Do you think we can try? I'm scared as hell, but—"

"Oh God, I love you." Angie began covering Vic's face with little kisses, kisses that were like tiny, electrifying sparks. Then she touched her forehead to Vic's and looked into her eyes. "I know what you're saying. And I do want to try. With you. And I promise we'll talk. We'll talk so much you won't be able to shut me up."

Vic smiled, the light back in her eyes.

"I won't clam up and be the tough, silent soldier type," Angie continued. "I promise you that. And I promise I'll be okay with making mistakes. Well, not okay with it, but...you know what I mean. We'll work through them. I won't try to be Miss Perfect all the time, or think the world is crashing in around me if things are not perfect all the time. There, you see how much I can talk?"

Vic laughed and kissed Angie's lips softly. "That's a very good sign. And I promise you that I won't put my blinders on. And that before I save the world, I make sure first that everything is okay with us."

They kissed again, deeply this time, and it made Angie feel like she could do anything, including conquering the world and presenting it to her lover on a silver platter. "I love you, Victoria Turner. I love you so much. With you, I feel like me, the real me, if that makes sense. And do you know the most important thing to me?" She wanted to tell Vic everything and all at once. "I respect you. I respect you absolutely." She'd never respected Brooke, and that was probably the very start of their problems.

"And I respect you, Angela Cullen. And I love you with all my heart, did you know that?"

"I didn't until now. I mean, I'd hoped." Angie wiped a tear that had appeared out of nowhere. "When did you know?"

"That's easy. That time I showed up at your family's winery and drank too much. You drove me home. You were so nice to me and I wasn't expecting that."

"That's when I started loving you too. You were more vulnerable than I expected. Human. And I realized I couldn't blame you for what happened. That you were as much a victim as I was."

Vic swung her leg over Angie and climbed onto her lap, straddling her. "I don't want to talk about that time anymore. In fact, I don't want to talk at all."

CHAPTER THIRTY-TWO

Vic threw her head back as Angie's lips found her neck. God, her kisses! They were soothing and incendiary at the same time. Fire and ice. Yielding and conquering. Whatever the two of them had meant by going slow together, well, *that* was clearly in tatters now, because Vic couldn't imagine not being loved, not being made love to, by this woman after they'd both laid bare their souls. Laid them bare and took them gently and lovingly into one another's hands. *I know what it's like to hold her heart in my hands, to possess it and cherish it, and I know what it's like for her to have my heart in her hands.* She wasn't scared by the thought so much as awed by it.

Angie's mouth hovered closer to her breasts now, her hands cupping the underside of them. It had to go, this bra, because she needed Angie's mouth against her skin. Needed it more than she needed to breathe. "My…I need to…"

"No," Angie whispered, her breath warm against Vic's flesh. "Let me, but not yet."

She could feel Angie's eyes caressing her breasts. She seemed to be inhaling Vic, breathing her in, and then her fingers moved with wondrous, slow exploration. First circling her breasts, then tracing the outline of the bra's fabric before ever so lightly brushing against her nipples. It was almost too much, except there was so much more she desired; they'd not even scratched the surface of their desire yet.

Breathless with desire, Vic urged her to kiss her breasts, hearing the pure need in her own voice and not recognizing her desperation. She'd never wanted another woman's mouth on her as much as she did Angie's.

Angie moaned softly, licked her lips and parted the fine fabric of the bra that Vic could only think about being ripped from her. Screw its ninety-dollar cost. A kiss as soft as a butterfly landed next to her nipple, and Vic wanted to scream. Scream and push Angie's mouth to her rigid flesh because she could hardly stand it anymore, her body clenching painfully, every cell clamping down as if to somehow gather more of Angie to her. Into her.

"Vic. You're so goddamned beautiful."

And then she moved that sexy mouth to Vic's nipple and took it gently, her tongue playfully suckling, her lips so soft and moist that Vic could barely press down enough on the gathering orgasm deep in her belly. God, that mouth. That mouth was surely one of the seven wonders of the world because it was doing things to her breasts she never knew were possible. She arched into Angie's mouth, felt Angie reach behind her and unclasp that damned bra.

"The bedroom," Vic managed. "We should move upstairs to the bedroom."

"No," Angie said, her voice all deep and gravelly and sex-fueled. "I can't wait that long."

Oh dear God. Vic inhaled a deep, shuddering breath as Angie's hand moved between her thighs, stroking higher and higher until they landed on her apex. Fingers teased her through her jeans, and Vic hardened at the combination of Angie's fingers and hand working in agonizing synchronicity.

"Angie, sweetheart…I don't think…I can…take much more of this."

"It's okay. I've got you."

She gently nudged Vic until she was lying down on the couch, and her mouth moved down to her stomach, making the muscles there twitch and jump at the exquisite little pulses Angie's mouth unleashed. She'd never made love on a couch before, it occurred to her as Angie's fingers tugged on the zipper of her jeans. *Why is that? Why have I never done that before?* Making love had always been a planned affair, acted upon like ticking off a checklist: bedroom first, clothes second, light on or off, bed, kissing, etc. But this, this had the shadow of something forbidden about it, something naughty and animalistic and too acute to be constrained by practicalities and rigid priorities. This was a raging fire that couldn't be extinguished.

Her jeans were down past her knees now, her matching black panties too. She could admit to herself that she'd dressed in these sexy underclothes today because somewhere deep in her mind she'd hoped this would happen with Angie tonight. Or soon, in any case.

Angie's fingers were on her, light and making circular patterns, and she was smiling, grinning at Vic. "God, Vic, I want you so bad. You feel so good, do you know that?"

Unable to speak, Vic shook her head lightly.

"Tell me what you want. Because I want to touch you everywhere, all at once, but I'm afraid it might be too much. Too fast."

"You…no…it's perfect."

"I want to discover every part of you. Love every part of you."

Vic's eyes slammed shut. She wanted Angie in and around and on every part of her too. She felt fingers dancing on her most intimate flesh, claiming her, expertly possessing her, like a piano player caressing familiar keys and making beautiful music. A finger slipped inside her, then another, and Vic pressed against them, began moving her hips in time to the short, quick thrusts. She was so wet, so close to coming, that it was all she could do not to. Yet.

"I want to suck you," Angie said, her voice throaty and dripping with desire.

"Oh God…yes. Please. Please, Ange."

"Please what, my darling?"

"Please…suck me." The dirty words ratcheted Vic's arousal higher, and the first touch of Angie's lips on her jolted her, sent white heat through her. When her tongue began moving in sure, rhythmic strokes, Vic was thrust to the edge, and then she was falling over it, throbbing and pulsing as her orgasm ripped through her, shattering her, making her its bitch, leaving her quaking and more in love with this woman than she'd been before.

"Oh, Ange. Come here, baby."

Angie was so ready to be touched by Vic, her body continuing to register her tense wanting. She'd been driven wild after making love to Vic, had almost come a couple of times, but it seemed important to save herself for Vic's touch.

She hadn't removed her own bra and underwear, so focused had she been on Vic's pleasure, but now Vic slowly began to peel the undergarments away, kissing the newly exposed skin and sending Angie into a new stratosphere of wanting. She slammed her eyes shut as Vic's mouth found her nipple, and oh! It was a thousand times better than the times she'd fantasized about Vic doing this to her. She quivered but tried to remain still as Vic's hands cupped her breasts, stroking their soft undersides. "Vic, you're so good at this."

"I'm only good because it's you, sweetie. All you."

Angie opened her eyes to lock into Vic's, which were ornamented with gold and green and gray specks. They were wide and moist and full of desire. And love. Definitely love.

"I love you, sweetheart," Angie whispered, choked up at the thought that finally she'd found what she'd wanted all her life but never allowed herself to hope for, because she never accepted or expected that she was worthy of such perfection, of such a gift. She was ready to take what she wanted, what she needed, to make herself whole.

"I love you too, darling. So much."

Vic kissed her way further south, tickling Angie's abdomen with her lips, her tongue. By the time she got to the hollow of her hip, Angie's body came alive with an abrupt jolt. She couldn't wait much longer; she was so ready, so wet. She pushed her hands into Vic's hair, silently celebrated as Vic took the hint and took her into her mouth. Gently at first, way too gently, but then she was plundering Angie with hard strokes, setting her flesh on fire. And Angie was gone, gone to a place where nothing else existed except the purest of pleasures and all of it immersed in the fine mist of unconditional love and reverent attraction. It was an explosive combination, her feelings for Vic and the physical sensations this woman unleashed in her. It wasn't long before she clenched and called out Vic's name, tossing her head back as her body convulsed in wave after wave of pleasure.

When Vic crawled into her arms, Angie was wrung out, exhausted but in the best possible way.

"Are you all right?" There was worry in Vic's voice. "Did I hurt you at all? Is your incision—"

"Whoa, no need to play doctor on me. Oh wait, what am I saying?" Angie growled playfully. "You can play doctor with me anytime you want."

Vic kissed her on the mouth. "I think I just gave you a pretty good exam, but I may have to do another one. Just to be sure."

"Mmm, I do like doctors who are thorough."

Vic gave her a scolding look. "Hopefully just *this* doctor."

"No need to ever worry about that, sweetheart." Angie's voice lost its playfulness. She hadn't wanted to bring Brooke and Karen into the bedroom with them. *Ever*. But it was too late now. "Vic." *Damn*. An unexpected roughness crept into her voice as the pain and humiliation of Brooke's betrayal hit her with fresh force. She'd only let Brooke's actions hurt her to a certain extent because, as she'd come to realize after a long and painful self-examination, she'd let Brooke be the bad guy. Let Brooke blow up their relationship because she'd not had the guts to. But this…this was different. A betrayal by Vic would absolutely destroy her. She'd never recover if she lost Vic.

Vic wound her fingers through a strand of Angie's hair. "Are you all right? You look sad, and I don't want you to be sad. Not tonight."

"Sorry, I'm not. Sad I mean. I'm happy, Vic. Happier than I've ever been in my life. And you need to know that I'll never intentionally do anything to hurt you. I might fuck up once in a while, but I'll never disrespect you. I'll never not love you and I'll never do anything to put our relationship in jeopardy."

There was not a trace of doubt in Vic's smile. "I believe you. And I'll never do anything to hurt you, to hurt us, either." Thickly, she said, "We're not *them*."

"No. We're not." Angie pulled Vic against her, wrapped her arm around her. "Do you think we have enough strength to make our way to your bed? I think you might have worn me out."

"If we help each other, I'm sure we can manage. And it's kind of nice to know that I was good enough to wear you out."

"Oh, trust me, you were good. But when I get my strength back, watch out."

"Is that a threat?"

"Nope. More like a promise."

Vic laughed, kissed Angie's cheek. "I love you, Angie. Now, take me to bed."

CHAPTER THIRTY-THREE

Vic rolled over, carefully opened one eye to check the bedside clock, then bolted upright. "Shit," she mumbled, tossing blankets aside and scrambling for her robe.

"Wait," Angie said in a slow, sexy voice. She grabbed Vic's wrist and hauled her back onto the bed, prompting Vic to squeal in delight. "I hope you don't think you can get away that easily after what I did to you last night."

"Trust me, I'd like nothing better than to stay here all day with you. But we—"

"But nothing, darling." Angie kissed her as deep and as languid as a lazy canyon river, her mouth instantly activating the fierce arousal to which Vic was defenseless.

Vic didn't find her voice again until Angie's lips had drifted to her throat and her hands began to wander over her terrycloth robe. "Trust me, there's nothing I'd like more, but we have somewhere to be in less than an hour."

Angie raised her head. "We do? Oh crap, not another doctor appointment, I hope. Well…" She grinned wickedly. "Unless you're the doctor and I'm the patient and this is the exam room. Yes?"

"No. Sorry, love."

Angie's face fell.

Vic kissed her on the tip of her nose. "I swear I'll give you all the exams you want as long as we're not late for our…our not-medical appointment. In the meantime, we really need to shower and get moving."

Angie flopped theatrically onto her back and sighed. "You're killing me here. You know that, right? You're supposed to be a healer, not a killer."

Vic hopped off the bed and playfully swatted Angie's bare thigh. "You'll survive it, I promise. And I also promise to make it up to you tonight."

Angie pulled herself to a sitting position. "Now you're talking. But we could share a shower to speed things up. Which would also give us a little time to make out *in* the shower."

Vic shed her robe as she padded to the bathroom. "Last one in's a dirty rotten egg!"

Minutes later, as they huddled together under the shower head to rinse the soap from their bodies, Angie's lips found the base of Vic's throat. It was such a sensitive spot, and Angie knew exactly what to do with it. Her mouth was gentle, her tongue ticklish and heating Vic from the inside. Vic threw her head back against the shower wall as Angie's mouth claimed a nipple, then the other one.

"Jesus, I can't say no to you when you do that." If they were late for their rendezvous at the dog breeder's with the rest of the Cullens, so be it, dammit. This, for the moment, was way more important. In fact, her brain was fast turning to mush under the onslaught of Angie's tongue.

Angie smiled up at her. "Good, because there's absolutely no reason for you to say no."

As the warm water sluiced over them, Angie slid down to her knees, and Vic began throbbing in anticipation of what was to come. Angie was so good at giving oral, a magician, really, that the mere thought or memory of it threw Vic into a volcanic arousal that had her seconds away from exploding. And begging for it. She was a goner as soon as Angie's mouth claimed her, gone weak in the knees, moaning loudly, wild colors zooming around behind her closed eyelids. As she thrust a final time into Angie's mouth, her orgasm shot through her, leaving her quaking and wanting more. She could do this with Angie all day, and she entertained the fantasy of both of them quitting their jobs so there would be no obstacles to their endless lovemaking.

Angie kissed her way back up Vic's body. "I am utterly addicted to you, do you know that? Do you suppose there's an antidote to such a thing?"

Vic threw her arms around Angie's neck and smiled against her lips. "If there is, I don't want it."

* * *

Fifty minutes later, Angie double-checked her seat belt as Vic roared through the streets of Traverse City and headed south along the lake. Fortunately it was a clear day and there was no discernable snow or ice on the roads.

"Are you really not going to tell me where we're going?"

"Nope, not until we get there. And not even wild horses could drag it out of me, so don't even try."

"How about wild tongues?" She stuck her tongue out and flicked it suggestively up and down.

"Stop it. Do you want me to crash?"

Angie crossed her arms in front of her and sighed. "I suppose not. Wait, you're taking us to the airport and we're catching a flight to the Caribbean for a week?"

"Ha, I wish!"

"Hmm, not a trip, huh? Oh, wait, we're going antiquing!" She clapped her hands in glee.

"It's pointless to try and guess, trust me."

Angie sighed again. "Fine. Be that way."

Minutes later, Vic pulled into a long driveway with a sign that read Edgewater Canine Breeders. When Angie saw her brother's pickup truck waiting for them, her confusion only grew. "What's Nick doing here?"

"Not just Nick. Claire and your parents too."

"No," Angie said as they exited the car. "They can't have a dog at the farm."

"I know. Allergies."

"So what are they doing?"

"You'll see, sweetheart."

Holding hands, they followed a sign that directed them to a separate door at the rear of the house, where barking could be heard. Inside, Angie's family waited for them, smiles swallowing their faces.

"Mom," Angie said, greeting them all with hugs. "You shouldn't be in here. Your allergies."

"I won't stay long. And besides, it's worth it. I took an antihistamine before I came, so it should be fine."

"You guys?" Angie said to Nick and Claire. "You're getting a puppy?" They lived in an apartment above the three-car garage at the homestead. Angie supposed they could have a dog there, as long as they kept it away from her mom.

"Nope." Nick grinned at her and inclined his head toward Vic. "We better let your girlfriend explain."

Ooh, girlfriend! Angie loved the way that sounded and she grinned stupidly in return. That her family loved Vic meant everything to her.

"Actually," Vic clarified. "It was Claire and Nick's idea. I just happened to jump all over it."

"Wait," Angie said. "What idea are we talking about exactly?"

Claire handed Angie a fuzzy yellow Labrador retriever puppy. It was chubby and wiggly and looked up at her with the most adorable chocolate brown eyes she'd ever seen. Angie held it against her chest and it began licking her hand.

"Oh my God, it..." Angie turned the puppy over to check out its bits. "She's adorable!"

The owner of the business, a pleasant-looking woman in her sixties with a leather apron that said "Labradors Rule" smiled and nodded at the puppy in Angie's arms. "She's the last of her litter. She's nine weeks, so she really needs a home soon."

The dog smelled mildly of grass and milk, and Angie kissed its snout. "I'd love to keep her, but I'm not in a position to right now."

"Actually you are, dear." Suzanne Cullen winked at her daughter.

"No, Mom. Your allergies. I can't bring this little girl home."

Roger stepped up to Angie and gently petted the puppy in her arms. "You think you're staying with us forever or something? One adult child still living at home is bad enough. But two?"

They all knew he didn't mean it. He was the biggest softie around.

"Actually," Vic said, placing an arm around Angie's waist and staring intently into her eyes. "I'd very much like you and the puppy to continue to stay with me. I mean, until you feel like getting your own place."

"Vic, are you sure about this? It might—no, it *will*—make messes on your floor. And cry and bark and maybe even break things."

"I'm sure. But the question is whether you want to be a doggie mother?"

Ever since Angie was a little girl she'd wanted a puppy. The military hospitals she worked in had regular therapy dogs visit, and some of the soldiers and veterans who came in for treatment were accompanied by therapy dogs. Angie had always made time for the dogs, petting them and talking to them and sneaking them treats, but that was as close as she got to having a dog in her life. Brooke would never have stood for having a dog; she was OCD when it came to keeping a tidy house.

"Are you guys serious about this?"

"Yes," Vic answered. "We all think a dog would be a great companion for you."

"But my shift work."

Claire stepped forward. "We'll all help with that. And you're off for another month, right?"

"Right." Angie held the puppy up to her face and locked eyes with it. It held her gaze, which was a good sign that it wasn't too timid, that it liked people. "What do you say, pup? Do you want to come home with me and Vic?" She tickled a chubby little hairless tummy that was impossibly soft.

In response the dog squeaked adorably and Vic took a turn holding it. "I think she's sure."

Thirty minutes later—paperwork signed, money exchanged, and the dog in a small carrier in the backseat—Vic wheeled the car onto the street. "First stop, a pet store to get food and a larger cage. And toys, of course. Second thing is to name her."

"Well, that's a no-brainer. We have to name her after an author."

"Sounds perfect to me. Your favorite is Zadie Smith and mine is Harper Lee. We could start with one of those. Unless you want to go with Flannery or Margaret or Alice."

"Flannery has possibilities, but Harper it is," Angie said. "Since this was all your idea."

"Uh-uh. You're Mommy Number One. I'm more like the crazy aunt. Or maybe stepmother. Zadie is perfect for her."

"Are you sure?"

Vic reached across the console for Angie's hand. "I'm sure. About all of this. Are you?"

Angie felt tears collect in her eyes. "I've always wanted a dog. How did you know?"

"Oh, a hunch. Plus a little birdie named Claire confirmed it."

"Have I told you lately I love you?" Angie raised their linked hands and kissed the back of Vic's.

"No, but you can never say it enough."

"Good. I love you, Victoria Turner."

"I love you too, Angela Cullen."

"Wait. I need to amend the puppy's name."

"What's that?"

"Zadie Lee Turner Cullen."

"That's a mouthful."

"I know. But it's perfect."

Vic laughed and squeezed Angie's hand. "You're right. It is perfect."

CHAPTER THIRTY-FOUR

Vic drew a line on the white board across the patient's name she'd just sent home with a prescription for antibiotics. February was always the worst for flu and respiratory illnesses, and lately the Emergency Department had been overrun with cases.

"What have you got for me next?" she asked Liv.

"Four-year-old boy. Sore throat, fever."

More of the same, Vic thought. *March can't get here fast enough.*

"And can I just say," Liv added with a grin, "that you look incredibly happy lately. I don't suppose having the last three weeks off work has anything to do with it. Nor the, ahem, roommate waiting at home for you."

Vic smiled back at her friend and colleague. "You'd be right on both counts. And thanks, Liv. For everything."

Vic strode into the treatment room, Liv trailing behind her.

"Hi," she said to the boy's mother. "I'm Dr. Turner. And you are?"

"Jessica Stone, and this is my son Devin."

Vic hoisted the boy onto the treatment table after shaking his hand. "You're not feeling too well, huh, Devin?"

He shook his head. He was alert but listless.

She checked his chart. His temperature had clocked in at one-oh-two when the nurse took it about fifteen minutes ago. "Can you open your mouth nice and wide for me?"

"It hurts," he whispered.

"I know it does, sweetie. You're a brave boy. Just try to open it as far as you can, okay? I need to have a quick look at it."

Vic pressed on his tongue with a wooden tongue depressor and peered at the back of his throat after shining the light from her penknife on it. It was purple and swollen and pus was visible. Strep throat was Vic's first guess, but she wanted to cover all the bases. When she was a medical student, one of the interns misdiagnosed epiglottitis in an eight-year-old girl. She would have died had an experienced resident not stepped in. Epiglottitis was a rare bacterial infection of the epiglottis that, if untreated, could completely cut off breathing if it swelled too much. Surgery—risky surgery—was the only option after that, and it had to be done quickly.

Vic explained to Devin and his mom that she was going to take a throat swab first and send it to the lab. But as soon as she extracted the culture, Devin's breathing became more labored and his eyes began to droop shut. He was barely conscious. *Dammit*.

"Liv," she said, keeping her voice steady so as not to alarm the boy and his mother. "Call for a pediatric anesthetist. Stat." Devin needed a breathing tube, and fast, because his throat was closing up, making it impossible for him to breathe and oxygenate his blood. Performing such procedures on small children was tricky. If he didn't get intubated in the next minute or two, his only remaining option at that point was a tracheotomy, which was not ideal.

Julie stepped into the room. "Can I help?"

"What's going on?" the mother asked, her voice tight with worry.

"Can you get an IV going?" Vic asked.

"Sure," Julie said, setting to work.

Liv returned with bad news. The only anesthetist on duty tonight was tied up in an emergency surgery. He wouldn't be free for at least another twenty minutes, and the on-call anesthetist was a good fifteen minutes out. The kid would be dead by then. *Shit.* Vic was going to have to do it herself. She ordered Liv to get her a laryngoscope and one of the smaller tube gauges they had, then ordered Julie to pump a mild sedative into the boy's IV bag and to start an antibiotic drip.

"Ma'am," Vic said to the mom. "I'm pretty sure your son has epiglottitis. It's a bacterial infection of his epiglottis at the back of his throat, and it's getting more and more difficult for him to breathe. We need to intubate him as quickly as possible. Once we do that, the antibiotics will kick in and attack his infection."

Frightened eyes darted from Vic to the boy. "Whatever you say, Doctor, as long as you make him better. Devin, honey?"

Devin flopped into Julie's arms, unconscious.

"We're going in," Vic announced, dropping the boy's head back and scooping his tongue out of the way before positioning the laryngoscope and exposing his epiglottis, which was swollen and angry looking. Carefully she aligned the tube and pushed it in. The epiglottis immediately bit down on it, but the tube was safely in. *Thank God.*

Within seconds Devin's color began to improve as air was pumped into his lungs.

"Is he going to be okay?" his mom asked, her eyes wide with shock and worry.

"Yes," Vic said, a little shaky from the adrenaline. "But we're going to have to transfer him to the pediatric ICU so they can keep a good eye on him."

"Well done," Julie said to her after Devin and his mom were escorted upstairs. "You're a rock star, Vic. I don't think I could have done that. Not under that kind of pressure. And how did you know it wasn't just strep throat or something run-of-the-mill?"

Vic shook her head. "You would have done it too if you'd had to. There were too many signs that his breathing was compromised. Plus I've seen it once before."

"Well, trust me, I'm taking notes on this one. Look. Your shift is over in fifteen minutes. Why don't you head on home? There's nobody else on the board and I'm sticking around awhile longer."

Vic was never one to leave early. As a supervisor, she preferred to lead by example. "Thanks, but no need."

"No. There is a need. You're only just back to work. Plus there's a patient waiting at home for you."

Vic smiled. She always smiled at the mention of Angie. "My patient at home is doing quite well, as a matter of fact."

"You never know. It's always best to keep as close an eye as possible on your very *special* patients."

Vic felt heat in her cheeks. Since she'd come back to work, Angie's absence in her heart was like a missing tooth her tongue kept trying to probe. She wanted to be with her as much as possible. "You're right. And I'd love to get home to Angie. Thanks, Julie. I owe you one."

Home and Angie in the same phrase. She could get used to that.

"Nonsense. See you tomorrow afternoon."

* * *

Angie couldn't be sure what woke her first: the drool on her chin, the puppy suddenly wiggling against her chest, or Vic kissing her cheek. Maybe it was all three. She remembered now; she and Zadie had fallen asleep together on the couch, having given up trying to stay awake for Vic to finish her shift. She rolled onto her back, keeping Zadie on her chest.

"Hey, sleepyhead." Vic pushed hair from her forehead and planted a kiss there.

"Hi, lover. You're pretty mushy for somebody who's just finished a ten-hour shift."

Vic edged herself onto the couch and petted Zadie, who looked up at her with sleepy eyes followed by a yawn that made her little yellow face disappear. "Aw, sorry for waking you, little girl. Do you have to go outside and be a good girl? Huh? You want to go outside and do your business?"

It amazed Angie how quickly the two of them had resorted to baby talk the minute Zadie had become part of their family. Zadie Wadie and Puppy Wuppy and worse.

"Yeah, she's probably bursting," Angie said, slowly sitting up. "I'll take her."

"No, let me. You stay put."

A few minutes later, Vic and Zadie returned, Zadie flopping down on the floor and Vic standing in front of Angie, wide-eyed and shifting from foot to foot.

"You're making me nervous. What's wrong?" She flicked her eyes to Zadie. "Is Zadie okay?"

"Everything's fine, it's just…"

Angie's heart started jackhammering in her chest. Even harder when Vic finally sat down beside her and took her hand. Her eyes were swimming and she had the weirdest look on her face. *Oh God.*

"The thing is…"

"Jesus, Vic, you're killing me here. You're good at killing me, come to think of it. I'm going to start calling you Dr. Mengele."

"Okay, that is *so* not funny." Then she laughed, mercifully erasing the tension in the room.

"Whew. You're laughing. Which means I may not have a heart attack after all."

"Oh, you." Vic's eyes took in Zadie, and she called the puppy over. Gangly and clumsy thanks to her rapid growth, Zadie wobbled over to them and Vic picked her up and placed her between them. "What I'm trying to say is…"

Time seemed to thicken. Words, or at least their meaning, traveled at a painstaking pace, and Angie found herself holding her breath again.

"What I'm trying to say is, even though words don't seem enough to do the trick, is that I love you so damned much. And this dog too. I can't believe how quickly she's wormed her way into my heart." She stroked Zadie's head, and in turn Zadie nuzzled the palm of her hand. "You see, when I came home tonight and saw you and the puppy curled up together on the couch, asleep, it made me realize something."

"What's that, sweetheart? Cuz you sure have my undivided attention right now."

Vic took a deep breath. "It made me realize that I don't want to be without the two of you. Ever. I want us to be a family."

Angie nodded slowly as understanding—and relief—dawned.

"I want," Vic continued, "for you to stay here. For good. To live with me. To be my partner. I don't want anything about what we have to be temporary or transient. Please say yes. Please tell me you want the same thing."

She touched Angie's cheek and her touch was exquisite and tender and like nothing Angie had ever felt before, because there were angels behind that touch.

"Oh, Vic." Her throat felt rough and dry and her eyes began to well. "Of course I want the same thing. Don't you know that?"

"No, I didn't." Vic was shaking her head and crying. Blubbering now. "I was afraid you were going to want your own place. You and Zadie…"

"Well, it's true Zades is pretty strong competition, with those big brown eyes and blond fur." Her voice went high and goofy. "Aren't you, girl? Oh and we can't forget that soft warm belly, can we?"

Vic laughed through her tears. "Um, is that a yes? Cuz I have a soft warm belly too. And blond hair."

Angie laughed, then leaned in and kissed Vic. And then kissed her some more until she was sure Vic was getting the message loud and clear. "Does that answer your question?"

"Yes. Mostly."

"Good. Because the other half of the answer is that I love you to the moon and back. And I hate the idea of ever *not* living with you. Are you kidding me? I was making myself sick worrying about you sending Zadie and me off to the doghouse. I mean… not literally a doghouse, of course, but making us get our own place. And that was definitely going to kill me."

"Well then, my love. Consider yourself not killed."

"And not homeless." Angie turned serious. "You rescued me,

Vic. You did. Without you…I can't imagine what my life would be like."

"We rescued each other." Vic pulled her close and they kissed again until Zadie whimpered between them and started licking them both.

Angie laughed. "Clearly she wants in on the act."

"Clearly. What do you say, little girl? Do you want this to be your forever home? Just the three of us, right here?"

The face licking intensified until Angie and Vic began giggling helplessly.

"She's so happy, I think she's going to wag that little tail right off," Angie said. "Do you suppose that's an actual thing?"

"I know it is." Vic stroked Angie's cheek again. "Because if I had a tail right now, I'd most definitely wag it right off."

Angie reached around until she found Vic's ass, which she squeezed lustily. "Just checking for a tail."

"Hmm, in that case, I have other things that need checking too."

"Oh, I am so on it, I'm already there."

Vic stood, gathered Zadie into her arms and held her hand out to Angie. "In that case, let's go up to bed."

Angie's heart was so big and so full, it actually hurt. But it was the sweetest pain she'd ever endured. Because her heart had, finally, found its forever home.

EPILOGUE

Ten weeks later

Vic circulated through the living room with a bottle of champagne, topping up glasses as she went. Angie was doing the same, but in the kitchen. The party was big enough that it had spread throughout the ground floor of their house. A few people had even spilled out onto the back deck, though the chill of winter continued to infuse the April evening air with its last breath.

She splashed more bubby into Julie's glass, then Shawna Malik's. The two hadn't left each other's side all night.

"Celebration seems to be in the air tonight," Vic said, tossing them a wink. "And you two definitely look like you're celebrating something."

"We are," Julie deadpanned. "We're celebrating you and Angie officially moving in together."

"And Zadie. Don't forget her."

Upon hearing her name, the yellow Lab sprang up from the floor, tail wagging, and enthusiastically nuzzled Julie's hand, looking for petting. Her limbs were long and gangly and her puppy fur was thickening. She was almost five months old now.

"Aw, how's my good girl," Julie said, petting Zadie's smooth head. Then to Vic, "It's your spotlight, my friend. Yours and Angie's. And might I add you both look very happy together. Congratulations."

"We are, thank you." Vic looked at Shawna, who would undoubtedly be blushing if her skin were lighter. "All right, spill it, Officer Malik. What's going on with you two?"

Shawna's grin said a lot more than her lazy shrug. "Julie's right, it's your day today. This party is for you and Angie."

"That's true, but I could really use an excuse to open another bottle of champagne. Now come on. Out with it."

Julie's hand crept into Shawna's. "We're officially a couple."

Vic feigned a swoon. "How shocking! I would never have guessed." She clinked glasses with each woman. "Well done, both of you. And a toast to the worst-kept secret around the hospital the last couple of months."

Angie snuck up behind Vic and threw her hands around her waist. "Hey, you. Okay if I crack that other box of champagne?"

"God, I hope so. Especially now that we have even more to celebrate."

"We do?" Angie rested her chin on Vic's shoulder. "Oh no, Zadie's not going to be a mom, is she?"

"Um, I think she's a little young for that."

"Good point. Plus she hasn't had her sex talk yet."

"You two." Julie grinned. "Good thing you found each other, 'cause I can't think of two people who are more suited to one another."

"With the possible exception of you two," Vic said, then to Angie, "They're officially a couple, in case you haven't figured it out."

"Ha, figured it out? Like everybody didn't know already, sheesh. Good thing you're not criminals, because you'd be pretty lousy at it."

Julie shook her head but couldn't seem to lose her smile. "Can't people get away with anything around that place?"

"Nope," Vic and Angie said in unison.

Moments later, Vic decided it was time for the official toast. Everyone was into their second or third glass of champagne and the plates and bowls of munchies were beginning to thin. If the party went on much longer, nobody would care about a toast or speeches.

Liv took her cue, clinked a spoon to her glass, and stood by the fireplace. "Welcome, everyone. And thank you all for coming to celebrate the official moving-in-dom of my best friend Vic Turner and her wonderful partner Angie Cullen."

"Is that even a thing? Moving-in-dom?" Angie's old friend Vinnie shouted from the back of the room. "If I'd known you could get a party like this without even getting married, I'd have been all over it!"

"Watch it, Vinnie," Angie warned, "or I'm telling your wife."

Next Liv went on to extoll the virtues of Vic and Angie, putting her arms around them both as she called a toast to their love and their good health and their future happiness. "And one final toast. I'd like to call a toast to Brooke Bennett and Karen Turner." A hush fell across the room as though a gavel had been rapped. "Because without them, Angie and Vic would never have found one another."

"Here, here," the gathering erupted in unison.

Angie's brother Nick stepped up next. He'd had more than a couple of glasses of champagne, Vic could see, as he launched into stories about Angie as a kid that were funny as hell but didn't exactly cast her in the best light.

"Jesus," Angie whispered. "This is worse than a drunken wedding toast by the best man."

Vic felt her face flush as a private vision floated through her mind. She was relieved when Claire—*thank God for Claire!*—nudged Nick out of the way and offered her heartfelt congratulations.

"Speech! Speech!" came the collective call.

Angie sent a silent plea to Vic; Angie hated public speeches.

"Okay, but you owe me one," Vic whispered and kissed Angie's cheek before turning back to the room. "Thank you,

Liv, Claire…and, ah, Nick I guess." The crowd laughed along with her. "And thank you all for sharing this moment in our lives and celebrating it with us. Two or three things before we polish off the rest of the champagne. The first is that my dear sweet Angie just received the news yesterday that she placed third in a statewide short story contest. Congratulations, sweetheart. I've always wanted to fall in love with a great writer, and now I have!"

The crowd whooped and hollered out to Angie, who was turning about three shades of red. She hated being singled out, and Vic sent her an apologetic wink. "But I'm not finished yet. Sorry, honey, you're going to have to withstand the spotlight a little longer." From her pocket she withdrew a small package wrapped in gold paper. "For you, my love."

Under her breath, Angie said, "Crap. I didn't get you anything!"

"You don't need to," Vic whispered back. "Now open it. I promise it's nothing embarrassing. You know, like a vibrator or something."

Angie tore at the paper. "That is so not funny."

"You're right. I'll save that one for a private moment."

Angie's face lit up as she held up the contents of the package—a fresh typewriter ribbon. "Cool! For my antique typewriter. Which I can tell you is very cool to look at but a bitch to type on. Thank you, darling. I promise to use it in good health."

"Good. See that you do. And now for the last item on my little agenda." Vic nodded at Liv, who then disappeared.

"What are you doing?" Angie whispered, more than a little desperately.

"You'll see."

"You're scaring me."

"I like keeping you off balance."

"So this is what I get to look forward to? The off-balance thing?"

"Yep."

"Shit."

Zadie snaked her way toward them through the parting bodies, tail wagging a mile a minute, a small velvet drawstring bag dangling from her mouth. She stopped in front of Angie, and with a motion from Vic's hand, sat and spat the bag out.

"What the…"

"It's for you," Vic said to Angie.

"Where's my gift, Zadie?" somebody from the audience yelled.

The expression on Angie's face—surprise, bemusement, embarrassment—was adorable. She was a good sport and opened the velvet bag, which contained a small ring box. As she popped it open, her expression melted into one of barely contained joy and excited surprise, and Vic's stomach did a pleasurable roll.

"Oh my God, you didn't!"

"I did. Will you marry me, Angela Cullen?"

"Um, aren't you supposed to go down on one knee?"

The crowd giggled with nervous anticipation.

"I'll do anything if it'll make you say yes." Vic dropped down to both knees and the crowd whooped. "Yes yes yes," they chanted.

"God, I'm to kill you," Angie said, but she was grinning and tears streamed down her cheeks. "Yes. Yes, I'll marry you, Victoria Turner!"

Vic leapt up, momentarily forgetting her forty-one-year-old knees, and took Angie in her arms to seal the proposal with a kiss. "You okay with a long engagement? Since my divorce will take a while longer to be finalized."

"I'll wait forever, if that's what it takes, darling."

Zadie was trying to crawl up their legs, so both women bent to pet her and drop kisses on her head.

Liv yelled over the crowd, which was still celebrating loudly. "Now that this has turned into an engagement party, folks, I say it's time to crack open more bubbly!"

Angie smiled at Vic and kissed her again. "Good thing you're marrying into a family winery."

"Exactly, since our friends and family are a bunch of boozehounds."

"If you think this is bad, wait until the wedding."

The air left Vic's lungs at the word "wedding." She never expected she'd marry once, let alone twice. But this time it was forever. This time she would give Angie and her marriage everything she had and never take a day of it for granted. This time she knew what she had and would do everything to keep it. "I love you, babe."

"I love you too, darling. Now let's get some more of that champagne so we can share a proper toast as an engaged couple."

"Ooh, I love the sound of that!"

Bella Books, Inc.

Women. Books. Even Better Together.

P.O. Box 10543
Tallahassee, FL 32302

Phone: 800-729-4992
www.bellabooks.com